BLACK HOLE SUNS AND REVELATIONS

Aaron A. A. Smith

Lobsterkreativ— San Diego, CA
Paperback ISBN: 978-1-7372477-1-5
eBook ISBN: 979-8-8691-5666-2
Library of Congress Control Number: 2025918291
Title: *Black Hole Suns and Revelations*
Author: Aaron A. A. Smith
Digital distribution | 2025
Paperback | 2025

This is a work of fiction. The characters, names, incidents, places, and dialogue are products of the author's imagination, and are not to be construed as real.

Published in the United States by New Book Authors Publishing

WHEN A LOBSTER WHISTLES ON TOP OF A MOUNTAIN THE BALLERINAS WILL DANCE

by Aaron A. A. Smith and Erin Camille Jackson

A valiant band of lobsters stage a daring escape from a restaurant on Valentine's Day. A miniature ballerina in a glass globe dances with a beauty that transcends time, space, and reality. A mild-mannered man is driven to violent madness by the machinations of an enormous spider who has invaded his home. A hard-nosed, hard-drinking detective tracks a talking *femme fatale* cat in a hardboiled kitty city. Temporal manifestations of the Four Horsemen of the Apocalypse struggle with familiarly human existential crises. A pair of hardened criminals fondly reminisce about their childhood friendship, each knowing that one must kill the other. Two doomed astronauts find bittersweet purpose in their final hours.

These are a few of the memorable themes and characters that appear- and sometimes reappear- in Erin Camille Jackson and Aaron A. A. Smith's short story collection *When a Lobster Whistles on Top of a Mountain the Ballerinas Will Dance.* In this evocative and eclectic anthology, Jackson and Smith expertly flow between genres ranging from existentialist literature and philosophy, noir, Kafkaesque fairytales, absurdism, Southern Gothic, poetry, and Japanese *mono no aware* to create a realistically surreal floating world of oddball humor, nostalgia, and ephemeral yet lingering beauty.

DEDICATION

To Aunto

We dug coal together. I wish you could be here to see the diamonds.

And to Ryker/Junior

What will you have after five hundred years?

PROLOGUE

It was there again. That stranger's face churning in the primordial tides. Its burning black eyes leered at Jimmie from behind the medicine cabinet mirror.

Jimmie had always felt like he was staring at the face of a stranger when he looked in the mirror. That freckled pink mask wasn't his real face. His real face was hidden somewhere deep inside the mirror. Somewhere he couldn't find.

This stranger's face was something different. Something Other. It was no reflection. It lived inside the mirror. And it wanted Jimmie to do something.

Jimmie pried open the medicine cabinet and swung the door wide until the mirror faced the wall. He tapped the cabinet's cheap plastic backing with a finger, then snatched his pills from the shelf. The pills didn't work. They were tin talismans like rabbit's feet or crucifixes. Maybe they were placebos. Maybe they were government tracking devices. Jimmie took the pills anyway.

He closed his eyes, clicked the medicine cabinet door shut, and gripped the sides of the porcelain sink. His chapped red hands welled white at the knuckles like the bones of a long-dead skeleton. His ragged fingernails were pale crescent moons drowning in a sky of blood.

He tightened his grip on the sink, took a series of shallow breaths, and opened his eyes. He gazed into the mirror, and the mirror gazed into him. Twin black hole suns fixed in hollow sockets glared into Jimmie's mind. Those eyes could see his thoughts, could shape his thoughts.

Beneath the burning black eyes, a dark maw spiraled in a perfect circle of night. The maw whispered to Jimmie like the voices in his head sometimes did.

The dark disk spun faster, and the maw's words pulled at Jimmie's mind with the crushing force of gravity. The call of the void echoed through every fiber of his being, rending and tearing his body, stretching and distorting his tendons and bones, shaping him like human clay into a long, grotesque husk.

The black hole suns burned their image into Jimmie's eyes, the last image they would behold. Jimmie's eyes seared and liquefied in their sockets. Flayed tendrils of his flesh reached out to cover the empty holes.

The maw gnawed at Jimmie's consciousness until his thoughts were no longer his own. He gave himself to the abyss.

The Other spoke in Jimmie's mind. He shared His word. His transparent truth. His burning darkness and cold revelation. At last, in the pure clarity of the darkness, Jimmie understood. At last, he was whole.

Without sight, Jimmie looked into the mirror again. For the first time in his life, he saw his own face. His true face.

It wasn't there.

CHAPTER 1

It was 9:48 on the night of June fourteenth. The world would end in five days, twenty-two hours, and twelve minutes. The doom of revelation was precise and inevitable. The fatal hands were ticking. The door was opening. The prophecy was in motion. Soon the sun would set and never rise again. The black hole sun would devour it whole and rise in its place.

Whitman Coe didn't know the world was ending. He didn't know his role in the coming apocalypse. For Whit, the end of the world was an irreversible truth. His world had ended three years ago on this very night.

Whit paced the shadowlands between the kitchen and the living room, fingers wrapped around a lukewarm can of beer. He still wore his wedding ring. As he paced, his wilted head and sinewy neck made Whit look like a vanquished bull in the *plaza de toros* awaiting the death stroke of the matador.

He took a pull on his beer and scanned the living room. His son Junior sat on the sofa scribbling in a pink Hello Kitty notebook and gnawing on his fingers. Next to the boy, a chonky gray cat was curled up and sleeping in a coil like a fluffy, obese nautilus. Her snub tail twitched as she dreamed her cat dreams. On the television, Luke Skywalker, Darth Vader, and the Emperor were engaged in their final showdown in the Emperor's throne room on the Death Star. The Emperor was attempting to win friends and influence Jedi via the subtle art of being a sardonic dick.

"Stop eating your hands, Junior," Whit said to his son.

Junior jerked his fingers out of his mouth and scratched the gray cat's head. The cat shifted, pinched her eyes shut, and purred. Junior looked up from his notebook. "Almost done, Dada," he said.

"Take your time," Whit said and sipped his beer.

Junior went back to his writing.

From an atmospheric perspective, Whit and Junior's Saturday night film fest painted a tableau of a contented little family of two.

But that wasn't the truth. A closer look around the house told a different story. The framed pictures hanging on the walls and perched on shelves told the story of three people: a father, a son, and a mother. A contented little family of three.

No. There were only two people in the room. The photographs were reflected images from long ago and far away. Captured moments from the lives of three people in memory.

"Okay, Dada, I'm done," Junior said.

"Do you want to read your story now or after the movie?" Whit said.

"You pick."

"I dunno."

"Okay, I'll read it now." Junior stood up, holding his Hello Kitty notebook in both hands.

Whit paused the movie as the Emperor went skydiving down the Death Star's reactor shaft without a parachute.

Junior flipped to the first page of his notebook and read:

"I was dreaming. I knew I was dreaming, but I couldn't wake up. My dada was asleep in his room. It had been three years since my mommy died.

"I heard a creak in the hallway and I woke up. A dark silhouette stood in the doorway. The man who gives me nightmares.

"I asked, 'Who are you?'

"He said, 'I have many names.'

"'You're not real,' I said. 'This is just a dream.'

"'Life is but a dream,' the silhouette said. 'And what a beautiful dream I can give you.'

"'What do you mean?' I asked.

"'Let me show you,' the silhouette said.

"The silhouette snapped his fingers, and I was in the living room. Dada and Mommy were sitting on the couch. I gave Mommy a huge hug and we started the day. We went to a baseball game, and to the zoo, and to a concert, and to a movie. And I was happy.

"The silhouette snapped his fingers again, and I woke up. I ran to the living room and looked at the couch, but Mommy wasn't there. It was only a dream.

"And the happy was gone."

Junior looked up at his father. Tears rippled in his eyes. Whit put an arm around his son's shoulder and pulled him close. Junior leaned against his father's chest and sobbed, his breath rising and falling in choked spasms.

"That was a really good story, buddy," Whit said. "Your mom would have loved it. And she would have loved the way you hold her in your memory. Your writing's really coming along, kiddo. Soon it'll be time for Dada to pass the torch to you. Then you'll be the writer in the family." He patted his son on the back. "Well, Junior. You wanna drink one last root beer and finish the movie before bed?"

Junior nodded. His tears had stopped.

"Okay, buddy," Whit said. He pressed play on the DVD player and chugged the dregs of his stale beer. He reached into the refrigerator, cracked open a root beer for Junior, and snatched a fresh can of suds for himself. "Cheers, buddy," he said, popping the tab of his beer can.

"To Mommy," the father and the son said in unison. They clanked their beverage cans together and sipped.

On TV, Darth Vader rasped his final breath.

"You know," Whit said, "when I was a kid and saw the original *Star Wars* for the first time, I never would have imagined that Darth Vader dying would've been so sad. Of course George Lucas hadn't given us his backstory yet."

"He is sad," Junior said. "He's angry, too, but I think he's mostly sad."

"He would be," Whit said. "He lost everyone and everything he loved. But then he found his son. That's what brought him back."

"Yeah," Junior said, "but Luke should've joined him so they could rule the galaxy as father and son."

"Sounds like a pretty good deal," Whit said.

Whit and Junior watched the movie until the Ewoks, hopped up on the glorious elation of victory in battle and the succulent flavor of spit-roasted stormtrooper flesh, finally partied themselves out and the credits rolled.

"Okay, Junior," Whit said. "It's bedtime. I'll read you a story, but first go brush your teeth to get all that soda off. Besides, you've got some serious pizza breath. Whoo!" He turned his head away from Junior and waved a hand back and forth in front of his nose. "You smell like a bag of garlic butts."

"You're a bag of garlic butts."

"Nuh-uh."

"Yeah-huh." Junior laughed and stuck out his tongue, then headed to the bathroom to scrub the root beer-pizza mélange off his teeth.

***

Junior burrowed beneath a tangled cocoon of bedsheets, sandwiched between a soft mound of stuffed animals and a bristling spear wall of spiny plastic Godzilla and dinosaur action figures. The rotund gray cat scrunched in a bread loaf pose at the foot of the bed, blinking at Whit as he read from a black-and-lime-green book with a lobster on the cover.

"Harlstons," Whit said, "leapt out of the window into the cool water. It splashed up in the air and sparkled with light." He closed the book and slipped it back into Junior's bedside bookshelf.

"That was a really good story," Junior said.

"It was," Whit said.

"It was sad, though. But it was also really beautiful."

"Sometimes the saddest things are the most beautiful. And the most beautiful are the saddest."

Junior thought about what his father had said for a moment, then nodded his head. "I guess I get what you mean," he said.

"Okay, buddy," Whit said, tousling his son's hair, "I think it's time for you to get some sleep."

"Okay, Dada."

Whit pulled the wadded covers over his son's shoulders and patted him on the head. "Goodnight, buddy," he said. "Get good sleep. I love you."

"I love you too, Dada," Junior said, his voice faraway and groggy.

Whit turned out the light and left the room. The bulbous gray cat followed.

Junior shifted his blankets and peeked over the edge of his comforter. He felt the presence of the dark silhouette. Somewhere close. Crouching in the chasmic maw of night.

He stared into the void until his eyes began to droop closed. As his vision blurred, a shadow beside the closet door started to waver. He focused his gaze on the shadow, and it took shape. The shape of a tall man in a black shroud.

Junior fought to keep his eyes open, but it was no use. The pull of gravity sealed them shut. He spiraled down, from darkness to darkness, into the labyrinth at the heart of the abyss.

CHAPTER 2

Stephen wandered through the labyrinth of mirrors. Through the sea of trees. Through the heavy mist and the hungry shadows that seemed to have swallowed the world whole.

The boy didn't know how long he had been lost in the dark woods. And it didn't matter. Time didn't exist here. There was only the maze. Only inescapable walls of mirrors and trees. Only left turns and right turns and paths he must choose. And each choice was pointless, because all paths led to the heavy mist and hungry shadows that would inevitably devour all time and space and memory. All paths led to the void.

A ragged blue-white light cast its beams downward through the gaps in the canopy of trees. It was a light that bit and rent through flesh and sinew and bone.

Stephen knew these woods. He had been here before. The tall pines eclipsing the night sky. The trickle of water flowing down a rock-hewn creek bed. The smell of wet stones, moss, and damp bark. He was somewhere deep in Ross Wood near the forbidden creek. But that wasn't really where he was. Not at all. He was trapped in a shadowland. A warped reflection of the familiar forest near his house.

Stephen came to the end of another straightaway. He stopped and scried into the mirror ahead of him, as though hoping the boy behind the looking glass could answer the riddle of the labyrinth. No answer came. Just the image of a small, frail boy, barefoot and dressed in astronaut pajamas.

A shrill caw reverberated through the canopy of trees. Stephen craned his neck to peek up. Perched in the crook of a gnarled branch, four crows glowered down at him. One of the crows cawed again. It sounded like a warning.

The crows studied Stephen a few moments longer, then leapt from their perch and darted into the black veil above the sea of trees. The beating of their wings echoed behind them.

Stephen chose the path on the right and marched deeper into the labyrinth. He staggered through the clag, pressing his fingertips against a mirror wall for guidance. The mirror squeaked as his fingers slid across its viscous surface. He snatched his hand away from the mirror and wiped his fingers on his pajama pants.

Something scuttled in the darkness. *K-tchikitikitik. K-tchikitikitik.* Stephen turned toward the sound, but he couldn't see through the mist. The sound came again. Closer this time. Faster. *K-tchikitikitik! K-tchikitikitik! K-tchikitikitikitikitikitikitikitik!* Stephen backed up, panting.

A disembodied groan rose from the fog ahead. A sound like sharp claws dragging across the face of a mirror. Glass shattering and tumbling to the damp soil. The crunch of footsteps treading on the broken shards.

A pale shape moved in the mist at the end of the corridor ahead. It lurched toward Stephen on two legs like a man, but the shape did not belong to any man or beast Stephen had ever seen. The shape loomed like a white shadow as it stalked forward, its gaunt limbs and body grotesquely elongated as though a violent force had stretched its skin and bones and tendons into their present nightmarish proportions.

The creature rounded its shoulders and hunched low. Jagged crescent-moon claws dangled from its knurled fingertips.

When the creature stooped down, Stephen glanced past its shoulder into the mirror at the heart of the labyrinth. A dark silhouette wavered behind the glass. The silhouette's eyes burned through the mirror like twin black hole suns.

The silhouette whispered into the fog, its voice floating on the cold wind. The pale creature bellowed and skirred toward Stephen, its claws screeching against the mirror walls.

As the creature drew near, its hideous form emanated from the mist. It was cadaver-white and completely hairless. Its withered skin draped over its contorted bones and shrouded the hollow pits of its eyes like an old and rotting rag. Its face was blank and fallow. A face that wasn't there.

Stephen stumbled backward into the slick surface of a mirror. He was cornered.

The creature took a final step forward. Its body tensed. It gaped its mouth wide and unhinged its jaw with a wet clattering.

An oozing row of scythelike fangs bore down on Stephen as he cringed against the mirror. The boy squeezed his eyes shut and turned his head away from the approaching beast.

Now Stephen could hear the low rumble of the creature's breath, could smell its stench. The stench of death and rancid flesh.

The creature hissed deep in its throat and lunged at Stephen.

Stephen stared into the abyss.

***

Stephen jolted awake in his bed. Eighty-five miles southwest, Junior did the same.

CHAPTER 3

Stephen scooted upright in his bed, jamming his back against the headboard. His pajamas clung to his skin, and his hair was plastered to his forehead. A furnace blast of sweltering night air rustled the curtains of his second-story bedroom window, but Stephen was freezing. He shuddered and wheezed. He reached into his bedside table drawer, pulled out his asthma inhaler, and took a deep drag of the bitter mist.

He cast about his bedroom. Perused the contents of his bookshelf. A few titles stood out in the moonlight: *Parallel Worlds* by Michio Kaku, *A Brief History of Time* by Stephen Hawking, *The Lord of the Rings* by J. R. R. Tolkien. He inspected the posters on his wall: *Godzilla: King of the Monsters*, Albert Einstein with his tongue sticking out, posters from all three of the original *Star Wars* films. Everything was in its proper place, and so must Stephen be.

Stephen could breathe again.

Then he heard a crash outside. This wasn't an unusual occurrence given how close Stephen's family lived to the woods. On occasion, a racoon, an opossum, or some other adventurous woodland critter would wander in from the tree line to rummage through the trash cans. But this crash sounded different. More savage. Somehow vicious. It sounded like the crash had come from old Mr. and Mrs. Coe's house next door.

A second, louder crash followed. Then a staccato of smashing sounds. Then something that sounded like wood snapping, followed by a muffled thud. Then silence.

Stephen's body went rigid. His heart bucked and fluttered like the desperate wings of a hummingbird in its death throes. He slunk out of bed and crawled to his open bedroom window. He pressed his face flat against the wall and listened to the darkness. Listened for the sound he dreaded to hear. The sound he knew would come for him.

K-tchikitikitik. K-tchikitikitik. Scuttling across the gravel drive between the Coe property and his parents' house.

The scuttling stopped.

Stephen pried his face from the wall and inched his head toward the window. He looked down.

The pale creature from his nightmare stood beneath the window. It tilted its head toward Stephen as if it had sensed the boy's movement. Leathery skin stretched like weathered tarps over the creature's brow ridge, sealing the hollow pits of its eye sockets. Hollow pits that stared up at Stephen. The creature parted its desiccated lips in a smile of recognition, revealing its fangs. They dripped wet with fresh blood.

CHAPTER 4

A frantic thud at their bedroom door shook Bob and Sarah Rockwell awake. The door swung open, the light switch clicked, and sixty watts of yellow glare stung their eyes.

"Mom, Dad!" Stephen shouted as he barged into the room.

Bob sat up, hunched over, and dangled his feet to the floor. He cupped his hands over his face and rubbed his eyes. "Why?" he groaned.

Sarah climbed out of bed and wrapped an arm around her son's narrow shoulders. "Oh, sweetie," she said. "Did you have another bad dream?"

"I did. But then it was real."

"My brain hurts," Bob said.

"What your father means to say is that we're not sure what you mean. Just slow down and tell us what happened."

"I was having a nightmare about a really scary monster—like really, really scary—and then I woke up and I heard a bunch of noises outside, and then I looked out my bedroom window and the monster from my dream was standing outside."

"My brain still hurts," Bob said.

Sarah shot a look at Bob from the corner of her eye, but Bob's face was still buried in his hands.

"That sounds like a very scary dream, sweetie," Sarah said. "But it was only a dream. You're a man of science. You know there's no such things as monsters, right?"

"Whatever it was, I was awake when I saw it out the window. I wasn't dreaming. It wasn't sleep paralysis or something. I was wide awake and cognizant when I saw it. Therefore I have empirical proof of its existence."

Bob had shaken the cobwebs from his brain, and his eyes had adjusted to the light. He straightened his back and looked at his son. "You said you heard some loud noises, right, Stephen?"

Stephen nodded. "Yeah, Dad."

"Can you tell me what they sounded like?"

"Like crashing noises and heavy things falling. Like wood snapping and glass breaking. And scraping sounds in the driveway. And then I looked out the window and saw the monster."

"Can you describe the monster?"

"It kinda looked like a man, but it wasn't. It was too tall to be a man, and its arms and legs and body were too long. It looked all stretched out. Its skin was all white and dried up like when you see a dead body on TV that's been dead a while, and its body was completely hairless, and it had sharp claws and fangs."

"What about the face?"

"It was pale like the rest of its body and it didn't have any eyes. It just had skin stretched over the empty holes. And it had thin lips and big fangs covered in blood. I know it sounds crazy, but I saw it, I swear."

Bob stood up and placed his hand on Stephen's shoulder. "Well, kiddo," he said, "that sounds like one scary monster. I hope hearing about it doesn't give me nightmares. Tell you what. Since we're both all shook up—as Elvis would say—why don't we go downstairs and have a couple bowls of ice cream, then head back to bed?"

"Two scoops?"

"You bet."

"With chocolate syrup?"

"Is there any other way to eat ice cream? What are we, heathens?" Bob tousled Stephen's hair and the boy giggled.

Bob raised an eyebrow at Sarah. "Would the Lady Sarah care to join us in the parlor for some refreshments?" he said.

Sarah blinked and yawned. "The Lady Sarah will join you for a cup of coffee, Sir Bob of the brew."

"Very good, milady. Then let us adjour—"

A metallic crash clanged outside.

"Trash pandas," Bob said. "Rabies weasels."

"It's the monster," Stephen said, eyes opening wide. "It came back."

"Rocky Raccoon came back."

"Who's that?"

"Before your time. But sounds like old Rocky knocked over the trash can. I better go pick it up and chase him off."

Without changing out of his pajamas or putting on socks, Bob sat on the side of the bed and laced up his boots. He stood up and winked at Sarah. "How do I look, darling?"

"Very dashing, Deputy Rockwell. You're an honor to the uniform. Or to the pajamas, anyway."

Bob narrowed his eyes, puckered his lips, and gave Sarah his best blue steel. She burst into giggles.

"Alright, chuckles," Bob said. "Alright, kiddo. I'll be right back."

"But Dad, aren't you going to take your gun?"

"I may launch a missile at a mouse, but using my service revolver on a trash panda or a rabies weasel would just be overkill." Bob reached into the bedside drawer and pulled out a flashlight. "But," he said, holding the flashlight aloft like a sword, "I shall not venture forth on my quest unarmed. I shall take with me the Holy Hand Flashlight of Antioch."

***

Bob toggled the switch on the side of the Holy Hand Flashlight of Antioch and spotlighted the overturned trash can. "Damn trash pandas," he said and bent to pick up the downed can. When he hefted the handle, something inside the can moved. "Still in there, huh, you little bugger." He dropped the handle. "Nightmare monster, trash panda, rabies weasel, or Houston Astros, you better get the hell out of my trash."

He circled the trash can and trained the flashlight beam inside the silver aluminum cylinder. Vacant green eyes flickered in the glare above a row of needle fangs. The opossum emitted a feral hiss and slingshot past Bob's feet into the woods.

"That's right, rabies weasel," Bob said. "Flee before the might of Deputy Robert of Rockwell and his Holy Hand Flashlight of Antioch."

He picked up the overturned trash can and cast a glance toward the Coe house next door. The front door gaped wide open, yawning in the dark like a fathomless gullet.

Bob shifted his grip on the flashlight and clasped it like a cudgel. He hunkered down and sidled heel-toe to the front stoop of the Coe house. "Hello," he called to the wall of darkness inside. "Mr. Coe? Mrs. Coe? It's Deputy Rockwell from next door. Is everything alright?"

He shined the flashlight inside the house. The beam split the gloom in the foyer and floodlit a zephyr of spiraling dust motes in the narrow corridor leading to the attic.

"Mr. Coe. Mrs. Coe. I'm coming in now," Bob said and crossed the threshold into the house for the first time since Whit Coe skipped town twenty-five years ago.

Despite the dry heat outside, it was cold inside the house. The air smelled like an abattoir, redolent with the scent of blood and butchered flesh. Bob felt a presence in the shadows. Something hiding in the dark. And it was watching him.

He spun and jerked the flashlight beam toward the presence. The beam caromed back into his eyes, blurring his vision with angry flares of light. He shielded his eyes with one hand and staggered a step into the living room.

Eyes still pulsing, he lighthoused the dining room: an oak table, six wicker-backed chairs, a hutch full of Hummels, a mirror on the wall facing him. He fixed the flashlight beam on the mirror. The beam ricocheted off the glass, glaring in Bob's face.

Scared of your own reflection, eh, Bob-O? Must be getting jumpy in your old age.

He started to pick up his right foot and realized it was mired in something wet and viscous. He pried it from the living room carpet with a moist *thwuck.*

Bob turned toward the living room and raised his flashlight. "Jesus," he said as the flashlight slipped from his grip.

The flashlight plunged into a dark crimson pool on the floor.

CHAPTER 5

Whit studied his face in the bathroom mirror. His beard stubble was looking a bit heavy tonight. He contemplated the act of shaving, but the thought alone made him feel exhausted. *Besides, it grows so damn fast anyway. Even when you're dead. Well, it doesn't actually* grow, *but as the corpse loses fluids and begins to desiccate, the skin shrinks, making it appear that the hair, beard, and fingernails have grown. Therefore Uncle Vania is a vampire and must be pinned to his grave with a wooden stake through his heart.*

He shook his head. He rubbed the stubble on the squared-off edge of his jaw with two fingers. "Fucking mirrors," he said and headed for the study. On the way, one of Alice's charcoal sketches caught his eye and he stopped. It was an abstract drawing of a woman, arms and legs crossed and clenched in front of her body as though she were trying to disappear into herself.

He went into his study, turned on the lights, and closed the door. He grabbed the bottle of whisky on his writing desk and poured a couple fingers into a clear crystal glass with a spiral motif. The glass had been a gift from Alice on the last birthday Whit would ever spend with his wife.

He downed the whisky in a single gulp, lapping the liquid fire. Smoky tendrils lingered in his senses.

He leaned his palms against the back of his red wingback chair and stared at his bare writing desk. Three years ago, it would have been cluttered with pens, pencils, notebooks, highlighters, research books—anything Whit deemed useful for writing his next novel.

He looked around the room. Everything made him think of Alice. The whisky glass. The music box ballerina Alice had given him to celebrate the publication of his first short story. A Kodak Carousel slide projector she had given him one Christmas. Relics and ephemera in a museum of memories.

Whit refreshed his whisky, belted it down, poured another. He dimmed the lights, sat in the wingback chair, and turned on the slide projector. The carousel went round and round, showing Whit his happy family memories. These memories were precious to Whit. But they were only memories. Those moments were gone, and he could never get them back.

Then the grief came again, as it always did, riving and unrelenting. Whit clenched his eyes shut and buried them in the palm of his hand. His features contorted. Tears breached through his closed eyelids and rippled down his cheeks. His throat constricted. His heart lashed the walls of his sternum, echoing in his temples. A clutching pain shot through the center of his chest. His breath came in spasmodic gulps. He tasted panic in his throat beside the whisky. He tasted death.

Whit turned off the slide projector and slumped against the backrest, shoulders rising and falling in soft, rhythmic breaths. And somewhere in those broken breaths, he sank into another memory.

***

"Hey, sunshine." Alice stood behind Whit's chair. She wrapped her arms around his neck and buried her face in his hair.

"Hey, babe." Whit placed his hands on top of hers. "What's up?"

"I'm going to the store. Want anything?"

"I'm almost done with the book," Whit said. "Just wait a bit and I'll go."

"Gotta go now," Alice said. "We're almost out of vodka."

Whit raised an eyebrow. "Uh-huh. Sounds like a real emergency."

"Yes," Alice said, nodding and raising her chin.

Whit grabbed the bottle of whisky on his desk. He held it up and sloshed it back and forth. "Have some whisky," he said. "Puts hair on your chest."

"Vodka." This time when Alice lifted her chin, she tilted her head to the side and smiled.

"Fine," Whit said. "Grab me a six pack. And maybe a bottle of champagne to celebrate the new book. Just be careful, okay?"

"Sunshine, we paid a lot of money to live in a safe, boring neighborhood. The liquor store's right down the street, but I'll drive there and park under a light. Everything's gonna be fine, you worrywart." Alice smiled and dipped her shoulder. "But I've got to

15

admit it's sweet the way you look after me. Now finish up that book so we can pop those bubbles."

"Okay," Whit said. "See you soon, babe. I love you."

"I love you too, sunshine," Alice said. She leaned in to kiss Whit goodbye. "More than anything."

***

Whit was in the zone that night. He lost all track of time as he churned through the final pages of his book. This was his favorite part of the writing process. That focused, almost unconscious drive to the finish line.

When he finished the novel, Whit dropped his pen on his desk and slammed a whisky. "Yes," he said, arching his back and stretching like a waking cat. His sense of time and space returned. He had been working a long time, but how long?

He stood up and hustled to the living room. Junior was asleep on the couch in front of the TV, but Alice wasn't in the room with her son. He checked their bedroom. Alice wasn't there either.

He felt his stomach drop as if he had fallen from a great height. A jolt like cold electricity surged up his spine. His head spiraled in a disorienting blur. He ran from the bedroom calling his wife's name. Only silence answered.

Junior staggered toward Whit rubbing his eyes with the heels of his hands. "Dada, what's going on?"

"I don't know. I can't find your mom."

Whit paced, rubbing his hands up and down his face. His breath came in gulping rasps like a fish that had been cast onto dry land to choke and die. "Alice," he said. "Alice! Alice! Oh, fuck, fuck, fuck!"

Whit crumpled forward, hands on his knees, shoulders heaving. He yanked his cell phone out of his front pants pocket and read the clock. "Two thirty-three? Fuck!"

He called Alice's cell. It rang six times, then cut to voicemail. He tried again. Voicemail again. He texted her: "Where are you? Are you ok?" He called again. This time the voicemail didn't kick in. The phone rang on. "Pick up the phone," Whit said. "Please, Alice, pick up the phone." The phone kept ringing.

***

The phone kept ringing. Ringing and buzzing on the desk next to Whit's head. "Ugh," he grunted, wincing. He flailed one arm across his desk like a drunken swimmer, peeled his face off the tabletop, and flung himself upright against the back of his chair. He twisted his body away from the phone, crossed his arms, and extended them toward the wretched device, as though the gesture would ward off the head-killing noise the phone was emitting.

He opened his eyes and looked out the window. The sun wasn't up yet. And the phone was ringing. The phone. Was. Ringing.

He fumbled for the phone and checked the caller ID.

"Too fucking early, Adam," Whit said and set the phone back on the desk. He leaned back in his chair and closed his eyes. The phone stopped ringing. Finally. Then it started ringing again.

"No," Whit said and tried to disappear into the padding of his chair. It didn't work.

Whit picked up the phone. "Goddammit, Adam," he said. "Bro, it's like Amish barn-raising early, so could you just—"

"Whit, oh sweet Lord Jesus!" Adam sputtered on the other end of the line. He was talking too fast and panting. "Oh God, Whit! I got some bad news! Real bad!"

"Adam, calm down," Whit said. "Just tell me what's going on."

"It's Dad and my mom, Whit. They're—" Adam's voice broke. "They're dead, Whit."

Whit sat upright. "What happened?"

"I dunno, Whit. Cops ain't said much yet, but they think some kinda wild animal or somethin got into the house last night and killed 'em."

"What?"

"Yeah, I know. Pretty far out, right?"

"Did the cops tell you why they thought it was a wild animal?"

"They said on account of the cause of death was lactation and extrangulation by fangs and claws like on a wild animal."

"You mean laceration and exsanguination?" Whit said.

"Yeah, that," Adam said.

Claws. Laceration and exsanguination. Last night.

"Adam, sit tight," Whit said. "I'll be there tomorrow." He looked at the purple-gray light spreading across his writing desk. "Or later today, I guess."

"Whit, I—" Adam began, but Whit had already hung up.

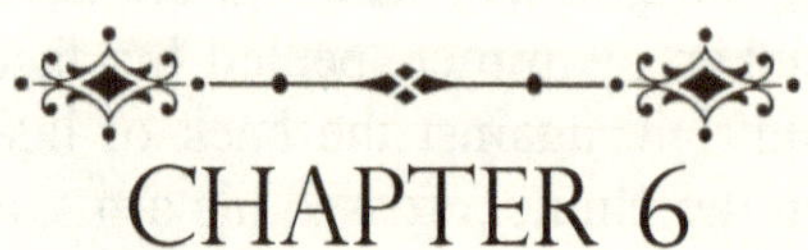

CHAPTER 6

Five days until the end of the world

Whit went to the kitchen and brewed a pot of coffee. He drank it black, cup after cup, and paced between the kitchen and the living room. He watched the shafts of sunlight slanting through the living room window. The light shifted from a gray-purple mist to a red-orange glow to the piercing headache-yellow of early morning.

He didn't want to wake Junior too early, so he turned the TV on low while he packed a duffel bag and fetched the cat carrier from the closet beside the front door. Then he continued to pace and sip black coffee until Junior came shuffling downstairs.

Junior looked at the duffel bag. "Dada, what's going on?" he said, rubbing his right eye with his palm.

"My dad and his wife died last night, so we've gotta go to the town where I grew up and take care of some things. It shouldn't take more than a couple of days. But we should probably head out this morning so we can get it over with."

"Oh," Junior said. "I'm sorry, Dada. Are you okay?"

Whit shrugged. "Yeah, I'm fine. Just gotta tie up some loose ends. It's a pain in the ass, but it'll be alright. Tell ya what, buddy, we'll treat it like a summer vacation. A lame-ass, boring summer vacation, but what the hell?"

"Sounds great," Junior said.

"Oh, good," Whit said. "You're finally getting the hang of sarcasm."

"Ha, ha."

"Exactly."

Whit and Junior laughed.

"Alright, buddy," Whit said and unhooked a cast-iron skillet from the kitchen pot rack. "I'll make some breakfast, then you can pack a bag. We'll drop off Goblin at the kitty hotel and grab some snacks on the way. Then we'll check into the Rockwell Town and Country Inn as soon as we get into town."

"Do they have a pool?" Junior said.

"Yep. And a swim-up tiki bar."

"Cool. I'll pack my swim trunks."

"For the tiki bar?"

"No, Dada," Junior said.

After Junior had crammed his gob with Eggos, scrambled eggs, and bacon, he stuffed some clothes and a toothbrush into his *Star Wars* BB-8 backpack. Little lights on the backpack blinked every time Junior shoved a new item into the pouch.

Whit put on a well-worn black San Diego Padres hat and pulled the brim low over his eyes. "Junior," he said, "there's gonna be a lot of sun on the drive. Put on your dickfish hat."

"Stop calling it a dickfish," Junior said. "It's an axolotl. It's an endangered Mexican salamander that never gets old."

"Looks like a dickfish. That joke never gets old."

Junior shook his head, but he was smiling.

"Okay, buddy," Whit said. "You ready?"

"I guess."

"Alright, let's go."

Whit slung his duffel bag over his shoulder. He opened the front door, but not into the morning glare. He opened the door into the darkness of that horrible night. Two policemen stood on the front porch. The lights of their squad car flickered red and blue against the black. The policemen removed their hats. "Mr. Coe?" one of them said.

Whit snapped back to the present. He stepped into a crystalline morning.

Junior lugged his backpack and the cat carrier to a black Audi in the driveway. Alice's Audi.

Whit turned back and stared into the half-shade of his empty house. He closed the door and locked the deadbolt.

Whit and Junior stowed their bags in the trunk and set the cat carrier in the back seat. The chonky gray cat crouched low, flattened her ears, and tucked her head into her fubsy body.

Junior turned around in his seat. "Sorry, Goblin," he said. "It'll be okay. It's just for a couple of days."

Whit turned the ignition. "Dead Man's Party" by Oingo Boingo blasted through the speakers.

"'Dead Man's Party!'" Junior shouted. "Turn it up, Dada!"

"Yeah, nothing ominous about that or anything." Whit boosted the volume. "You know, the first concert I ever went to was Oingo Boingo. My dad took me."

"I thought you didn't get along."

"We didn't. Especially after—We got along less and less over the years and eventually we had a big fight and stopped talking altogether. I think that was easier for both of us. Family's complicated. It's not all good memories or all bad memories. But memories have weight. And when it came to me and my dad, that weight tipped too far to the bad side. What matters most with family is love and memory. How much you love each other and how strong the good memories are. Now for me, the greatest love and the best memories of my life were with you and your mom. Better than anything I ever shared with anyone else. Better than anything I could've imagined. I didn't grow up in the kind of family your mom and I made for you. Most of my memories growing up weren't so good. But Oingo Boingo was a good memory. That make sense, buddy?"

"I think so," Junior said.

***

Whit and Junior dropped Goblin off at the kitty hotel and stocked up on snacks and soda. And booze. Whit was going to need a lot of booze.

Thirteen punk and new wave hits later, Whit felt a lurch in his stomach. He and Junior had entered the pull of the suburban gravity well known as Rockwell, California. In a few exits, they would spiral down its event horizon.

"Hey, Dada," Junior said, grinning. "What do you call bread that doesn't exist?"

"Bread that doesn't exist… I don't know, what?"

"Naan bread." Junior giggled. "Get it?"

"Oh, an existentialist pun this time. That'll get you some bonus points, although Dr. Samuel Johnson did say that puns were the lowest form of comedy."

"Who's Dr. Samuel Johnson?"

"Some guy who hated puns."

Whit checked the exit signs dangling over the highway until he spotted a Fenway-Park-green sign that read, 'ROCKWELL 3RD AVE NEXT RIGHT.'

Four crows perched on top of the sign.

Whit tightened his grip on the steering wheel. He took the exit.

On the radio, "It's the End of the World as We Know It (and I Feel Fine)" by R.E.M. kicked in.

CHAPTER 7

Whit peeled off the interstate and rolled into Rockwell for the first time in over twenty-five years.

Rockwell was a small-time, middle-class double-Dubuque of a burgh with pretensions toward affluence. Its indigenous inhabitants had abandoned the land in the early nineteenth century for unknown reasons. Whit thought they'd had the right idea. But at least Rockwell had a leg up on its neighboring town Isabella Creek. In 'the Crick' it was easier to find a bag of meth or a bottle of Oxy than a mouth with a full set of teeth.

As Whit cruised down Third Avenue, he watched the bustle of Rockwell's main drag. He barely recognized it. Almost all the old mom-and-pop businesses were gone. In their place stood a fungible row of craft breweries, gastropubs, and other hipster haunts. These invading eateries were either painted a blinding white like a dentist's office in Heaven or were decked in dark wood tones amidst a labyrinth of nonfunctional exposed brass pipes and rails. The clientele of these new businesses sported skinny jeans and overgroomed beards. All the street parking was metered now.

Gentrification. It didn't represent the banality of evil. It represented the evil of banality.

Whit hung a left on Camino del Rio and slowed the car as he approached the site of the Rockwell Town and Country Inn. A craft brewhouse and gastropub stood on the inn's grave.

"Well, shit," Whit said. "So much for that tiki bar."

CHAPTER 8

Whit curbed the car in front of his father's house. "Jesus," Whit and Junior said in unison.

The door of Whit's childhood home yawned open, yellow crime scene tape stretched across its threshold. A forensics investigator stood on the lawn talking to two cops—one short and wiry, the other tall and husky. Even twenty-five years on, Whit recognized the two men.

Three squad cars and a forensics van were parked in the gravel drive between Whit's dad's place and the Rockwell house next door. Bob and Sarah Rockwell stood on the edge of their lawn next to a boy about Junior's age, while Adam yammered and twitched in front of the group in a rhythm known only to junkies or ex-junkies who had partied so long that the junk had hardwired itself into their DNA.

"There's no place like home," Whit said. "Come on, Junior. Let's click our heels." They got out of the car and headed up the drive.

Bob was the first to see them. "Whitman F. Coe," he said, sauntering out to meet Whit and Junior. A wide smile spread across his face. He splayed his hands like a Southern preacher.

"Hey, Bob-O," Whit said.

Junior watched as the woman, the boy, and the twitchy man spun to look his way. He froze when the twitchy man turned around. The man had no face. Just leathery white skin stretched over gnarled bones and hollow eye sockets.

Junior closed his eyes and counted to five. He opened his eyes. The empty face was gone. True, there was still an emptiness in the twitchy man's face. But it was a normal emptiness. A human emptiness. Two gray-blue eyes, a nose, a mouth. Dusty orange hair and freckles.

Whit and Bob shook hands and half-hugged.

"Whitman F. Coe," Bob said again. "The prodigal has returned. While I do regret the circumstances of that return, I'm still damn glad to see you again, old buddy."

"Glad to see you too, Bob."

"Hey, bro," Adam said. He bounded forward and hugged Whit. "Man, thank Jesus you're here. Everything's all jacked up. You look good. Got some gray hairs in your beard, though. Hey, is that Junior?"

"No, that's just some random kid I hire for public appearances."

"Oh."

"Of course that's Junior. Junior, this is your Uncle Adam."

"What's up, little man?" Adam said.

"Hi," Junior said.

"Handsome kid," Adam said to Whit. "Looks just like you in the old pitchers from when you was that age."

"Well, Whitman," Sarah said. "You gonna give me a hug or not?"

"Have you ever known me to refuse a hug from a beautiful woman?"

"Old charmer," Sarah said.

Whit bent down to hug Sarah.

"Whit, I'm sorry for everything you've been going through," Sarah said. "If there's anything Bob and I can do, just let us know."

"Thanks, Sarah." Whit let go of Sarah and put an arm around Junior's shoulder.

"Junior, you've already met your Uncle Adam. This is Bob and Sarah. We were all friends since we were younger than you."

"Really?" Junior said.

"Yep. Bob and I grew up right next door to each other. Bob grew up in that house." Whit pointed at Bob and Sarah's two-story-Cape-Cod-gray craftsman. "And I grew up over there." He flicked his head toward his dad's house but didn't look at it.

"And this young gentleman," Whit gestured at Stephen, "must be the heir to the Rockwell crown."

"No," Sarah said. "He's just some random kid we hire for public appearances." She smiled at the corners of her mouth. "Whit, this is our boy Stephen."

"Nice to meet you, Stephen," Whit said. "This is my son Junior."

"Hi, Junior," Stephen said. "Cool hat. Do you like axolotls? Of course you like axolotls. I mean you have an axolotl on your hat. Hey, do you like *Minecraft*?"

"Yeah," Junior said. "It's super fun."

"I know." Stephen smiled. "Hey, I have a rare green *Minecraft* axolotl plush in my room. You wanna see it?"

"Sure," Junior said. He looked up at Whit. "Can I, Dada?"

"That's fine with me," Whit said. "As long as it's okay with Stephen's parents."

"I think that's a great idea," Sarah said. "You boys have fun."

"Not too long, though, Junior," Whit said. "We still need to find a hotel before it gets dark."

"Oh, hush," Sarah said. "You and Junior can stay with us while you're in town. It'd be downright inhospitable if we let you boys stay in some rat-trap motel eating fast-food takeout. Besides, I think it might do Bob and Stephen some good. They don't have any other boys their own age to play with."

Junior bounced up and down. "Can we, Dada?"

"Yeah," Bob said, bouncing along with Junior. "Can you, Dada?"

"You and Junior can stay at my place," Adam said. "I got three dogs and a tank full of African sickletts, and there's a buncha farrel cats that run around the yard. You could prob'ly catch one for Junior and take it home."

Whit consulted the Adamspeak-to-English translator app in his head. Adam had three mangy dogs, a tank of African cichlids, and a pack of feral cats in his yard. And the cats were up for grabs. Awesome.

"Then it's decided," Sarah said. "Stephen, help Junior get settled in your room. Bob, you can get Whit set up in the guest room when you're done here. I'll bring out the air mattress for Junior."

"Oh, baby," Bob said. "I get all tingly when you take charge like that."

"I know you do," Sarah said, glancing over her shoulder at Bob as she went up the walk to the house.

"Alright, Junior," Whit said. He handed Junior the keys to the Audi. "Get your backpack out of the car and follow Stephen to his room."

"Okay. Thanks, Dada."

Junior and Stephen shot for the Audi.

"And give me the keys back on your way inside," Whit called after Junior. "Don't forget and lock them in the trunk like that one time."

Junior popped the trunk, slung on his backpack, and clunked the lid shut. He and Stephen scampered across the lawn toward the house. He tossed the car keys underhand to Whit as he ran past. They landed in the grass three feet short of Whit's shoes.

Whit slumped his shoulders and stared at the car keys. "Really?" he said and bent down to pick up the keys.

The boys raced up the walk and hurdled the porch steps.

"Hey, Stephen!" Bob shouted at his son's back. "Don't run in the house!" But the boys were already inside, the front door clapping behind them. Bob raised his hand above his head and let it fall to his side in the international semiotic dad code for never mind. This is futile. Fuck it.

***

Stephen's room was neat. Tidy. Almost German in its order and precision. His bookshelves were organized by genre—one shelf for science, one for science fiction, another for fantasy—and sorted alphabetically by author. His Einstein, *Godzilla*, and *Star Wars* posters were spaced three inches apart on the wall and lined up ruler-straight at the tops. On the plain of a crisp blue bedspread, assorted plushies stood in Prussian battle ranks, poised to invade Belgium and drive the Schlieffen line to Paris. The lone hint of disorder was a pile of Godzilla and dinosaur action figures strewn across a patch of carpet in the far corner. A solitary independent Bohemian principality ruled by sovereign reptiles.

Stephen plucked one of the plushy troops from its place in the battle formation. "Here's the rare green *Minecraft* axolotl," he said, handing the stuffed animal to Junior.

"Hey, buddy," Junior said to the axolotl and stroked its head. He gave the room a once-over. "Cool bedroom," he said. "Hey!" He pointed at one of Stephen's *Godzilla* posters. "*Godzilla: King of the Monsters*! That's my favorite!"

"Mine too," Stephen said. "But the original *Godzilla* is pretty classic."

"Yeah. And *Godzilla vs. Destroyah*."

"That one's really good too. But sad."

"Poor Godzooky," Junior said. "Hey!" He reached for his backpack. "I brought a *Godzilla vs. Kong* movie book with me. Wanna see it?"

"Does Godzilla have nuclear morning breath?"

Junior unzipped his backpack and pulled out the Godzilla book. He handed it to Stephen.

Stephen looked at the cover. "Cool," he said. "It's an art book."

26

"It's got lots of art for battle sequences, and there's character profiles for the cast."

"Sweet," Stephen said, leafing through the pages. "Now that's a good battle shot." He tapped a picture of Godzilla and Kong squaring off on an aircraft carrier.

"Hey, Stephen," Junior said. "Can I ask you a weird question?"

"How weird on a scale of one to ten?"

"Maybe like a seven."

"So pretty weird, but not super weird."

"I guess," Junior said.

"Okay," Stephen said. "Shoot."

"Have we ever met before?"

"I don't think so. Why?"

"You just seem really familiar to me. Like I've seen you someplace before. But it's all foggy."

"Huh," Stephen said. "Have you ever been to Rockwell before?"

"No."

"And you live in San Vaes, right?"

"Yeah."

"So I've only been to San Vaes once when my parents took me to the zoo. Have you ever been to the zoo there?"

"Yeah, my dada takes me all the time."

"In that case it's possible, however unlikely, that you actually did see me on the day I was there. It's also possible that I just happen to look like someone you've met before." Stephen scratched his temple. "Or you could have temporal lobe epilepsy."

CHAPTER 9

Forensics packed the last cardboard boxes from the Coe scene into the back of a van and clanged the sliding door shut. One of the investigators leaned in, said something to the two cops, and handed a set of keys to the husky blond one. The cop slipped the keys into his front shirt pocket.

The forensics investigators piled into the van and drove away.

The cops turned and headed toward their squad cars, the smaller one favoring the leg he had shattered twenty-five years ago. It dragged behind him as he walked across the drive, scraping dirt and kicking gravel.

The husky blond cop hooked his thumbs in his belt loops and swaggered wide-legged like a John Wayne caricature. He had a high-and-tight haircut, a walrus mustache, ruddy skin, and a beer belly that drooped over his belt buckle. But nobody ever noticed these features. The only thing people noticed was the eye. It was white and milky, covered in a pale film. Beside the dead eye, a faded scar ran down his cheekbone in mottled tendrils.

Both men had earned their scars on the same night.

When the cops saw Whit standing with Bob and Adam, they pulled up like an invisible choke chain had yanked them back in place. The smaller man's mouth drooped open, then rose in an easy grin. The husky man recoiled and dropped his eyes to the ground.

The smaller man hobbled forward.

"Deputy Ross," the husky man said. "Hold up. I wanna have a little powwow with you and Deputy Rockwell."

"Yes, Chip," Deputy Ross said.

Chip bowed up on Deputy Ross and glared down his nose at the smaller man.

Deputy Ross fidgeted with his fingernails. "I mean yes, Sheriff Gustafsson," he said.

"Now that's better. Deputy Dave." Sheriff Gustafsson wedged two fingers between his lips and whistled. "Deputy Rockwell!" He waved Bob over. "Let's huddle up."

"Go, team," Bob said to Whit out of the corner of his mouth and crossed the drive to join Chip and Dave.

Chip shuffled from one foot to the other, widened his stance, and dug his thumbs deeper into his belt loops. "Okay, boys," he said. "Here's what we got. Deputy Rockwell, you were first on scene, so you know how fucktangular shit is in there. Me and Deputy Ross just got done talking to forensics. They won't know for sure until the coroner gets done with his exam, but they think that sometime late last night a wild animal entered the premises and fatally mauled Mr. and Mrs. Coe. They don't know what kind of animal yet, but they said it could be a bear or a mountain lion based on the tooth and claw marks on the vics. The ME's calling in some kinda animal expert in the morning, and hopefully they'll have a report for us sometime tomorrow afternoon. If it was an animal attack, we turn the file over to wildlife and our work is done. But for the time being, this is an open police case. Now I know you boys' old butt buddy is back in town and it's his old man on the slab, but do not fuckin inseminate any official police information to a civilian under any circumstances. You boys got me?"

"I think you mean disseminate, Chief," Deputy Ross said.

"Don't tell me what I fuckin mean, Dave. I know what I mean, shitbird. Now let's try this again. Do. You. Boys. Got me?"

"Yes, Chief," Bob and Dave said.

"Good," Chip said. "Now I'm gonna go grab a Whopper, take a big dump, and head back to the station. Dave, if you ain't there by the time I get back, you're off this case and on meter-maid duty for two weeks. Bob, stay home and see if you can get somethin more reliable from your kid's witness statement than 'a fuckin monster ate the neighbors.' And here." Chip reached into his shirt pocket and passed Bob the set of keys forensics had given him. "These are the keys to the Coe premises. Give them to Mr. and Mrs. Coe's next of kin. Forensics is done with the scene."

"Yes, Chief," Bob said.

"Now if you boys'll excuse me," Chip said, "I got a hot date with a Burger King bathroom." He slid into his squad car, pulled out of the drive, and headed for his aforementioned assignation.

"Whit Coe," Dave said, broad smile returning as he skipped, stiff-legged, to greet his old friend. He shook Whit's hand and clapped him on the shoulder. "Damn, it's good to see you again, Whit. I'm sorry—I mean I know you're here because of your dad and all, but… I just mean…" Dave lifted his shoulders and waggled his head back and forth. "Damn it's good to see you again, Whit."

The corner of Whit's mouth curled in a lopsided grin. "You too, Dave," he said and swatted Dave on the arm.

"Whit," Bob said, holding up the keys to Whit's dad's house. "Forensics is done with the house. It's all yours and Adam's now."

"Okay," Whit said, taking the keys. "Adam. It's all yours." He dangled the keys in front of Adam.

"What do you mean?" Adam said.

"The house," Whit said. "It belongs to you now."

"You mean you don't wanna move in or sell it or nothin?"

"Nah, I'm good. I just want to take some of my mom's and my sister's stuff if it's still there."

"Alight, then. Thanks, bro." Adam took the keys.

Whit nodded. "So," he said, "you want to start sorting shit at the house tomorrow? You don't have to if you're not feeling up to it yet. I can get started on my own."

"Naw, Whit. It's sad. I seen a lot of death. I lost a lot of friends. Now I lost my mom, and we lost our dad. But we'll see our loved ones again after we fulfill God's destiny. We just gotta take care of business. I'll swing by in the mornin and we'll knock it out, bro."

"Alright," Whit said. "In that case, you better head home and get some rest. I'll see you in the morning. Just not too early."

"So, like six am?"

"Fuck you."

Adam laughed and climbed into his beat-up gravestone-gray Chevy pickup. He waved and backed down the drive, tires crunching over loose gravel.

"I should head out too," Dave said. "I gotta get back to the station before Chip gets back from taking a shit."

"Okay," Whit said.

"But, hey," Dave said. "Let's get a drink while you're in town."

"Sounds good. I'm staying with Bob and Sarah, so you know where to find me."

"Cool. Seeya soon, then, Whit. Seeya tomorrow, Bob."

Dave took a right on Cedar. Adam took a left. Whit watched the paint-splattered bumper of Adam's truck as it faded down the road.

"He staying out of trouble?" Whit said to Bob.

"Well, he hasn't been in one of my cells in a long time. Most of his old junky pals are either dead or in Corcoran, so they can't drag him down into their shit anymore. I think he's off the meth and the Oxy. Just smokes a lot of weed from what I hear. And that's legal now. But, you know, once a junky…"

"Yeah, I know. Once you've got that hungry ghost on your back, it'll ride you into the grave."

CHAPTER 10

"So," Whit said, leaning back in his chair. He turned to Junior. "This was a long time before you were born, so bear that in mind." He took a pull of beer from a brown bottle and looked across the dinner table at Bob and Sarah. "Anyway, Alice decides she wants to go barhopping before we hit the grocery store. Just completely out of left field. We go to three or four bars, and we're planning on hitting one more. This filthy little tetanus trap on Fifth called Mumu's. But on the way, Alice sees a playground and decides we're gonna go play on the equipment."

"Oh, no." Sarah turned her head away and winced.

"Oh, yes," Whit said.

Bob and the boys leaned forward in their seats.

"So we stop at the playground," Whit said, "and I run up this slide, but there's a rail blocking the entrance, so I can't get to the top. I turn to go back down and I slip on a wet patch. My feet slide right out from underneath me and I go straight down on my left arm. Hard." He slapped the long white scar on his forearm.

"By the way," Whit splayed his hands, palms out, "this was a moisture-related accident, not an alcohol-related accident. Just for the record."

"Sure," Bob said. "Just for the record."

"Thank you, Officer," Whit said. "Anyway, I get up and my arm is buzzing with pain all the way up and down. So I take off my hoodie to get a look at my arm, and it's split wide open. The sharp part of the bone must've cut all the way through the skin because everything that's supposed to be on the inside is hanging on the outside. And there's this stringy white tissue just dangling—"

Sarah squeezed her eyes shut and pinched her face like she'd just sucked on a lemon. She shook her head back and forth and waved her hands in front of her face. "Oh, no no no no no," she said.

"You want me to stop?" Whit said. He tossed up his hands and grinned.

"No!" Bob and the boys shouted.

"God, no," Sarah said. "This is too damn good." She took a sip of beer. "Go on." She twirled her index finger.

Whit rubbed the stubble on his chin and looked up at the dining room chandelier. "Now where was I?" he said. "Ah, yes. The juicy bits, as Alice called them. The juicy bits are dangling out of my arm and I'm bleeding like a stuck pig. Now we were pretty poor back then and we didn't have health insurance, so going to a hospital was out of the question. So with my arm in this… state, I manage to drive to a Rite Aid. Alice gets out of the car and runs into the store. She runs back out a few minutes later with a bag of supplies. She sprays the wound with this antiseptic that might as well have been lighter fluid, butterfly tapes the skin back together—well, more or less—, then wraps my arm up in gauze.

"Now about this time, normal people would have thrown in the towel and gone home. But then again, normal people don't tend to find themselves bleeding out in a Rite Aid parking lot on a casual night out. And besides, Alice and I were on an adventure and we still had two more stops to make: a grubby little dive bar and a grocery store."

"You didn't," Sarah said.

"Of course he did," Bob said, raising his beer. "He's Whitman fucking Coe." Bob slapped a hand over his mouth. "Sorry, kids."

The boys looked at each other and giggled.

"I don't think they mind," Sarah said.

"That's okay, Bob," Whit said. "That's what the 'F' in Whitman F. Coe stands for. It's on my birth certificate."

Sarah and Bob laughed along with the boys, who were still giggling at Bob's spontaneous outburst of profanity.

"But yes," Whit said. "Yes, we did. We went into that dirty little dive bar—and it really is a wonder I didn't get tetanus—and at some point Alice put on my hoodie, but my blood had soaked all the way through the sleeve. And while we're waiting for our drinks, Alice leans up against the bar. So when she gets her drink and stands up, there's this big wet blood smear on the bar. But it's so dark in there, and everybody's so wasted that nobody notices.

"So we get our drinks and go out on the patio for a smoke, and some frat boys notice my bloody bandage and ask me about it. I tell them what happened, and they think it's such a cool story they buy us a round of drinks. So Alice and I ended the night smoking and drinking with a bunch of frat boys. Then we hit the grocery store and headed home. Adventure accomplished."

Whit raised his forearm and flashed the craggy scar under the light of the dining room chandelier. "And that's the story of how I got this scar," he said.

"Whoa," Stephen said. "That's badass."

"Yes, thank you, Whitman, for that lovely dinner-table tale," Sarah said.

"Hey, you asked." Whit grinned and took a swig of beer. He ran a finger along the edges of his scar. "Huh," he said. "Looks like it's healing."

"That's the good thing about scars," Sarah said. "They heal."

"Only if the wound closes," Whit said.

Junior swallowed a mouthful of mashed potatoes and looked up at Whit. "You and Mommy used to smoke?" he said.

"Yes, Junior," Whit said. "I'm glad you took some edification from that story."

CHAPTER 11

"**G**odzilla: King of the Monsters or classic Godzilla?" Stephen said.

Junior reclined on the air mattress in Stephen's room and smooshed a handful of Cheesy Poofs into his mouth. "I think," he said, crunching a mouthful of enriched orange cornmeal, "King of the Monsters because he's bigger and his atomic breath is stronger."

"Yeah, I think you're right," Stephen said.

Junior shook the bag of Cheesy Poofs at Stephen. Stephen leaned forward in his desk chair and scooped up an atomic-orange handful.

"Okay, uhh…" Junior searched his internal Godzilla character database for potential monster matchups. "I know, Godzilla 2021 or the original Mechagodzilla?"

"Hmm." Stephen rubbed his temple. "Well, Mechagodzilla is really powerful. But I think the new characters are stronger than the old ones, so Godzilla 2021."

"Uh-huh," Junior grunted through another mouthful of Cheesy Poofs.

Three taps pattered on the bedroom door.

"Candygram for Mongo," Whit's voice came from the other side of the door.

"Come in," Stephen said.

Whit opened the door and stood under the lintel.

"Who's Mongo?" Junior said.

"Nobody," Whit said. "It's from an old movie."

"What's a Candygram?" Stephen said.

"Well, back in the old days, sometimes people would send candy to a friend or a loved one, and they'd send a telegram—like a little note—with the candy."

"Oh," Stephen said. "Weird."

"Kinda, yeah," Whit said. "Anyway, I just wanted to say goodnight. Junior, do you have everything you need?"

"I think so, Dada."

"Okay, then. Goodnight, boys."

"Goodnight, Mr. Coe," Stephen said.

"Goodnight, Dada," Junior said. "I love ya."

Whit smiled. "I love you too, buddy. Sleep tight."

Whit closed the door and dogtrotted downstairs to the kitchen. He popped the tops off three bottles of beer and rejoined Bob and Sarah on the front porch. They were sitting on the porch swing, still holding hands like they had when they were high school sweethearts.

Whit held out two beers. "Your soldiers look depleted," he said. "Here's some reinforcements."

Bob swished the dregs at the bottom of his beer bottle. "Good man," he said. "Just in time." He and Sarah drained their old beers and grabbed the new bottles.

Whit stretched his back and ambled to the porch rail. He stared into the night. Country night, black and impenetrable. "I'd forgotten how quiet it was out here," he said. "Except for that one fucking cricket over there. That loud bastard's gonna keep me up all night. Doesn't it keep you guys up?"

"Well, shit," Bob said. "I hadn't noticed it before, but now it will. Thanks, asshole."

"Any time," Whit said, raising his beer.

Sarah, Bob, and Whit chuckled.

Sarah took a long pull on her beer bottle. "Speaking of sleep," she said, standing up, "I should start my bedtime routine. My *Father Brown* mystery novel's starting to pick up."

"You mean you're not reading Whitman F. Coe tonight?" Whit said.

"We've read every Whitman F. Coe novel and loved them all. I think Bob's read most of them at least three times. Which reminds me, you need to sign some of our copies while you're here."

"Sure. It'd be my pleasure."

"Good. They'll fetch more on eBay," Sarah said.

"Oh yeah," Whit said. "You should be able to get at least half the original cover price."

"Oh good, then. A solid return on my investment. Anyway, I'm heading up. It's wonderful seeing you again, Whit." Sarah gave Whit a quick hug, then leaned down and kissed Bob.

"I'll be up soon," Bob said. "Just one more beer."

"Uh-huh," Sarah said and cocked her head. "Take your time. You boys get caught up. Get in some man time." She lowered her brow and pounded her sternum with her fist.

"Ungh, ungha," Bob grunted and repeated his wife's gesture. "Thanks, babe. Seeya in a bit."

"Good night, Sarah," Whit said. "Thanks for everything."

"Of course, Whit," Sarah said. She patted Bob on the shoulder and stepped into the house.

The men sipped their beers in silence for a while, then Bob hopped off the porch swing and stood next to Whit. He raised his beer bottle. "Cheers, old buddy," he said. "It's great having you back."

"Cheers, Bob-O."

They clinked their bottles and swigged.

"Man," Bob said. "Feels just like old times."

"Yeah," Whit said. "I mean if you can forget about the grisly maulings and the suburban sprawl. At least the developers haven't taken out all the trees yet." He gestured with his beer toward the tree line behind the house.

"Nope," Bob said. "Not yet. My old man used to say those trees were like hairs on a mean ol' giant's ass. You can try to trim 'em and tame 'em, but they're just too damn thick and rough to ever clear out."

Whit and Bob chuckled again.

"Yeah," Bob said, "some things about this town never change. But then again…"

"What?"

"Something just feels different these days. I'm not talking about gentrification or nostalgia for the good old days. It's something else."

"Like what? Werewolves? A new Church of Scientology?"

"More like the Pied Piper," Bob said.

"You mean you've got a diddler with a flute running around town?" Whit said.

"I don't think the Pied Piper was a—never mind. That's not the point. The point is over the last three years there's been a string of missing persons cases." Bob darted his eyes to the side and leaned closer to Whit. "And there's a pattern."

"What kind of pattern?"

"All the missing persons are male," Bob said. "All in their late teens to mid-twenties. And there's a cycle to the disappearances." He took another pull on his beer. "June thirteenth, almost exactly three years ago, the first kid, Jimmie Macomber, age twenty-two, disappears without a trace. He doesn't say goodbye to his family or friends. Nobody sees him leave town. He doesn't even leave a note behind or pack a bag of clothes. He's just gone. Poof!" Bob snapped his fingers. "Nobody in town ever hears from him again, not even his old man. June seventeenth, same thing happens again. Paul Harris, age twenty-one, vanishes into thin air. Doesn't leave a note. Doesn't tell anybody he's leaving. Doesn't pack a bag. Nothing. June twentieth, Chuck Cunningham, age twenty-three, disappears just like the others. Then there's not another case until this past December thirteenth, when Patrick O'Hearn, age twenty-six, goes missing. Again, doesn't say goodbye to anyone, doesn't take anything with him, doesn't leave a note. Nobody sees him leaving town, nobody in town ever hears from him again. December seventeenth, Marko Thompson, age eighteen, pulls a Houdini. Followed once again on the twentieth by James Novak, age twenty-seven." Bob raised his finger. "Now from then on, three kids from Rockwell have gone missing every month. One on the thirteenth, one on the seventeenth, and one on the twentieth."

"So the first kid," Whit said. "Jimmie Macomber. You said he went missing on the thirteenth of June, three years ago, right?"

"Right," Bob said.

"Bob, the Macomber kid went missing the day before Alice's death. My old man and Barbara," he nodded toward his dad's house, "were killed exactly three years after Alice. To the day."

"Fuck me," Bob said.

"And," Whit said, "San Vaes Forensics determined that Alice's cause of death was a single claw slash to the jugular. But they couldn't match the claw mark to any known species of animal."

"The claw marks. That's why you're here, isn't it?"

"Yep." Whit took a long drag from his beer bottle. He needed whisky.

"So what does it all mean?" Bob said.

"I don't know," Whit said. "You wanna help me find out? I'm sure Chip told you not to talk to me about the case, so I understand if—"

"Fuck Chip," Bob said. "I'm with you, old buddy."

"Thanks, pal," Whit said. "I appreciate ya."

Bob slapped Whit on the back and said, "Okay, let's solve this thing, brother." He paused a beat, then said, "Whit, I'm sorry to ask, but what else can you tell me about what happened to Alice?"

"Not much. Like I said, forensics determined the COD was a single claw mark from an animal but couldn't match it to any known species. I hired some outside forensics experts, but they couldn't get a match either. No reliable witnesses. All San Vaes PD could scrounge up was a guy who was working at the flower shop across the street from the liquor store where it happened. But what the guy said was ten kinds of crazy, so…"

"Crazy how? What'd he say?"

"He said he saw a monster climbing over the wall in the liquor store parking lot."

"A monster?"

"Yup," Whit said. "A tall white shadow monster with no eyes."

"Jesus," Bob said. "It's the monster from Stephen's nightmare. It's real."

CHAPTER 12

Whit didn't sleep that night. He didn't dream. Again. For a while, he sat beneath the glow of the desk lamp in the guest room and read *Kafka on the Shore* by Haruki Murakami, periodically taking a swig from a bottle of Bushmills. After a while, his eyes grew too tired to read, but he didn't lie down and close them.

He sat on the edge of the bed, took another hit of whisky, and thought about Alice. Whit still talked to her every night, even though he knew she couldn't hear him.

"Alice," he said. "I miss you. I wish you were here. I wish a lot of things."

He stood up, took another pull on the whisky bottle, and peeled back the window curtains. Almost dawn.

Whit glared at his father's house.

He crept out the door, crossed the lawn, and climbed the porch steps of his childhood home. He hesitated on the top step, staring at the polished brass doorknob. He turned it.

The living room lay in coal-gray shadow. And in that shadow, a presence waited for Whit. It had always been waiting for him. Its unseen eyes watched as he entered the house.

Whit reached in the dark for the light switch. The bulb clicked to life.

The living room looked like a butcher row set in a doll house. The cozy middle-class furniture had been smashed and slashed to pieces. Whit's father's reclining chair had been overturned and split in two. Craggy claw marks ran across the wooden frame of the chair back. Stuffing protruded from the cushions and spread onto the floor like viscera. A deep black-red spray spattered the room like a grotesque Jackson Pollock painting. The red covered the furniture, the floors, the walls, the coffee table.

Whit felt the shadow presence in the darkness behind him. He spiraled his body and glanced over his shoulder into the mirror on the dining room wall. Something in the mirror whispered to him. A dark energy pulled his mind into the depths of the glass.

The glass flashed white, and the mirror showed Whit the living room as it had been when he was a child. It showed him a forgotten memory. Whit and his twin sister Astrid were four years old. They stood side-by-side, clutching their new matching teddy bears. The children's heads were bowed and tears ran down their cheeks. Tears ran down Mommy's cheeks too. Daddy was angry again.

"I told you not to buy any more toys!" Daddy shouted at Mommy. "We can't afford it!"

"Can't afford it?" Mommy said. "They're children, Allan. Our children. And you just went yachting with your yuppie college buddies last weekend. Can we afford that?"

"Fuck you! I'm outta here, you ball-breaking bitch!" Daddy snatched his car keys off the coffee table, slammed the front door, and sped away in his sports car.

Mommy doubled over and sobbed. Whit and Astrid wrapped their arms around her.

"It's okay, Mommy," Whit said.

The looking glass flashed white again, and the memory was gone. The mirror reflected the living room as it was now: a tableau of blood and gore and violent death.

Whit looked at the mess and put his hands on his hips. "Fuuuck," he said. He snapped his fingers. "Cleaning supplies."

Whit ducked into the kitchen, yanked open the cupboard beneath the sink, and pulled out a bottle of bleach. He set the bottle down at the edge of the living room where the blood spatter stopped, then headed down the claustrophobic hallway to the garage.

Hungry shadows enveloped the corridor, devouring the path ahead of Whit. As he wandered further into the corridor, the shadows draped deeper, inching closer along the walls. He felt the grip of the passageway tightening. Then a dizzying wave of vertigo as the hallway lurched and the path ahead expanded, stretching into the eternal darkness of the void. He felt the presence again. Heard its whispering drone drowning out the world.

Whit snapped back from the fog and realized he had stopped walking toward the garage. He was standing directly below the attic, eyes glassy and fixed on the trapdoor. He shook his head and walked on.

He opened the garage door, punched on the muddy tobacco-yellow light, and heaped his arms full of cleaning supplies: toolbox, two-gallon paint bucket with mesh screen and roller, two-gallon can of primer, TSP, box-cutter, a roll of plastic sheeting, and a paint-specked transistor radio. He set the supplies next to the bottle of bleach and surveyed his serial-killer starter kit. "Beer," he said.

Whit straightened his back, shot a glance at the mirror, and left the house. Behind the glass, burning black eyes watched him leave.

CHAPTER 13

Four days until the end of the world

Junior and Stephen huddled together in the kitchen studying two parallel rows of pancakes cooking on a cast-iron griddle.

"Let's flip them," Junior said. "I like them soft. And I'm hungry."

"We can't," Stephen said. "They haven't solidified enough yet. The bottoms will get stuck on the griddle and they won't flip."

"Solidify faster, pancakes," Junior said. "Hi, Dada!"

"You're up before eleven *and* you're making breakfast?" Whit said, stepping through the front door. "Who are you and what have you done with my son?"

Junior giggled. "It's me, Dada."

"That's just what a Pod Person would say. You sure you're not Donald Sutherland?"

"I'm sure, Dada."

"That's what I was afraid of." Whit turned to Sarah and Bob, sitting at the dining room table, sipping coffee and perusing the morning paper. "Hey, Sarah. Bob. I have confirmation. That kid in the kitchen is in fact my son. Whatever he told you, he doesn't know how to cook. Your house is about to look like Faulkner's barn."

"Well, then," Sarah said, "I'm glad we ponied up for Faulkner coverage in our insurance policy."

"Yeah," Bob said. "We're covered for fire, theft, flood, zombie apocalypse, tornados to Oz, lions and tigers and bears."

"Oh, my," Whit said.

"Here," Bob said, folding a section of the morning paper and offering it to Whit. "Want the sports page?"

"Nah. I'm just popping in to grab a case of beer. I gotta hustle and clean up the mess at my old man's place before Adam gets there. You know how twitchy he gets. Just give me the highlights."

"Alright, then," Bob said, placing the sports page on the table and taking a sip of coffee. "Padres lost, Dodgers won."

"Well, shit, Bob. You got any good news?"

"We're still not as bad as the Rockies."

"I feel nothing," Whit said and padded to the kitchen. "Morning, boys," he said to Junior and Stephen. "How's the breakfast line-cook shift going? Have you set anything on fire yet?"

"No, Dada." Junior looked up at Whit and smiled.

"Good," Whit said. "Have you dunked each other in pancake batter yet?"

"Not yet," Stephen said, brandishing a batter-coated stirring spoon at Junior.

"Hey, Stephen." Junior pointed at one of the pancakes. "I think that one's ready to flip."

"Ten seconds," Stephen said. "Let's count down."

The boys counted down from ten, then Stephen said, "Liftoff! Flip it, Junior!"

Junior took a spatula and flipped the pancake.

"Touchdown!" Stephen said.

"Nice one, buddy," Whit said. "That's one small step for pancake, one giant leap for breakfast."

"What?" Junior said.

"That's what the first man on the moon said when he stepped onto the moon's surface," Whit said.

"One small step for pancake?" Junior said.

"Actually," Whit said, "it's one small step for man, one giant leap for mankind."

"Oh, okay. That makes more sense. That's funny, Dada. I'll save this pancake for you."

"No time, kiddo," Whit said, pulling a case of PBR from the fridge. "Too much work to do."

"Hey, Dada, can me and Stephen go birdwatching in the woods today?"

"Stephen and I. But, sure. Have fun. See if you can find a Norwegian blue parrot out there. Just stay on the trails. It's really easy to get lost in those woods. And be home before dark."

"Okay, Dada. Thanks."

Whit put an arm around Junior's shoulder. "Love you, buddy. Seeya soon."

"Love you too, Dada."

"Seeya, Stephen," Whit said.

"Bye, Mr. Coe."

Whit toted the case of beer into the living room. "Alright, kiddies," he said to Bob and Sarah. "Off to the coal mines."

"Watch out for cave-ins and black lung," Sarah said.

"Fire in the hole!" Bob said. "Hey, Whit, I'll call you as soon as I get the results from the coroner's report."

"Thanks, Bob," Whit said. "You're an officer and a gentleman."

Bob saluted and crammed an entire strip of bacon into his mouth.

CHAPTER 14

Whit navigated the radio knob through the waves of static and disembodied white noise until he found the '80s station. "Dear God" by XTC cued up.

"That'll do," he said and stood up.

He looked at his father's transistor radio. At the paint spatters dotting its face. Then he looked at his father's living room. At the blood droplets decorating the walls. Red rain on white snow.

He chugged a beer and set to work.

Whit drudged through the rabota with semiautomatic singularity of purpose: slap a coat of primer over the crimson spray on the wall. Bleach and scrub the blood-soaked floors. Sweep up the shattered tchotchkes. Heft the broken bits of furniture outside for later disposal.

When he'd finished his task, he downed another can of beer and inspected his work. On the gallery walls, abstract gray rectangles gessoed over the red splatter painting. The room was bare and empty.

He drummed his fingers on the hollow beer can and peeked down the hall at his old bedroom. The door was half open. He crumpled the beer can, flipped it into an empty paint bucket, and slunk into the bedroom.

It wasn't his room anymore. If it ever had been. The walls were beige. An oak rolltop desk had replaced Whit's bed. A cigar humidor sat on one end of the desk, a crystal decanter filled with brown liquid on the other. A scant handful of books lined the top shelf, all leatherbound editions of the classics. Not a memory of Whit remained.

He took a slug from the decanter. Brandy. He downed another gulp and followed his twin sister's memory down the hallway. He stood outside her door.

Whit heard a whisper in the air. His eyes followed the voice down the hallway to the trapdoor in the ceiling. Something in the attic beckoned him.

He shook off the pull of the void and opened the door to Astrid's room.

Nothing had changed. The room remained a dollhouse shrine to a little girl who had died long ago. Teddy bears and stuffed unicorns nestled together on a pink bedspread. A music box ballerina reposed on the bedside table. Across the room, a pink My Little Pony perched beneath a vanity mirror on a child-sized desk.

The mirror flickered white, wavering into another memory.

Whit and Astrid were little, four or five years old. Astrid was dressed as a princess in a tiara and a pink tutu. Whit was dressed as a knight with a green blanket draped over his shoulders like a cloak. He held an empty roll of wrapping paper aloft as a sword. They were talking and laughing, but Whit couldn't hear their words.

The mirror burned white again. Nine-year-old Astrid was lying in her little pink bed. Her face was pale and gaunt. Her long black hair was gone, and she wore an iridescent scarf on her head. She had oxygen tubes in her nose and a feeding tube in her stomach.

Astrid turned her head and looked at Whit through the mirror. She opened her mouth to speak.

The mirror blazed again. Astrid was gone.

Whit slumped on Astrid's bed and buried his face in his hands. When he looked up, the thick blue spine of a photo album in Astrid's bookshelf caught his eye. He pulled out the photo album and thumbed through its pages.

Footsteps thumped across the floor outside the bedroom. Whit looked up. The doorknob turned.

"Hey, bro," Adam said, barging into the room. "There ya are. Sorry I got here so late. I ain't slept that long in ages. All that shit yesterday musta burned me out, ya know what I'm sayin? Anyways, looks like you went to town in the livin room. Save some work for me, bro."

"Careful what you ask for," Whit said. "We've still got some heavy lifting to do. You down to load up the truck and make a dump run?"

"Yeah, I'm down to get loaded and take a dump." Adam leaned back and brayed to himself.

"Yeah, yeah," Whit said. "Let's get moving, asshat." He closed the photo album.

"Hey, whatcha got there, Whit?" Adam asked.

"Nothing," Whit said.

CHAPTER 15

About a half mile down the trail, the woods gave way to a clearing. Junior and Stephen hunkered down on a fallen tree trunk and Stephen unslung a gray 'NASA SPACE EXPLORER' backpack from his shoulder. He unzipped the backpack and pulled out a pair of Ziploc baggies stuffed with bologna sandwiches and orange wedges. He handed one of the baggies to Junior, who attacked his meal with a devastating flurry of kaijuesque chomps.

Stephen ate half of his sandwich with measured bites, sealed the remaining triangle in a Ziploc, then said, "Hey Junior, you wanna play Dungeons and Dragons when we get back?"

"Sure," Junior said through a wad of sandwich. "How do you play?"

"You mean you've never played DND before? Oh, man, you're gonna love it. You get to create different worlds and come up with your own stories. And you can be all different types of characters. You can be a knight or a bard or a wizard. You can even be a humanoid cat. My character is a cleric because they're the most—"

A chorus of caws cut Stephen short. A black ring circled in the sky above the heart of the forest.

"Crows," Junior said.

"A murder of crows," Stephen said. "A big one."

The boys stood up and drifted toward the trail, eyes fixed on the dark disk swarming the horizon.

"Hey, Stephen," Junior said, "what do you call a big murder of crows?"

"What?"

"A mass murder. Get it?"

Stephen grinned. "Yeah. That's pretty good," he said.

"What do you think they're doing?" Junior said.

"Crows are carrion scavengers. They probably found a dead animal in a clearing over there."

"That's not disturbing or anything," Junior said. "Hey, what's a crow's favorite rock song?"

"What?"

"Carrion, my Wayward Son. Get it?" Junior giggled.

"Oh, like that song from *Supernatural*," Stephen said. "Yeah, that's a pretty good one too."

"My legs are getting tired," Junior said. "Maybe we should head back and eat lunch."

"We literally just ate lunch. How can you still be hungry?"

Junior shrugged. "I don't know."

"Okay," Stephen said. "My legs are a little—"

A high-pitched shriek pinged in the trees ahead.

"What was that?" Junior said.

"It's a bird," Stephen said. "Sounds like a big one. Maybe the Norwegian blue parrot."

The boys jogged down the trail toward the sound of the bird call. The bird shrieked again.

"That way!" Stephen pointed into the shadow shroud of the forest. "Come on Junior!" He scudded off the trail and plunged into the dark sea of trees.

Junior started after Stephen, then stopped at the edge of the trail. He looked at the line between the trail and the forest. He watched his friend disappear into the underbrush.

Junior left the trail.

As the boys coursed through the forest, the scrub and the shadows clamped around them like a gorging gullet. The sunlight and the trail faded behind them.

The bird shrieked again in the dimness. It was close.

Junior and Stephen pulled up next to a flat gray stone that looked like an altar. Stephen looked at Junior and raised a finger to his lips. He cocked his head and cupped his palm beside his ear.

The forbidden creek rumbled behind a dense thicket of bracken.

A shrill cackle echoed in the treetops on the far bank of the creek. Something stirred behind a veil of pine needles.

"There he is," Stephen said, pointing at the pine tree.

The boys clambered through the bracken and sloshed through the shallow creek to the far bank.

A rock hissed past Stephen's head and thunked against a tree. Junior and Stephen slid to a stop on the muddy ground.

Four older boys swaggered out from behind a cluster of bushes—a wiry blond boy, a gangly boy in a Jim Beam trucker hat, a blotchy-faced boy, and a buck-toothed boy in a camo T-shirt.

"You're trespassin," the blond boy said. "This side of the creek belongs to us. Now you gotta pay the toll, nerd."

"We just wanted to see the bird, Deuce," Stephen said.

"Oh, ya hear that, boys?" Deuce said. "They just wanted to see the bird."

The older boys whooped and snickered. "Oh, the little birdie," gangly trucker hat said. "They just wanted to see the bird." He flapped his arms and strutted like a rooster.

"Here's a bird for ya," Deuce said, extending his middle finger. "See?"

The older kids hooted and pranced back and forth, middle fingers raised at Junior and Stephen.

"Hey, nerd," Deuce said to Stephen. "Who's your new faggot friend?"

Stephen stammered, "He's—his name is—"

"Shut up, nerd," Deuce said. "He—his, buh-buh-buh." He looked at Junior. "What's your name, faggot?"

Junior didn't answer.

"What are you, retarded? What's your *name*, kid?"

"Junior."

"Junior, huh?" Deuce said. "You mean like Whopper Junior?"

"Whopper Junior," blotchy face said, sneering.

"Hey, Whopper Junior," Deuce said. "What are you hanging out with Stephen the nerd for? You lose a bet or somethin?"

"Me and my dada are staying with Stephen's family until my grandpa's funeral is over."

"Your dada?" Deuce said. "Your fuckin *dada*? What are you, like three years old? Oh, shit. Wait a minute." Deuce snapped his fingers. "Old man Coe's your grandaddy?"

"Yeah."

"So your daddy's that poetry-writin faggot writes all them satanic books."

"Actually, they're horror novels."

"Actually. Aaaaactuuuaaalyy," Deuce said and rolled his eyes. "Bullshit. All books are for faggots. Says so in the Bible. And my mama said your daddy's books was straight from the Devil, and one day Jesus was gonna come and strike your old man down."

"Your mom isn't even in town anymore," Stephen said. "She left with that truck driver five years ago."

Deuce turned away from Junior and mad-dogged Stephen. He bowed up to the smaller boy and leaned down until they were face-to-face.

"What did you say, nerd?" Deuce said. "What did you fuckin say?" Stephen could smell rotten beef jerky and cheap liquor on Deuce's breath.

"No-nothing," Stephen said.

"Bullshit. You said somethin, nerd. Somethin *real* stupid. And I thought nerds was s'posed to be smart." Deuce stood upright and cracked his neck. "Ya know what, nerd? You got a big mouth. You know what we do to little kids with big mouths on this side of the creek?"

Deuce reached into his back jeans pocket and pulled out a folding knife. He unfolded the knife and held it to Stephen's face. Stephen staggered backward. Buck-toothed camo T-shirt snatched him by the collar.

"No, please, Deuce," Stephen said. "I didn't mean it. I'm sorry."

Junior took a step forward. Blotchy face and gangly trucker hat grabbed him by the arms. "Stay out of it, new kid," blotchy face said. "Or you're next."

"I'll tell my dad," Stephen said.

"Your daddy works for my daddy," Deuce said. "You ain't gonna do shit, and he ain't gonna do shit. And besides…" He pressed the tip of the knife against Stephen's chin. "How you gonna tell your daddy what happened if you ain't got no tongue, little man?" Deuce widened his eyes and grinned.

"Come on, Deuce," gangly trucker hat said. "Let's ditch these little bitches and go to my house. My daddy ain't home. We can drink some of his Thunderbird."

"Shut the fuck up, Skunk," Deuce said. He pointed the knife at Skunk. "We ain't done here yet. The nerd still ain't paid the toll."

Deuce hooked the knife blade under Stephen's binocular straps. "Hey, nerd. Gimme them goggles."

"But my parents gave me those for my birthday," Stephen said. "And I need them for birdwatching."

"You know the rules, nerd. Pay the fuckin toll. Now."

Stephen handed Deuce the binoculars. Deuce slung them over his neck.

"What's in the backpack?" Deuce said.

"Just a birdwatching guide and half a bologna sandwich," Stephen said.

"Fork it over."

Stephen handed the backpack to Deuce. Deuce fished out the half-eaten sandwich and let the backpack drop into the mud.

"Now as for that big mouth of yours," Deuce said. He dunked the sandwich in the creek and smeared it in on the muddy ground. "Open up, buttercup."

Stephen squirmed, but he couldn't break free of the bigger boy's grip. Deuce smashed the muddy sandwich into Stephen's mouth. Stephen sputtered and coughed. The older boys crowed.

Deuce backed away from Stephen. "Travis," he said to buck-toothed camo T-shirt. "The nerd's paid the toll. Let him go. For now." Travis let go of Stephen's collar and shoved him down into the mud.

Deuce turned to Skunk and blotchy face. "Skunk, Billy, let the new kid go." Skunk and Billy pushed Junior into the mud next to Stephen and giggled.

Deuce reached into his back pocket and pulled out a playing card. He flicked the card at Junior and Stephen. The Deuce of Spades landed faceup on the ground between the two boys.

The older boys hiked up a small crest toward the woods. Deuce turned around to face Junior and Stephen. He unslung the binoculars from his neck and smashed them against a rock on the ground. "Guess I didn't really want these anyways," he said. He flashed his knife at Junior and Stephen. "And next time you little bitches cross over to my side of the creek..." He ran the blade in front of his mouth from ear to ear. "I'll cut you a permanent grin."

CHAPTER 16

The swinging doors to the Rockwell County Coroner's exam room hinged open, and two men in sea-green scrubs emerged. The older man squinted and rubbed the back of his neck. The younger man tented his fingers and pressed them to his chin.

Chip wolfed down the ass end of a bear claw and heaved himself out of the waiting room chair. He swaggered up to the medical examiners, smacking his lips and chewing his cud.

Bob stood up and joined the party.

"Well, Doc," Chip said to the older man. "You done with the stiffs?"

"Yes, Sheriff," the older doctor said. "My medical examiner's report is on the books."

"So whatcha got?"

"I think," the older man said, "I should turn that question over to Dr. Planck." He indicated the younger man. "Dr. Planck is an expert consultant in the field of forensic zoology, based in San Vaes. He's an expert in the biology, physical characteristics, and behavioral patterns of animals, as applied to crime scene investigation." He took a step back and nodded at Dr. Planck.

Chip widened his stance and folded his arms.

"Thank you, Dr. Ellicott," Dr. Planck said. "Officers. I began my examination of the bodies of Mr. and Mrs. Coe at ten forty-three a.m. I was able to corroborate Dr. Ellicott's findings that—"

Dave came hobbling into the room, one shoe chirping as it dragged across the polished linoleum floor. "Sorry," he said and looked at the linoleum.

Chip half-turned and peeked over his shoulder. "Bring out the gimp," he said. "What kept ya, Deputy Dave? Foot pursuit of a little-old-lady jaywalker?" Chip pushed his beer belly forward and snorted.

Bob ground his teeth.

"As I was saying," Dr. Planck continued, "I was able to corroborate Dr. Ellicott's preliminary findings that Mr. and Mrs. Coe were killed late on the night of June the fourteenth, and that the cause of death was exsanguination by laceration. The victims' jugular veins and all major arteries of the head, neck, and torso were severed by a series of powerful claw slashes and bites. These wounds confirm Dr. Ellicott's finding that Mr. and Mrs. Coe's deaths were the result of an animal attack."

"Animal attack," Chip said, smirking at Bob and Dave. "Just like I told you boys. Case closed. Wrap it up in a bow and ship it off to wildlife. Simple."

"Actually, Sheriff," Dr. Planck said, "this is where things get complicated. The animal that inflicted these wounds belongs to a species entirely unknown to science. The animal's incisors are jagged and of irregular size and shape, somewhat like the teeth of a shark. The canines are curved and fanglike, approximately eight inches in length, more analogous to those of a mountain lion or other large cat. Based on the depth of the bite wounds, I estimate that the animal is capable of a bite force of approximately thirteen hundred pounds per square inch—comparable to that of a bull shark or a gorilla."

"A gorilla?" Dave said.

Dr. Planck smiled. "Yes, Deputy," he said. "Primates can be quite ferocious. Now on to the claws—and this is the key. The animal possesses five long, jagged, slightly hooked claws. Very distinct and unique. Again, entirely unknown to science." He raised a finger and looked at the cops, each in turn. "However, not entirely unknown."

Bob knit his eyebrows. "You mean somebody's seen claw marks like these before?" he said.

"Yes, Deputy," Dr. Planck said. "As a matter of fact, *I* have. Three years ago when I was called in to consult in the death of a young woman named Alice Coe."

CHAPTER 17

Stephen poked his head out his room door and meerkated down both sides of the hall. He stuck his head back inside the room and closed the door.

"Dude," Junior said. "Who the hell were those douchebags?"

"The blond kid's name is Deuce Gustafsson—well his real name is Merril, but he calls himself Deuce. Sheriff Gustafsson's his dad, so he thinks he can do anything he wants around town. Which is pretty much true. He's always picking on other kids, beating them up, taking their money and stuff. He even shoplifts from the gas station and Mr. Kim's grocery store all the time. Chip knows about it, but he doesn't care. I think he kinda encourages it."

"Wait, wait, wait," Junior said. "Hold up. You mean the sheriff is named Chip? Like the little teacup from *Beauty and the Beast*?"

The mental image of Sheriff Gustafsson as a Disney cartoon teacup, still dressed in his police tans, sent Stephen into a wild giggle fit. He doubled over, face contorting. His shoulders jackhammered. He reached for his inhaler and sucked in a deep puff of mist. It tasted bitter. Somehow gray.

"Oh, man," Stephen wheezed. "I can't remember the last time I laughed that hard. But, anyway, the sheriff's named Merril too. Merril Gustafsson the Third, to be exact."

"Which makes Deuce Merril Gustafsson the Fourth? Fancy." Junior raised his hand and gave Stephen the royal wave.

Stephen erupted in a second bout of giggles, then pulled on another puff of mist from his inhaler. "Dude, you should be a comedian when you grow up," he said. "But anyway, that's Deuce. Those other kids are his cousins from across the creek—Skunk, Billy, and Travis McGee."

"Skunk? What's his real name?"

"That's the best part. Skunk is his real name." Stephen fell forward giggling again.

Junior squinted. "No way," he said.

"No, I'm serious," Stephen gasped. "Like on his birth certificate."

Junior joined Stephen in a fresh round of giggles. "Oh, that's so messed up," he said. "No wonder he's such a dick."

The boys hunched up, lungs heaving, faces red, tears streaming down their cheeks. When the giggle storm had passed, Junior wiped his eyes and said, "But seriously, what is wrong with those guys?"

"Inadequate prefrontal lobe development," Stephen said. He tilted his head and raised one narrow shoulder. "They're jerks. Bullies. The McGee kids are like bullies in every town. They're pretty bad. They like to hurt other kids, take their stuff, scare them. Makes them feel tougher than they really are. Standard bully stuff. Now Deuce…" The corner of Stephen's mouth twitched upward. "He's worse. He's a straight psycho. I think he wants to hurt people really bad."

Junior nibbled on his fingernails. "Hey, Stephen," he said. "If I tell you something really weird, do you promise to keep it a secret?"

"Promise," Stephen said, crossing his heart.

"Okay, well…" Junior looked away and took another chomp at his fingernail. "Ever since I was little, I've been able to see things about people."

"You mean like intuition?"

"No, it's something different. It feels more real. It's like I can feel the bad in people. It's like this black spot starts burning in the back of my brain. And sometimes I can even see flashes of the bad things that person has done. Kinda like pictures. When I got close to Deuce in the woods today, that black spot in my brain started burning. Worse that I'd ever felt in my whole life. And I saw flashes of the things he's done. Horrible things." Junior winced and pressed two fingers flat against his temple. "So you're right about him, Stephen. He's worse. He's so much worse."

CHAPTER 18

Chip waddled up to the Rockwell PD reception desk. "Any calls while I was out, Lucy?" he said.

"Six," Lucy said and tapped her pencil on a memo pad. She was sitting under the AC vent wearing a China-blue argyle sweater. "Five from Mrs. Foley about her missing Pomeranian Evita, and one from Ralph Corcoran about Mrs. Foley's missing Pomeranian Evita."

"So Ralph found the dog?"

"You could say that."

***

Chip could smell it even before he opened the door of the squad car. The sickly-sweet perfume of rotting flesh roasting in the June sun. When he cracked the door, a fresh wave of stench and a furnace blast of hot air slapped him in the face. He coughed and clapped a hand over his muzzle, then walked up the steps to Ralph's porch.

Ralph was waiting on the porch in a half-rusted folding metal chair holding a can of Schlitz against the side of his head. Sweat and moisture from the beer can beaded on his sun-and-cigarette-wrinkled skin. When he saw Chip, Ralph smiled at the corner of his mouth, reached into his cooler, and held up a beer. Chip waved off the offer.

Ralph got up and eased down the steps. "Hey, Chip," he said. "How ya been?"

The men shook hands.

"Well, I smelled better," Chip said and wiped his brow. "How you been keepin, Ralph?"

"Can't complain, buddy. Workin steady. Forty hours a week."

"That come with a mule?" Chip said.

Ralph smirked. "Shiiiiit," he said and gulped his Schlitz. "You sure you don't want a beer, Cap? It's hotter than a two-dollar pistol out here."

"Thanks," Chip said, "but I'm on duty and I wannna be outta here before animal control shows up. Lucy said there's something on the dog I might want to see?"

Ralph glanced down and nodded. He flicked his head toward the dirt lot behind his house. "C'mon, Cap. It's out back."

They cut through the side yard of Ralph's property. As they walked, the stench grew stronger, the putrid miasma burning in the air like mustard gas. They stopped at the edge of the dirt lot.

A dead Pomeranian rotted in a dusty patch of brown earth. Dried red-black blood caked the dirt next to the dog. The dog's eyes were shriveled and sunken into its skull. Its tongue dangled from its mouth. A long incision ran up its body from its groin to its throat.

Chip knelt down beside the dog and inspected its tags. They were shaped like little hearts. The front inscription read: 'Evita.' Chip flipped the tags over. Mrs. Foley's name, address, and phone number were engraved on the back.

"Fuck me," Chip said, turning his head and dropping the tags from his fingers.

The tags brushed against something in the dog's fur. Something Chip recognized at once. Like some twisted magic trick, Chip pulled the playing card from the dead dog's fur. He held the card between two fingers and stared at it in the sunlight.

It was the Deuce of Spades.

CHAPTER 19

Whit and Adam heaved the last stacks of cardboard boxes into the bed of Adam's pickup.

"That should be about it," Whit said.

Adam tapped the top box. "Hey, Whit," he said. "You sure you don't wanna take none of Dad's stuff for yourself. Even the old pitchers with you in 'em?"

"I'm sure, Adam. They're not my memories."

"Alright, then." Adam bobbed his head for no apparent reason. "Hey, bro," he said, "you wanna come over to my place for a bit? You gotta see my aquarium. Those African sick-letts are killer. And I got a ton of weed growin in my back yard. It's primo shit, bro. Primo, primo."

"Maybe some other time," Whit said. "Right now I'm beat." He looked at the dirt on his jeans and on his hands. "And I need to take a shower."

"No problemo, bro. You could—"

Whit's cell rang.

"Bob," Whit answered. "You got anything?"

"Yeah," Bob said, "but I'm not entirely sure what. First thing, the ME's done with his exam, so your dad and Barbara's bodies have been released to you and Adam. They're en route to Willoughby and Son funeral home right now. Should be there within the hour."

"Thanks, Bob. I'll head out to Willoughby's right after I hose off. You want me to pick up dinner while I'm out? It's the least I can do. Maybe some good old-fashioned junk food? Pizza, burgers, wings."

"You had me at junk food."

Whit chuckled. "Sounds good," he said. "Is O'Malley's still there or has it been devoured by a microbrewery?"

"It's still there. And so's Jim. His old man passed about seven years ago, so Jim's running the whole pub."

"By himself?"

Bob laughed. "Yeah, I know," he said. "But yeah, why don't you swing by? I know Jim would love to see you."

"Will do." Whit flashed a side glance at Adam and stepped away from the pickup. "What about the coroner's report?"

"That's where things get tricky. The local ME called in an outside consultant. Some forensic zoologist from San Vaes. Says you hired him to work Alice's case. Dr. Planck?"

"Planck? Yeah, he's one of the consultants I hired for Alice's case. Kinda weird, but he definitely knows his shit. Anyway, what did he say?"

"Basically that you're right. Whatever this thing is that killed your old man and Barbara, it's the same thing that got Alice. Planck matched the claw marks from both cases. But he still doesn't know *what* this thing is. Or where to find it."

"Or how to kill it?" Whit said. He stayed silent for a long time.

"Whit?" Bob said. "You okay, buddy?"

"Yeah, I'm good," Whit said. "Hey, Bob? Do you still think this creature is connected to those missing kids you were telling me about?"

"I do. I don't know how, but I know it."

"In that case," Whit said, "we just might have a lead on it."

"What's that?" Bob said.

"If this creature is connected to the missing kids, and the cycle of those disappearances holds up, we might be able to catch its trail tomorrow when—"

"When another kid disappears."

CHAPTER 20

Whit shed his dirty clothes onto the bathroom floor of his old house and hopped into the shower. Despite the glaring afternoon heat, he cranked the hot water and let the steam envelop the room in a veil of mist. He watched the dirt slough off his skin and spiral down the drain like Janet Leigh's blood in *Psycho*, then scrubbed himself clean.

He opened the sliding glass door and froze.

Behind the murky surface of the cabinet mirror, a face watched Whit. It stared through the glass with burning black eyes.

Whit tilted his head to the left. Then to the right. The face in the mirror didn't move.

He climbed out of the shower. He approached the mirror. He stood in front of the glass and looked at the wavering face beyond. He reached out his hand.

Whit swiped the foggy surface of the mirror with his palm. The face that met him was his own. Nothing but his own reflection in the mist.

But when I moved, the reflection didn't.

CHAPTER 21

The man in the black suit looked like a hedgehog. It was because of his hair. It was mousy brown and burred straight up at the ends like quills, or as if he had just rubbed a balloon across the top of his head.

"Good afternoon," the hedgehog man in the black suit said, folding his hands. "Welcome to Willoughby and Son Funeral Home. My name is Peter Willoughby. How may I help you?"

"I'm Whitman Coe," Whit said. "My brother Adam should be here shortly. We're Allan and Barbara Coe's next of kin. I understand they've recently arrived here."

"Ah, yes," Peter said and shook Whit's hand. "I'm so sorry for your loss. Your loved ones are downstairs with my restorative artist Edward as we speak. They're in good hands. Please come in, Mr. Coe." He swept his arm in a practiced gesture of welcome.

Whit followed Peter into the foyer. Across the shiny hardwood floor. Past a display table topped by an arrangement of purple, white, and pastel-colored flowers. Past the potpourri smell of the blooms.

They entered the sitting room. Its color scheme seemed to be bridesmaid dress meets Neapolitan ice cream. Past the sitting room, nonfunctional pillars gave way to an alcove decked in a faux-finish blue sky. Like a convalescent-themed Italian restaurant in Disneyland.

"Please have a seat, Mr. Coe," Peter said, indicating a gray sofa with a pink floral vine print. He picked up a clipboard and a laminated binder from a low coffee table and sat in a chair facing Whit. He drew a pen from the clipboard holster and scanned a document clipped to the board.

"I see," Peter said, "that your loved ones have a pre-need contract with us. That means that they have already reserved a plot at Rockwell Cemetery and have made all the necessary funerary arrangements. Resting vessels, service arrangements, all paid-in-full up front. A very tasteful package. However, if you would care to upgrade—"

Whit waved Peter off. "Sounds like they knew what they wanted. I'll stick to that."

"Of course, Mr. Coe. Now when would you like to schedule the internment and funeral service at the cemetery?"

"Can you do it tomorrow?"

Peter wrinkled his forehead and blinked. "We can, however we usually recommend the bereaved family takes some time to—"

"Time is what I'm thinking of," Whit said. "I'd like to get this over with."

"I understand, Mr. Coe." Peter stood up. "In that case, I'll get some paperwork from my office and make a phone call to the cemetery. I'll be back shortly. In the meantime, feel free to grab a cup of coffee or stretch your legs. The viewing room is unoccupied and quite peaceful." He swept his hand toward an adjoining room in that same practiced manner, then ducked out of the waiting room.

Whit slipped the clutches of the pink sofa vines and got to his feet. He stretched. He clip-clopped across the hardwood floors. He inspected a stale pot of coffee percolating on a side table, then ambled into the viewing room.

He walked down an aisle between two rows of folding chairs and stopped in front of a lacquered mahogany display casket. He gazed into its gleaming veneer.

The reflection on the surface of the casket shimmered and flashed white. Whit saw himself standing above Astrid's tiny casket. The thick flesh-toned makeup on her face and the vibrant rouge brushed on her cheeks made her look like a doll.

The reflection wavered and flashed white again. Whit stood above his mother's casket. She wore a white dress. She was younger than Whit was now. Her face looked serene. The hint of a smile curled the corners of her mouth. In life, Whit's mother had never found peace. But in death, she had.

The image rippled away like an ebbing tide beneath a fathomless sea. The burning white light eclipsed Whit's senses again.

He stood over Alice's casket. A spill of dark hair cascaded down the shoulders of her blue dress. She wore a yellow ribbon around her neck.

Whit caressed his wife's cheek and bent down to kiss her forehead. He hunched over Alice's casket and wept the violent yet fragile tears of unutterable grief.

With a final flash of white, the vision was gone. Whit stood in the empty viewing room brooding at his own image, warped and unfamiliar, reflected in the mahogany casket. He unhunched his shoulders and wiped his eyes.

A pale shape loomed in the reflection behind Whit's shoulder, spreading like a shadow over the casket. The faceless creature opened its jaws and reached its knurled white hand toward Whit.

Whit growled and spun to face the creature. He grabbed it by the neck and squeezed. Then he let go.

Adam slumped over coughing. "Damn, bro," he said. "It's just me." He straightened up and snickered. "Man, Whit," he said. "You look like you just seen a ghost."

CHAPTER 22

Whitman Coe left the town of Rockwell without a word on the night of his high school graduation over twenty-five years ago. Twenty-five years. A quarter of a century. It sounds even longer ago and farther away when you think of it like that.

***

Whit sat on the hood of his hunter-green Buick boat, one arm draped around Maggie Bell's shoulders. Maggie wore Whit's letterman jacket and leaned her head against the bulk of his chest. She slugged a sip from Whit's whisky flask, then passed it back. Whit took a pull and breathed in the warm summer air—the air of freedom after four years of high school. He tilted his neck back and looked at the stars.

Sputtering footsteps clacked behind the car. Whit and Maggie spun their heads toward the sound.

"Whit, come quick!" Sarah panted as she sprinted for the car. Her shirt was ripped. "Chip and the McGee boys grabbed Bob, Dave, and Jim. They're really drunk, Whit. They said they're gonna throw them off the water tower."

"Oh, shit," Whit said. "Stay here. I got this." He bolted for the tower.

Whit was slashing through the bushy trail to the water tower when he heard a scream. A scream of terror. Then more screams. Screams of agony.

Whit charged into the clearing. Dave Ross was writhing on the ground clutching his leg. The shattered bone of his tibia was jutting through the skin like a primitive blade. It shone pale white in the moonlight.

"Oooh!" Chip and the McGee boys cheered. "Touchdown!" Chip said, raising his arms over his head. Chip and McGees bellowed laughter and exchanged high fives.

"One down, two to go," Chip said.

"Looks like we got a drumstick on this one," Tails Only Tommy McGee said, grinning. "Let's see what we get next. How's 'bout a wing?"

"So which little piggy's gonna try to fly next?" Lanky Lewie McGee slurred.

Chip tightened his grip on Bob's shirt collar. "Eeny, meeny, miny, moe." He waggled his pointing finger back and forth between Bob and Jim. "Aw, fuck it. I say it's Bobs away." The McGee boys whooped and cackled.

"No, please," Bob said.

"Chip, don't," Jim gasped through Tommy's choke hold. "Please. I think Dave's really hurt, man. He needs help. We won't say anything. I swear. We know you boys were just drinking and letting off some steam and things got a little out of hand. Please, Chip. Let's just get Dave some help."

Chip scratched his Chin, miming the act of pondering. "Nah," he said. "Dave'll be fine. I wanna see if baby Bobby bounces or breaks."

The McGee boys cackled again, and Chip pitched Bob off the water tower's platform. Bob screamed as he fell. His stomach lurched and his head spiraled in a nauseating whirl. His eyes rolled back in their sockets. The whole of Bob's consciousness was a plummeting blur. He squeezed his eyes shut and braced himself for the excruciating pain ahead. Then everything went black.

Bob never landed.

His freefall came to a sudden stop as if a powerful hand had jerked the brakes on a roller coaster.

Whit rasped out a harsh breath and lowered his outstretched arm. Bob plopped the last few inches to the ground unscathed.

"What the fuck?" Tails Only Tommy said, snatching the trucker hat off his head and scratching his greasy scalp.

"I didn't hear no thump," Lanky Lewie said. "Did he even hit the ground?"

"Course he hit the ground, you idiot," Chip said. "Lucky bastard musta hit a soft patch."

"Looked like he stopped before he hit the ground," Tommy said.

"And they let you graduate?" Chip said. "That ain't how gravity works, you fuckin retard."

"But, Chip, it looked like—"

"Looked like nuthin. We're up too fuckin high. It's too fuckin dark. And you're too fuckin drunk and stupid. Now shut the fuck up and let's toss ol' Jimbo. Maybe he'll bounce better. Aw, shit."

Whit scudded to Bob's side. Bob was unconscious but breathing.

Whit knelt next to Dave. "Hang on, buddy," he said. "I'm gonna clear these fuckers out, then we'll get you some help. I know it hurts, but you're gonna be just fine, okay?"

Dave trembled and writhed on the ground. "Okay, Whit," he said. The words chattered though his teeth.

"Whit, look out!" Jim shouted.

Tommy and Lewie grabbed Whit by the collar. Whit drove his heels into the ground and shoved himself to his feet, flinging the smaller boys off his back.

Whit cracked Tommy square on the jaw with a left hook. Tommy whiplashed to the dirt. His eyes glassed over and stared into the darkness above.

Chip gave his best swing, an overhand right that caught Whit flush across the left cheek. Whit's head barely moved. He was in a cold white rage. He felt nothing. Nothing but the rage. He glared into Chip's eyes. Past them.

Chip raised his hands and tried to back away. Whit pounced on him.

Chip thudded onto his back. Whit straddled him and began to pummel his face. Chip's vision blurred white. The same white as Whit's rage. The night burned white and red. The warm summer air smelled like copper.

Lanky Lewie backpedaled, wheeled, and fled down the trail.

Tails only Tommy drifted in and out of consciousness. He caught fragmented images of the night sky. Of Dave writhing on the ground. Of Whit hammering away at Chip's face with his fists. Then Tommy's reeling gaze fixed on Whit's eyes and he felt a terror he had never known in his existence. It was an inhuman terror. But Whitman Coe was no human. Of that Tommy was sure. He was sure as he looked into Whit's solid black eyes. He was sure as his vision began to fade again. He was sure as he slipped back into unconsciousness.

Whit continued to bludgeon Chip's face. The flesh around Chip's left eye was a shredded sack of meat. His cheek was sliced open and oozing a stream of blood into the dirt.

Whit no longer felt any sense of self. He could see everything he was doing to Chip. He could see the torn flesh and the welts rising under Chip's eye. He could hear the sickening wet thumps. But he couldn't control what he was doing. He couldn't stop. It was like he was hypnotized.

Whit felt a meaty hand touch his shoulder. "Whit," Jim said. "He's out. You gotta stop, buddy. You're gonna kill him. Whit, you gotta stop now. It's okay. It's over. Bob's okay. Dave needs help. Whit, we gotta help Dave."

Whit snapped to. The cold white rage was gone. He looked at his clenched fist, painted in blood. He looked down at Chip. The left side of his face was a mangled pulp, but he was breathing.

Whit stood up and surveyed the carnage. Tails Only Tommy was out cold. Lanky Lewie was gone. Bob, Maggie, Sarah, and Jim were gawping at Whit, faces blank like they'd just walked away from a bomb blast. Even Dave had stopped writhing on the ground to watch him.

Whit ran a hand through his hair and staggered backward. It wasn't Chip's mangled face that haunted him. It was the faces of his friends. The horror in their eyes.

Whit turned away. He didn't speak. He didn't look at his friends. He just stared into the night. Then he wandered away like a sleepwalker.

That was the last time Whit would see Bob, Sarah, Jim, and Dave for twenty-five years. And he would never see Maggie again.

***

"Do you have any idea what time it is, Whitman?" Allan Coe said the microsecond his son stepped through the door. He turned off the TV and swiveled in his recliner to face Whit.

"No," Whit said and closed the door behind him.

Allan checked his watch, then turned the watch's face toward Whit. "Two thirty-three. Two thirty-three in the fucking morning. And what time is your curfew?"

"Midnight."

"Riiiight," Allan said. "Now I know math isn't your best subject, but can you see how two thirty-three is *past* midnight?"

"Dad, I'm tired," Whit said. "Can we do this later?"

"No, Whitman." Allan got out of his recliner. He put his hands on his hips and stood looking up at Whit. "We're both up. You need to stop putting things off. That's why you never get anything done. Now have you picked a college yet?"

"No, Dad, I already told you. I worked the last three summers at O'Malley's to save up enough money to take a year off and travel. I want to see the world while I still have the chance. Maybe I'll write about it."

Whit's father rolled his eyes and snorted. "Like you're going to be Mark Twain or something," he said. "High school is over, Whitman. It's time for you to grow up, get your head out of the clouds, and go to college. Start a normal life and quit being such a weirdo. If you want to be a bum, fine. Do it after college."

"I get it now," Whit said. "This isn't about college. You didn't graduate until you were thirty-four. It's about appearances. You want me to appear normal. Respectable. Successful. But not too successful. Average like you. You're not afraid I'll fail. You're afraid I'll succeed. Your ego never could take being overshadowed, especially by your own son."

Allan Coe flipped his son the bird and yelled, "Fuck you!" He sneered and tossed up his hands. "You know what, Whitman? Fine. You just do whatever the fuck you want. You want to travel? Travel. Right fucking now. Travel your lazy ass out of my house right fucking now." He shook his head. "You know what, son? I'm disappointed in you."

"Yeah, I'm well aware. Kinda loses its meaning after you've heard it enough times. I'll just pack my shit and get out of your hair. Or what's left of it anyway."

As Whit turned to leave the living room, Allan noticed his son's scratched and bloody knuckles.

"Jesus Christ, Whitman. Have you been fighting?"

"Yes."

"Have you been drinking?"

"Yes."

"Drunk and fighting on grad night? Really mature, Whitman."

"I'm not drunk. I've just been drinking."

"Whatever, Whitman. I'm done with you." Allan wiped his hands together. "You want to throw away your life? Fine. I don't care anymore. But I'm so disappointed in you. And you know what? Your mother would have been disappointed in you too."

Whit felt the hypnotic rage burning in his mind again. Flooding his neurons with white flame.

He leaped across the room, grabbed his father by the neck, and slogged him against the wall. Whit held his father by the throat and squeezed. Allan Coe's face turned red, then purple. His eyes bulged in their sockets. He clasped Whit's wrists and struggled to pry himself free.

Whit heard a clatter down the hall. He looked up and caught a glimpse of himself in the living room mirror. His eyes were completely black.

He closed his burning black eyes and rasped a long breath. More with his mind than with his body, he forced his hand open.

Allan Coe slid down the wall and landed hard on his backside. He clutched at his throat and gasped for air. He looked up at his son, eyes still red and bulging, then raised his palms and stared down at the floor. Whit's own father was afraid of him. And rightfully so. If he hadn't seen his reflection in the mirror and snapped out of his trance, Whit would have killed him.

What kind of man kills his own father?

Whit backed away. The fog in his head had cleared.

Adam and Barbara were huddled in the hallway. They stared at Whit through the same masks of horror his friends had worn earlier that night. Adam trembled and clung to his mother. He had wet his pants.

Without a word, Whitman Coe walked into his bedroom, packed a single duffel bag, and drove out of Rockwell, he hoped, for the last time.

CHAPTER 23

Whit slid Alice's Audi into a space in the parking lot behind O'Malley's Pub. He got out of the car and stared at the Victorian house looming on the other side of the road. Its exterior was painted a rustic country yellow with hunter-green trim. The same as it had been when Whit had last seen it.

The house had three stories and a widow's walk perched at the top like a castle turret. Looking at the widow's walk had always struck Whit with a pang of melancholy. Maybe it was the image that came to his mind when he looked at it—a solitary woman in a high-collared black dress, hair pinned up, pacing the walk like a hungry ghost. Forever waiting for a love who would never return to her. The woman grew old as the years went by, but she never stopped pacing the widow's walk every day, long after she had given up all hope of her lover's return.

When Whit was growing up, the other kids in town had thought the house was haunted. And perhaps it was, after a fashion. Haunted by the passage of time. A ghost of days and memories now lost. And some of those days and memories belonged to Whit.

He closed the car door and walked into O'Malley's. The late afternoon light cut a rectangular beam through the open doorway, casting a gleaming yellow brick road straight to the bar. The rest of the bar lay in the dank half-light characteristic of all dive bars at that waning time of day. Neon Coors, Guinness, and Jameson signs glowed on the walls. San Diego Padres, Kansas Jayhawks, and Alabama Crimson Tide banners dangled from the rafters. A row of arcade games and a pinball machine stood snubbed in a corner like wallflowers at an eighth-grade dance while the jukebox played "Gigantic" by the Pixies.

Three day-drunks sat at one end of the bar drinking Night Train. They spun a dreidel and placed bets on which side would turn up. At the other end, a rheumy-eyed old man in a Budweiser hat stared at the suds in his half-empty bottle of beer.

Whit sat down at the bar. A young woman in a Blondie T-shirt smiled at Whit and walked up to take his drink order.

"What can I get you, Whitman F. Coe?" the bartender said.

"I'll go with a Bushmills," Whit said.

"Good choice," the girl said and poured a glass.

"Good song." Whit took a swig.

"I've got the jukebox rigged." The girl reached into her jeans pocket and pulled out a quarter. It had a tiny hole drilled through it and a string looped through the bore hole. She dangled the quarter from the string. "I drop the coin in the slot. Leave the string hanging outside the machine. Then yank it right back out by the string. Infinite jukebox playlist."

Whit looked at the day-drunks at the bar. "That's probably for the best," he said. "To paraphrase the song," he pointed at the speaker on the wall behind the bar, "is there a big, big lug around here, goes by Jim?"

The girl laughed. "The big, big lug's in the kitchen stuffing his big, big face. I can't wait to see the look on his big, big face when he sees you, Whitman Coe."

"You seem to have me at a disadvantage," Whit said. "You know me, but I don't know you."

"Everybody in this town knows you, Whit Coe. Your books are banned in every school."

"Here's to that," Whit said and belted down his whisky. "I guess some things never change. Not that I'm exactly up on local events. I've been out of the loop for a while."

"So they say."

"They say lots of things."

"That's true," the bartender said. "Another?" She swirled her index finger in a circle.

"Please," Whit said.

"And such a polite boy," the girl said. She poured Whit a fresh glass of Bushmills. "But still at a disadvantage."

"That's hardly sporting," Whit said.

"Fair enough. I'll give you a clue." The girl leaned forward and rested her elbows on the bar. "Do I look just a wee bit familiar to you, Mr. Coe?"

"You do," Whit said. "Of course we couldn't have met here because I left town twenty-five years ago and you're—"

"Are you trying to ask a lady her age, Mr. Coe?" The girl raised an eyebrow.

"No. I only meant that—"

"I'm kidding, Mr. Coe," the girl said, grinning. "Such a serious man."

"Okay, I give," Whit said. "Why do you look so familiar to me?"

"Do you watch porn?"

"What?"

"Kidding again." The girl laughed and shook her head. "You're too easy, man. Okay, Mr. Whitman F. Coe." She leaned into Whit and raised her chin. "Take a good look at my face." She tilted her head, batted her eyelashes, then looked up and to the side.

Whit narrowed his eyes and studied the girl's face. His stare softened and he sat upright in his seat. "You look like…"

The girl winked. "Ladies and gentlemen, we have a winner! I'm her daughter."

"You're Maggie's girl," Whit said. "I didn't know."

"Like they say, you've been out of the loop a while. Pleased to meet you, Whitman Fitzgerald Coe. I'm Zelda Bell Sloan." She held her hand out, palm down and knuckles raised, like an old-timey lady presenting her hand to be kissed.

Whit squeezed Zelda's hand. "Pleased to meet you, Zelda Bell Sloan," he said and slammed his whisky. "Goddamn." He set the empty glass on the bar. "Same again, please, Zelda Bell Sloan."

Zelda poured another Bushmills. "Sorry about all the teasing, Mr. Coe. I wouldn't normally bust a perfect stranger's balls like that, but between reading all your books and hearing my mom's old stories about you, I guess I kinda feel like I know you. At least a little. And you're just too funny, man. So serious." She knit her brows and jutted out her chin.

"Yeah, yeah," Whit said. "Well, if you can bust my balls like an old buddy, you can call me Whit. You calling me Mr. Coe makes me feel old."

"You're not old, dude." Zelda leaned across the bar and squinted. "Although," she said, scratching the stubble on Whit's chin, "your kitty whiskers are getting a bit gray." She tapped the side of Whit's whisky glass. "Now finish your drink, kitty," she said and swished her finger in a circle again.

Whit did as he was told, and Zelda poured him another round.

"You're weird," Whit said.

"You're weird," Zelda said.

They looked at each other and giggled.

"New friend!" Zelda clapped, then scratched Whit's chin again. "Nice kitty."

"Okay, new friend," Whit said. "Let's catch up. How's your mom been?"

Zelda cast her eyes down, poured herself a shot of whisky, and took a heavy gulp. "I hate to be the one to tell you this, Whit," she said, "but my mom passed away about eight months ago. Cancer."

"Oh," Whit said. He slumped his shoulders. "Jesus. I'm so sorry. I didn't know."

Whit and Zelda took a silent slug of whisky together.

"I'm sorry too," Zelda said. "About your wife. My mom cried when she read about it in the paper."

"Why?"

"She said she was reading your obituary. She said in spite of that hard shell you show to the world, you feel things more deeply than anyone she'd ever met. And that hearts like yours don't break into big pieces you can glue back together. They shatter into tiny shards and scatter to the winds."

"All these years I was afraid that Maggie blamed me for the way I left. That she wouldn't understand. She deserved better. All my friends did. But her most of all."

"She never blamed you, Whit. She blamed your dad. She blamed this fucking town. But never you. She knew you were struggling with something she couldn't understand, and that you left the way you did to protect her and your friends. She said this town was too small and too evil for you. And if you'd stayed it would have crushed you. Or worse."

"Maggie always was the smart one," Whit said. "She was right. This fucking town. It's like a black hole that sucks you in and never lets you go. It slowly crushes you and all your dreams and everything you could ever do or become until there's nothing left. And there you are, frozen in time and space wondering what happened to your life. Where did it all go?"

Zelda glanced at the day-drunks out of the corner of her eye. "Or you just finally snap and kill someone."

"Well, there's always that."

Whit and Zelda chuckled.

"Holy shit, she smiles!" a husky man in a flannel shirt said as he popped out from behind the swinging kitchen doors. He was crunching on a basket of onion rings. Little crumbs nestled into his bird's nest of a beard. "Why aren't you scowling at the punters like usual?" He folded his arms across his chest and made a pouty face.

"Well, I just was a few seconds ago," Zelda said.

"And contemplating murder," Whit said.

"Fuck me," the burly bear man said. "No fucking way, man! No fucking way!" He lumbered around the bar to greet Whit. "Could it be?" he said with a big grin. "It can't be. It is! Whitman mother-f-ing Coe!"

Whit stood up and the bear man clasped him in a bear hug.

"Hey, Jim," Whit said.

"Hey, Whit," Jim said. "Goddamn it's good to see you, man."

"You too, buddy. But Jim. I can't breathe."

"Me neither, man. I just can't believe—"

"No, literally, Jim. You're crushing my lungs."

"Oh." Jim let go. "Sorry, Whit." He clapped Whit on the back. "Man it's been a stretch."

"It has."

"But man we had some good times back in the day."

"We did."

"I heard about your old man today," Jim said. "I know you two weren't exactly close, but I'm sorry, brother."

"Word travels fast."

"It's a small town, Whit. You know how it is. Anyway, I know you've been through some tough shit over the past few years, and I wish I could say something to make it all better, but I know I can't. So I'll skip the bullshit platitudes and pour you a shot of whisky."

"Thanks, Jim," Whit said. "That's probably the wisest thing anyone's said to me on the subject. And the whisky doesn't hurt."

"And if I claim to be a wise man, it surely means that I don't know," Jim said. "Double Bushmills?"

"Double wise. Carry on."

Whit finished off his current glass of whisky while Jim ducked back to the business side of the bar.

"I got it," Zelda told Jim, snatching the bottle of Bushmills.

Jim threw up his hands and retreated from the whisky bottle. "Yes ma'am," he said. "Mind if I have one too?"

Zelda kanpied her whisky and poured three more. She slid one to Whit. "There you go, kitty," she said.

"Slainte," Whit said.

"Slainte," Zelda and Jim said.

They drank.

Jim scratched at the ladybug tattoo on the inside of his left forearm.

"New ink?" Whit said.

"Nah," Jim said. "It's about three years old. Almost exactly three years old now that I think about it. On the summer solstice. Only reason I remember it was the solstice is because my tattoo guy, this real hippie-dippie, keeps saying how getting a ladybug tattoo on the solstice is like divine luck or destiny or something. I don't know. But the weird thing is that it always itches around this time of year. Damndest thing." He slapped the tattoos on Whit's upper arm. "I see you got some ink yourself, buddy. Celtic stuff, right?"

"Yep," Whit said.

"Yeah, I recognize that swirly symbol on your shoulder. What's it called?"

"A triskele."

"Right," Jim said, snapping his fingers. "Anyways, you want some grub, Whit? Menu hasn't changed."

"Good," Whit said. "I hate change. I'll take three pizzas—one cheese, one pepperoni, one Hawaiian—two dozen wings, three orders of chicken tenders, and four orders of frings to go."

"You got a tapeworm or is it just your cheat day?" Jim said.

Whit chuckled. "My son and I are crashing at Bob and Sarah's place while we're in town. I'm the pizza delivery guy tonight."

"Hey, I've got nothing but respect for pizza delivery guys," Jim said. "They're the backbone of the independent film industry."

"Jim," Whit said, "I think that's a different kind of film industry."

"Huh," Jim said. "That explains a couple of things. But seriously, man, say hi to Bob and Sarah for me. And tell Bob that prohibition's been over for like a hundred years, so he won't get collared if he happens to swing by the bar for a drink sometime."

"Will do," Whit said.

"Speaking of drinks," Zelda said and belted down her whisky. "Come on boys. Catch up."

Whit and Jim gulped down their whiskies.

Zelda was about to pour another round when Tails Only Tommy and Lanky Lewie McGee staggered in. They plopped down on a couple of stools at the corner of the bar and slouched against the bar top.

Jim and Zelda angled to face the McGee brothers, Jim sliding a hand under the bar to grip a weathered Reggie Jackson model baseball bat. Whit slid to the edge of his barstool and planted his feet on the ground.

"Nope," Jim said to Tommy and Lewie. "You boys know you're eighty-sixed for life. I told you, no drugs and no fighting in my bar. You broke the rules. You lost your privilege to drink here. Now get out." Jim pointed at the door.

"Shut up, fat tits," Tails Only Tommy said to Jim. Tommy and Lewie cackled. "Tell ya what. You want us to leave, why don'tcha make us leave?"

Jim tightened his grip on the bat but didn't make a move.

"Yeah, that's what I thought, pussy," Tommy said. He leered at Zelda. "Hey, little girl. Since fat tits over there ain't got the sack to move his fat ass, why don't ya bring us a couple of Schlitzes and two shots of Jim Beam? And while you're at it, how 'bout you slide down under the bar and suck my—"

Whit cut Tommy's sentence short by bouncing his face off the bar. Tommy made a gurgling sound in his throat as he choked on the blood streaming from his broken nose.

"Oops," Whit said. "How clumsy of me."

"Goddammit, asshole!" Tommy lurched to his feet. "You 'bout to get fucked u—" Tommy wheeled around, right hand cocked in a fist behind his ear. He dropped his hands when he saw Whit towering over him.

"You gonna finish that sentence, Chinatown?" Whit said, running a finger along the bridge of his nose.

"Whi-Whit? That you?" Tommy said and pinched his bleeding nose.

"In the flesh," Whit said.

Tommy and Lewie shuffled a couple of paces toward the door.

"Well, shit, Whit," Tommy said. "I wasn't 'spectin to see ya here."

"I can see that, Tommy."

"So what brings ya, Whit?"

"Shut the fuck up, Tommy." Whit took a long slow step toward Tommy and Lewie. He looked down and sized them up. "Tails Only Tommy and Lanky Lewie McGee. You boys haven't changed a bit. Still gotta learn everything the hard way. So here's an etiquette lesson for you." He cuffed Tommy, open handed, across the face, then did the same to Lewie. "Lesson one. My friend asked you nicely to leave. The polite thing to do is leave. So leave. Now. Or I'm gonna ask you to leave myself. But I won't ask so nicely."

"Whoa, whoa, whoa, Whit," Tommy said. He raised his hands and backed toward the door. "Everything's cool. We ain't lookin for no trouble. We was just foolin around. We'll be on our way."

"Well look at that," Whit said. "Looks like you boys learned something after all. Now I've got one more lesson just for you, Tommy." Whit slapped Tommy across the face again. Harder this time. "Keep your mouth shut and your vile suggestions in your pants." He cuffed the back of Tommy's head.

Whit flicked his head toward the door. "Now drag your sorry asses out of here," he said, "and don't ever come back. Unless you want another lesson."

"Sure thing, bro," Lanky Lewie said.

"It's all good, Whit," Tommy said. "We're leavin and we ain't never comin back. Swear to Jesus."

"Swear to Jesus," Whit repeated, cocking his head. "I'll take that as an oath, Tommy. So how about you, Lewie? Do I have your word?"

"Yeah, Whit," Lewie said. "You got my word."

"That's good," Whit said. "A man's only as good as his word, and an oath is a sacred thing. You know, about fifteen years ago I was in a museum, and they had this exhibition of medieval torture devices. Fascinating stuff. Did you boys know they had specific torture devices to fit each crime? And they had two different devices used to punish a man who broke his word. One was called the pear of anguish. It's this little pear-shaped device made up of metal segments. The metal segments are attached to a screw. Now they'd take this metal pear and jam it into the oathbreaker's mouth and turn the screw. And as they turned the screw, the metal segments would open up like a flower in bloom. And bit by bit, the oathbreaker's teeth would shatter and his jaw would break. Now what do you boys think that would feel like?

"The second device was pretty straightforward. It's called a tongue tearer, and—even you boys should be able to guess—it was used to tear out the oathbreaker's tongue. You see the tongue tearer looked like a long pair of iron scissors. They'd hold the tongue tearer in a fire until it got red hot. Then they'd clamp it on the oathbreaker's tongue and twist it. And the tongue tearer was so hot from the flames that after about three turns the tissue of the tongue would just sorta melt and stretch off like saltwater taffy. You boys have had saltwater taffy before, right? Now what do you boys think that would feel like?"

Whit took a step forward and stared down his nose at the McGee brothers. "Now Tommy, Lewie," he said. "You wouldn't want to learn the hard way happens when you break an oath to me, would you?"

Tommy and Lewie shook their heads.

"Good," Whit said. He leaned close to Tommy and Lewie and said in a voice low enough that Jim and Zelda couldn't hear, "Because if you boys even *think* about breaking your oath and bothering my friends again, I'll know it. And I'll reach right into your little brains and tear that thought out. I'll just tear it right the fuck out of your skulls. Now what do you boys think that would feel like?"

For a brief flash, Tommy thought he saw Whit's eyes flicker black.

***

Tommy peeled his pickup truck onto the road.

"This is bad," Lewie said.

"No shit, dipshit," Tommy said.

"Every time that man come around, everything goes straight to Hell."

"He ain't no man, Lewie," Tommy said. "But you're right on one account. More right than you know. Whitman Coe will send us all straight to the fires of Hell if we don't stop him."

Lewie scratched his head. "What you meanin, brother?"

"I mean he ain't no man. He's a demon from the fiery pits of Hell. And the righteous Christian man must stop him at all cost. The Lord Jesus shall show me the way."

"What you sayin, Tommy?"

Tails only Tommy looked his brother in the eye. "Whitman Coe must die."

CHAPTER 24

Deuce throttled his bicycle brakes and skidded across his father's lawn, leaving a long, crooked scar across its pristine green surface. He fishtailed the bike to a stop, leapt off, and trotted up the front porch steps into the house.

His father was standing in the foyer, one hand resting on his hip, the other holding a Budweiser. "So whatcha been up to, boy?" Chip said.

"Nothin, Daddy," Deuce said. "Just hangin out by the creek with Skunk and them."

"Nothin, huh?" Chip chugged his beer and set the empty bottle on an oak console table beside the doorway. "Just hangin out with the boys. That it?"

"Yessir."

"You ain't got up to no mischief?"

"Nossir."

"Don't shit a shitter, boy. I know what you been up to and I know when you're lyin to me. I'm your old man and I'm a cop. So don't even try to bullshit me, boy."

"If you already know everything, what you askin me all this shit for?"

"I'm just testing how dumb you are, boy. And you failed the test. So you wanna tell me what you really been up to?"

"Daddy, I already told you—"

Chip slapped Deuce across the face. "What did I just say about lyin to me?"

"Not to."

"Then why the fuck are you lyin to me right after I just told you not to, you fuckin idiot?"

"Daddy, I—"

Chip raised his hand. "Were you about to lie to me again, boy?"

"Nossir."

"Good." Chip folded his arms over his chest. "Now for the last time, what you really been up to?"

"Shit. I shoulda knowed that little Rockwell nerd woulda ratted me out."

"What the fuck are you talkin about?"

"Nothin, Daddy."

"Boy," Chip said.

"Me and the boys was just mindin our own business chuckin rocks by the creek when Stephen and that new kid come across the creek into our turf. Me and the boys was just—"

"What new kid?"

"That Coe kid with the grandaddy just got wasted next door to Stephen's house. The one with the daddy writes all them satanic books."

"Goddamn sonofabitchin Bob." Chip hooked his thumbs in his belt loops and grit his teeth. "Merril, you best just stay clear of Stephen and that Coe kid. You and your cousins just leave 'em be. You hear me?"

"Yeah, Daddy."

"I mean it, Merril. Bob works for me. That means he's under my wing, shitbird though he may be. And that Coe kid'll be gone in a couple days. Him and his psycho old man. That whole family ain't right. So stay clear. You hear me? Stay clear of them all."

"You're scared of that poetry-writin faggot," Deuce said.

Chip grabbed Deuce by the neck of his T-shirt and scudded him against the wall. "You got no idea what you're talkin about, boy."

Deuce could smell stale Budweiser and beef jerky on his father's breath.

"Right now," Chip said, "it's *you* oughta be afraid of *me*. 'Cause you're about two words away from an ass whoopin, son." He stared into Deuce's eyes and saw his own reflection. Deuce looked away.

"Yeah, that's what I thought." Chip let go of his son's shirt. "Little pantywaist."

Chip sauntered back a step and drew himself to his full height. "Now let's get to the fuckup I wanted to talk to you about in the first place before you brought me a whole new fuckup." He reached into his back pocket and pulled out the Ace of Spades card he had found on Mrs. Foley's dead Pomeranian. "Here's a magic trick for ya. Was this your fuckin card?" He flicked the card into Deuce's face. The card bounced off the boy's nose and fluttered to the floor.

"Daddy, I don't know nothin—"

Chip cuffed Deuce across the face again. "What did I *just say* about *lying* to me!"

Deuce looked at his shoes and pressed his back against the wall as though he could disappear behind it.

"You know where I found this?" Chip pointed at the card on the floor.

Deuce didn't speak. He shuddered against the wall and sobbed.

"Yeah, you know where I found it. You know who does shit like this? Ted Bundy. Jeffrey Dahmer. Fuckin serial killers, Merril. Just what the hell is wrong with you? Never mind. I don't even wanna know. Just stop it. Right fuckin now."

Chip took a half step back and ran his stocky fingers through his crewcut. "You're sick, boy. And just lookin at you makes me sick." He pointed down the hallway. "Now go to your room. Go on. Get out of my sight. And if you ever do anything like this again, I will beat the skin off of you. You hear me?"

"Yessir."

"Good. Now go to your room and don't come out. You're grounded until further notice."

Deuce slunk down the hallway. His cheek still stung where his father had slapped him and his back ached where it had cratered into the wall. He smeared tears from his face as he walked. He went to his room and slammed the door behind him.

"Fuck you, old man," he said under his breath.

***

Deuce paced in his cramped bedroom. He fidgeted with his pocketknife. Pulled the skin mag out from under his mattress and lay down on his bed. Turned the pages and ogled the naked women. And felt nothing.

He wanted to feel something. He had tried many times. He just couldn't.

He slid his hands down the front of his boxers and fiddled with himself. Still nothing. He was as soft as a wad of cookie dough melting in the sun.

Only one thing worked for Deuce. And he needed it.

He got out of bed and stood in front of the bedroom door. He pressed his ear against the door and listened. He could hear the exaggerated shouts of the wrestling announcers blaring through the living room speakers. Deuce smirked. His old man would be zoned in on the matches for a good hour or so, blissfully unaware of everyone and everything else.

Deuce turned his bedside radio to the local heavy metal station, loud enough that his father would hear it if he passed by in the hall, but low enough that he wouldn't tell Deuce to turn it down. He wrapped his hand around the doorknob and turned it as quietly as he could manage. He inched the door open and peeked his head out. All clear.

Now for the tricky part. He skulked into the kitchen and eased open the fridge. He always kept a couple of opened cans of tuna in the otherwise unoccupied veggie crisper drawer for occasions like this. Couldn't always risk the noise of the can opener. He grabbed a crusty fork from the sink and scraped the tuna into a Ziploc baggie, then slipped out the kitchen door as his father cheered at the wrestling match. Operation jailbreak successful.

The sun was starting to set when Deuce reached the woods. He wandered through the brush. Searching. Hunting. No luck. He crossed to the far side of the woods and popped up in a dirt clearing spotted with weeds and scrub.

And finally found what he needed.

A brown striped cat materialized from a weed thicket. It wafted forward and regarded Deuce with fear and hunger in its eyes. The cat licked its lips, gave Deuce a sidelong glance, and began to trot toward the woods.

Deuce opened the Ziploc bag of tuna. "Here, kitty, kitty," he called. He pinched a wad of tuna between his fingers, bent down, and extended his hand toward the cat. The cat slithered forward and stared at the fish. "Here, kitty, kitty. You hungry, boy?"

The cat lowered its head, revealing bony shoulders beneath its patchy fur. It edged toward Deuce, then stopped just beyond the boy's reach. It peered up at Deuce, then sniffed the tuna on his fingers. Deuce didn't move. Didn't breathe. The cat licked at the fish, probing and tasting. Then it began to nibble at the tuna, eyes closed and head bobbing with each bite.

Deuce reached into the Ziploc and scattered a handful of tuna across the ground in front of the cat like some bizarre fish-planting Johnny Appleseed. The brown striped cat chowed down ravenously, lost in its meal.

"Nice kitty," Deuce whispered as he drew his pocketknife. "Nice kitty."

CHAPTER 25

"How are you not drunk?" Zelda said to Whit and poured another round of Bushmills.

Whit shrugged. "Years of practice, I guess."

"I know what it is," Zelda said. "You've got that writer's metabolism. They all drink like fish."

"And then they die," Whit said.

"That's dark," Zelda said.

"You're dark."

"Shut up." Zelda smacked Whit on the chest with the back of her hand.

"Hey," Jim said. "I can drink like a fish. Wanna see?"

"No," Zelda said.

Whit spread his hands and raised his shoulders. "Well, now that you've built it up…"

Jim grabbed a clean shot glass, pulled the soda gun, and squeezed a spurt of club soda into the glass. He took an egregious gulp, filling his cheeks, and spat the club soda out in a stream from the corners of his mouth. He placed his hands against the sides of his neck and flapped them back and forth like gills. "See," he gurgled. "I'm drinking like a fish."

"Dude, gross," Zelda said.

"You get it?" Jim said. "Because of the gills and… No?"

"Oh man," Whit said. "Jim O'Malley, you haven't grown up one day."

"That's because I'm a Toys R Us kid."

"What?" Zelda said.

"It's an old ad from—Never mind," Whit said.

"I won't grow up. I'm gonna stay a kid forever," Jim said.

"Well, you're doing a bang-up job so far," Zelda said.

"Like a big Baby Huey," Whit said.

"An adolescent Sasquatch," Zelda said.

"A juvenile Wookiee."

Whit and Zelda giggled.

"Yeah, ha, ha," Jim said. "Y'all look like if Aquaman and the goth chick from Beetlejuice went back to the eighties and formed a rock band." He strummed an air guitar and chortled to himself.

"Laugh it up, fuzzball," Whit said. "Beetlejuice was from the eighties, ya goober."

"Hey, Jim," Zelda said. "You wanna join our eighties rock band?"

"Hell yeah," Jim said.

"Awesome," Zelda said. "I always wanted to be in a band with Saxsquatch." She mimed playing a saxophone.

Whit, Jim, and Zelda broke into a wave of laughter, then Jim said, "Oh, man. Good times." He wiped his eyes with a bar napkin and gulped at his whisky. "Just like old times. Ah-hah. Speaking of..." He raised a finger. "Zelda, give me your magic quarter."

Zelda passed Jim the quarter on a string, and Jim hared off to the jukebox.

"What's he doing?" Zelda asked Whit.

"I'm not sure, but I'm pretty sure you don't want to know."

Jim punched some numbers into the jukebox and jogged back to the bar. He passed the quarter back to Zelda and looked at Whit with a big shit-eating grin.

"What did you do?" Whit said.

"Just wait for it." Jim held up a hand and gestured at one of the wall speakers. "Any second now. Any second. Aaaannd…"

A honky-tonk piano melody chimed through the speakers.

"No," Whit said.

"Yes," Jim said.

Zelda flicked her eyes back and forth between the two men.

"Lookin at your watch a good time," Michael Stipe sang in an exaggerated twang.

"Waitin near the station for the bus!" Whit and Jim shouted along.

When the song hit the chorus, Michael Stipe sang, "Don't go back to Rockville," but Whit and Jim sang their version: "Don't go back to Rockwell!"

By the second time the chorus kicked in, Zelda had learned Whit and Jim's alternate version of the song and joined in. When the song faded out, they all clapped, high-fived, and drained their glasses of whisky.

"Oh my God," Zelda said. "Where did you find that and why, Jim, did you never teach it to me?"

"Fuckin Whit the wit, man. When we were in high school, he was always listening to these obscure old CDs. And one day he played this one in his car after school and he starts singing his version of the chorus. Course I'd never heard the song before, and Whit's singing louder than the car stereo, so I thought the song really was 'Don't go back to Rockwell.' Like for months."

"That's awesome," Zelda said. "Was that R.E.M.?"

"It was," Whit said. "Good ear. It's not in their usual style. Actually, I heard the song started out as kind of a joke. You know, just the band goofing off. But it turned out to be a pretty good song."

"Well, buddy," Jim said to Whit, "much as I hate to break up the party, your food oughta be about ready, so I'll go back and check on it. But I couldn't let you go without playing that blast from the past."

"It's a good memory," Whit said.

"We did have our share," Jim said. "Oh, I meant to ask: when's your old man's funeral?"

"Tomorrow."

"That's efficient."

"I'm sure my cat misses me."

"Right," Jim said. "Anyways, if you want to throw a wake for your old man or just get some guests together afterwards, feel free to use the pub. Mi casa es su casa, buddy."

"You sure?" Whit said.

"He's sure," Zelda said. "Kitty come visit!" She tented her hands and clapped her fingers together.

Jim raised his eyebrows and cast Zelda a sidelong glance. "What she means to say is it's no trouble at all and we'd be more than happy to host y'all."

"Well in that case, how can I refuse?" Whit said.

"You can't," Zelda said.

"Then it's settled," Jim said. "Wake at O' Malley's tomorrow. Rockwell's gala event of the century."

"Dead man's party," Whit said. "Who could ask for more? Thanks, Jim."

"What are juvenile Wookiees for?"

Zelda bounced up and down and clapped her hands. "Yay, yay! Kitty comes back to play!"

Jim glanced at Zelda out of the corner of his eye again. "Girl, you're weird today," he said. "I've never seen anyone so excited for a wake in my life. Anyways, Whit, it's been great seeing you again, old buddy. I haven't had this much fun in a long time. Lemme grab your order. I'll be right back." He flipped a quick wave at Whit and popped behind the swinging double doors into the kitchen.

"One for the road?" Zelda said.

"Why not?"

Zelda grabbed two clean glasses and filled them with whisky. "Slainte," she said.

"Slainte," Whit said.

They clinked glasses and took a swig.

"I'm really glad we met," Zelda said.

"Me too," Whit said.

"You know," Zelda said, "you're exactly like I always pictured you from your writing, and from what my mom told me about you."

"What did she say about me?"

"Well for one thing, she said you were easy on the eyes." She tilted her head toward Whit and raised an eyebrow. "She said you were really funny in a dark, deadpan sort of way. That you were a good friend. Loyal. She said you cared more than you let on. She also said you had one hell of a temper." She raised an eyebrow again. "But you only turned it on bad people. Like you did tonight with those McGee assholes. That reminded me of something she once said about you that always stuck with me, though I didn't understand what she meant until tonight."

"What was that?"

"She said you were the shepherd who eats the wolves."

CHAPTER 26

Whit hunched at the edge of the guest room bed flipping through the photo album he'd taken from Astrid's room. He paused on a picture from Halloween when he and Astrid had been seven or eight. Whit was dressed as a knight. Astrid was dressed as a princess—or a hincess, as Astrid had said when she was little. Always a knight and a princess. Always the sword and the tiara.

Whit looked at his sister's smiling face and pressed his fingers to his forehead.

A knock at the door shook Whit to attention. He snapped the photo album shut and set it on the bed.

"Hey, Dada?" Junior twisted the doorknob.

"What is your name?" Whit grated at the closed door.

Junior swung the door open and said, "I am Arthur, King of the Britons."

"What is your quest?"

"To seek the Holy Grail."

"What," Whit said, "is the airspeed of a swallow?"

"What do you mean?" Junior said. "An African swallow, or a European swallow?"

"I don't know that. Ahhh!" Whit flung himself back onto the bed.

Junior raced across the room and pounced on his dad, laughing.

Whit sat up smiling. "Hey, buddy," he said. "Come to say goodnight?"

"Yeah, I'm getting tired."

"That's because you ate like sixteen chicken tenders and a whole basket of frings."

"It was worth it." Junior pointed at the photo album on the bed. "What's that, Dada?" he said.

"Oh, nothing," Whit said. "Just an old photo album from when I was a kid."

"Can I see it? I've never seen pictures of you when you were a kid. How come?"

"Because when I left this town, I had to leave everything behind."

"Why?"

"Long story. Doesn't really matter now."

"Oh. Okay, Dada. So can I see the pictures?"

"Sure, buddy."

Junior picked up the photo album and leafed through the pages. "Hey," he said, pointing at a picture of Whit in a baseball uniform, "that looks like me. Is that you?"

"Yep. A very long time ago."

Junior thumbed through a few more pages. "Who's the little girl in all those pictures with you?" he asked.

"That was my twin sister Astrid. She died of Leukemia when we were nine."

"I didn't know you had a twin sister."

"Yeah, I guess there were a lot of memories I'd been trying to leave behind. Does that make any sense?"

"I think so, Dada. Did Mommy know you had a twin sister?"

"Of course. She knew everything about me. She was the only person who ever really knew me. And she loved me anyway."

"I know you pretty well, Dada. And I love you."

"I love you too, buddy," Whit said. "More than anyone in the world." He wrapped an arm around Junior's shoulder.

Junior gave Whit a big hug. "Goodnight, Dada," he said.

Whit squeezed his son. "Goodnight, buddy. Now get some sleep. We've got an early day tomorrow."

"Okay, Dada. Seeya in the morning."

"Sweet dreams, buddy."

"You too, Dada."

CHAPTER 27

*W*hitman. *Whit.* The voice sounded small and far away. It was a little girl's voice. *Whit.*

Whit opened his eyes. He was sitting slumped forward on the edge of the bed. The first thing he saw was a pair of tiny red shoes. Ruby slippers. He sat upright and raised his head.

Astrid was standing in front of him at eye level. Her eyes were black and her skin was grey blue as though she had been someplace very cold for a very long time. She wore a pink princess gown and a plastic tiara.

Astrid pressed her fingers to her lips and motioned Whit to follow her. Then she turned and walked into the darkened hallway.

Whit followed. He followed Astrid down the hallway and across the living room. Out the door and into the night. Across the lawn and up the porch steps of their childhood home. He followed her inside the house. Into the darkness.

Shadows clasped Whit in their coils as he entered the living room. The house was as claustrophobic as a sepulcher. Pure dark.

An otherworldly red-orange glow burned in the corridor. A single beam of light shone down through the open attic door like a spotlight calling Whit to his place. The ladder to the attic was down. The spotlight illuminated its steps in craggy chunks.

The little girl's hand reached down from the dark rectangle of the attic trapdoor. She crooked a finger, beckoning Whit. He followed as though he were sleepwalking. His feet seemed to carry him of their own will to the hellish spotlight below the attic.

Whit tilted his head back and gazed into the red-orange light and the darkness that surrounded it. He peered down the corridor ahead. At the yawning walls that extended into the chasm without end. He looked back over his shoulder. The path he had taken was gone. It had been replaced by a cold black chamber stretching into eternity. The abyss stared at Whit from all sides.

The sound of scraping claws echoed down the corridor. *K-tchikitikitik. K-tchikitikitik.* Ahead and behind. There was only one way Whit could go. Still moving like a sleepwalker, he climbed the ladder and edged his head through the attic door.

Astrid was standing in the corner at the far end of the room. Her limbs and torso burned vermillion in the glow of the phantasmal spotlight. Her head was completely engulfed in shadow, making her look like the specter of a decapitated little girl. A pale shape loomed beside her.

Whit cleared the top of the ladder and planted his feet on the rickety wooden planks of the attic floor. One of the boards groaned beneath his weight. He could see Astrid's face again. It was expressionless. Hollow. Whit examined the pale shape beside Astrid—a flat, oblong object covered by an old white sheet that had faded to a soiled yellow.

Astrid looked up at Whit, then at the object beneath the sheet. She looked at Whit again, waiting.

Whit reached out and flung the sheet aside. He looked underneath. And saw himself. His image reflected in a mirror. *The* mirror. His mother's antique looking glass that had hung on the living room wall until she died, and Whit's father secreted all her belongings in the attic.

Whit gazed into the mirror as though spellbound. Then he gently picked it up and carried it in his arms like a lost lover to the living room. He placed the mirror back on the wall where it had once hung. Where it belonged.

Whit stared through the looking glass, and it stared through him. Through the Other's eyes. Through the burning black holes set into that unfathomable face.

The black maw spiraled inside Whit's head. Drawing closer. Opening wider. Springing open to eclipse Whit in the black hole sun.

CHAPTER 28

Three days until the end of the world

*H*ey, sunshine.
Sunshine, warm and white, spilled through the bedroom window and came to rest, though not peacefully, on Whit's closed eyelids. He stirred under the glare but didn't open his eyes. Not yet.

He had been dreaming of Alice again. He knew this because he could still hear her voice in his head. An echo of love and welcome.

Hey, sunshine.

He knew this because he could still smell her hair and the charcoal-gray hoodie she so often wore. He knew this because he could still feel the soft brush of her fingers as she took him by the hand and led him to a time and place he had once known. A time and place now gone, except in dream and memory. But most of all, he knew this because he felt a desolate sese of loss. A sinking emptiness collapsing at his core.

This was how Whitman Coe woke up almost every morning.

Whit turned his face away from the window and sat up. He slumped forward and snatched the overturned whisky bottle off the floor. He swallowed his morning medicine.

He looked at the black suit draped over the back of the desk chair. It was encased in plastic like a corpse in a body bag. Today was his father's funeral. Whit wasn't sure how he felt about that.

After three cups of black coffee, he went through the motions of getting ready for the funeral—shower, shave, suit up, help Junior with his necktie. On the way out the door, he checked his hair, straightened his tie, and took a hard look at the face in the mirror.

***

The face in the mirror looked the same. Except for the eyes.

Whit hadn't bothered to go to bed last night. He couldn't get used to sleeping in that big bed without Alice. So he'd sat in the red wingback chair at his writing desk with a bottle of whisky until the sun came up on the day he buried his wife.

He made scrambled eggs, pancakes, and toast for Junior, but ate nothing himself. Then he put on his black suit, helped Junior tie his necktie, and studied his face in the mirror before they left for the service.

He reached for Alice's car keys on the hook beside the door. They weren't there. He searched the coffee table, the kitchen table, his writing desk, the bedside table. He flung the couch cushions onto the floor.

"Fuck, fuck, goddamn keys! Where are the goddamn car keys!" He clawed at his tie and gulped for air. "Where the fuck are the fucking keys!"

"Dada." Junior laid his hand on his father's shoulder.

Whit looked down at his son.

"Dada, they're in your hand."

Whit unclenched his fist. Alice's car keys were in his palm, snagged on his wedding ring.

"I'm sorry, buddy," Whit said. "I guess Dada kinda freaked out there for a minute."

"It's okay, Dada," Junior said. "I'm pretty freaked out too."

***

Alice's hearse led the funeral procession through a granite rain. Whit and Junior trailed the hearse in Alice's car.

"Don't let her get away, Dada," Junior said. "We can't lose her."

"I won't, buddy," Whit said. "Promise."

The procession wended its way along the damp gray streets and through the cemetery gate to the sloping green hillside where Alice would be laid to rest.

Whit and Junior stood together on the hillside, staring at Alice's gleaming black casket. Its surface beaded with droplets of rain.

Whit wrapped his arm around his son's shoulder as the funeral ceremony began.

***

Whit wrapped his arm around his son's shoulder as the funeral ceremony ended. The sun glinted off the oak veneer of Allan and Barbara Coe's coffins, stinging Whit's eyes.

"And now may the Lord bless thee and keep thee," a minister in a black robe and clear-rimmed glasses said. "May the Lord make his face shine upon thee, and be gracious unto thee. May the Lord lift up his countenance upon thee, and give thee peace. Amen." He signaled the faithful that the eulogy was over by spreading his arms wide, palms facing skyward like Christ the Redeemer overlooking Rio. He stepped back from the caskets and gazed out at the gathering, a practiced beatific smile on his face.

Adam applauded and shuffled forward to face the mourners. "Dearly beloved," he said, "we are gathered here in the sight of God and his son Jesus to celebrate the lives of my father Allan Coe and my mother Barbara Coe. They were good people. Salt of the earth. Good Christians. And I know they're lookin down on us from Heaven. For they believed in the Lord Jesus, and all whosoever believeth in Jesus shall be saved, for Jesus saves."

"And Moses invests," Whit said under his breath. Bob, Sarah, Jim, and Dave giggled, earning a scowl from an old woman with an unconvincing red-orange dye job.

"And I'm sure," Adam said, "my folks are real glad to be lookin down and seein all you come out to pay your respects. When I look around me here, I see a lot of love and respect and Christian fellowship. And I wanna thank y'all for bein here to share in that love and respect and Christian fellowship.

"I also see a lot of headstones. Sometimes I feel like all I see is headstones. Most of my friends are dead. And now my parents. Me and my brother Whit have seen too much death."

The corners of Whit's mouth tightened. He scraped his thumbnail along the edge of his index nail.

"Even before I was born," Adam said, "Whit had lost loved ones. He lost his twin sister and his mother when he was a kid. He was way too young to go through that. And now…" Adam paused and looked at Whit.

Don't say it. Don't you dare fucking say it.

"He's lost his wife and soul mate Alice."

Whit glared at Adam from underneath his eyebrows.

"Whit, stay strong, bro," Adam continued to testify. "Keep fightin. You will be with your loved ones again after you have fulfilled your destiny. Love and respect."

Whit placed two fingers beside his right eye and pressed hard.

"In conclusion," Adam said, "I wanna thank you all again for bein here and showin your love and respect for my mother and father. Mother, Father," he looked at the caskets, then up at the sky, "I love you and we'll be together again in Heaven someday."

Adam gestured at Whit. "And now I wanna welcome a very special speaker. My brother Whit the writer would like to say a few words."

Whit shook his head and waved his hands back and forth in front of his body.

Adam waved Whit forward. "Come on up, bro," he said. "Don't be shy."

"No, Adam," Whit said.

"Aww, come on, big bro. I'm sure everyone would like to hear some words from you. C'mon up." He waved again. "Come o—"

"Goddammit it, Adam!" Whit shouted. "I said no! Stop including me in your pity party and stop talking to me about God and Jesus and all that bullshit! And stop pushing me! It's not all about you! Fuck!" He looked around at the mourners. Saw the stunned expressions on their faces. "I'm sorry," he said.

Whit placed his hand on Junior's back and led his son to the car.

Beneath the shade of a yellow flowering tree, a tall old man in a gray tweed suit watched them drive away.

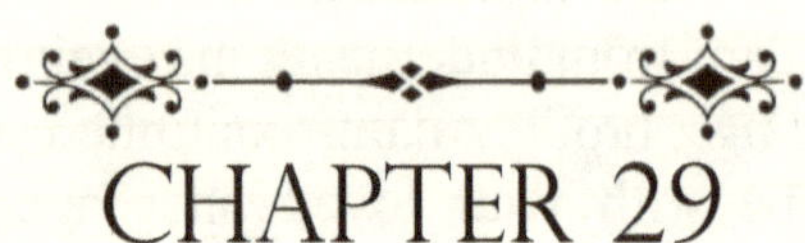

CHAPTER 29

Adam's pickup clunked across the cratered blacktop bridge into Isabella Creek. Past ramshackle trailers and abandoned dirt lots. Past packs of feral dogs and shirtless children. Thunking over potholes that pitted the streets like the scars of artillery shells until he rolled onto the dirt sidewalk in front of Mike Forester's decaying single-wide trailer.

Adam skipped up the cinderblock steps to Mike's trailer and knocked on the rust-corroded screen door. A hollow buzz rattled through the frame. He tried to peek inside, but the layers of grime encrusting the tattered mesh screen blocked his view.

A scattered rustling and what sounded to Adam like a beer bottle toppling rose from the murk inside the trailer. Then the shuffle of footsteps as the outline of a short, scrawny man approached.

"Well, I'll be dipped in shit," Mike said, swinging the door half open. "Adam Coe, 's that you?"

"Hell yeah, it's me, M.F."

"Well, damn, son! It's been a coon's age, yo!" Mike swung open the layers of dust that served as his front door. "C'mon in, bro."

Adam stepped into the trailer. It was decked out in modern hillbilly couture. A torn brown faux-leather sofa leaned against the near wall. Some of the tears in the cushions had been patched with duct tape, others had been ignored. Yellow-brown foam stuffing protruded from the unmended tears like the innards of a gutted animal.

On the floor beside the sofa, a haphazard pile of *Penthouse* and *Easy Rider* magazines threatened to Jenga-slide in a scree of Harley Davidsons and hooters. In keeping with the themes of Harley Davidsons and hooters, Mike's wood-chip walls were plastered with centerfolds and Harley Davidson mirrors.

An uncovered yellow-and-brown-stained mattress lay on the floor in the center of the room. Mike had disassembled the bedframe and shoved it into a corner. He had also disassembled two old televisions, a stereo, a rotary phone, a Tandy computer, and a CB radio. Their guts were strewn around the trailer in a Boschian scene of electronic carnage. And the piece de resistance was a two-foot-deep pile of empty toilet paper rolls piled up in the back corner like a barrow mound.

Adam eyed the pump shotgun dangling in Mike's grip.

Mike smiled. A few of his teeth were still left. "Don't worry, dog," he said. "This ain't for you." He wedged the scatter gun back into the corner between the screen door and the wall. "Can't be too careful these days, ya know? So, what can I do ya for, bro?"

"Same ol'. Twenty crystal, sixty Oxy."

"Hell yeah, bro. No problemo." Mike grinned his mostly toothless grin again. "I'll be right back."

Mike went into the back room, rummaged around for a few seconds, and came back with a pair of Ziplocs—one filled with pills, the other with rough white powder. Adam handed Mike four twenty-dollar bills and Mike handed Adam the Ziplocs.

"I kicked in a little extra crystal for ya, bro," Mike said. "Special friends-and-family discount 'cause you always been a real good friend to me."

"Thanks, bro," Adam said and shook Mike's hand.

Mike slapped Adam on the back. "Any time, brother," he said. "It's been way too long. I missed ya, bro."

"Me too," Adam said and shoved his fix down the front of his black funeral pants.

CHAPTER 30

Zelda's face lit up when she saw Whit and Junior walk into the bar in their matching black suits. "Hey, boys," she said. "Nice costumes."

"Actually," Whit said, "we're Agents Plant and Paige." He reached into his breast pocket, pulled out his wallet, and flashed it like a badge. "FBI."

"Right. So what can I get for you, Agents?"

"Can I have a Shirley Temple?" Junior said.

"Of course you can, Agent." Zelda poured a glass of Bushmills for Whit, then whipped up a Shirley Temple for Junior.

Whit and Junior thanked Zelda for the drinks.

"So, Agent," Zelda said to Junior, "what's your real name?"

"I'm Junior."

"Nice to meet you, Junior. I'm Zelda."

"Oh, cool! Like *the Legend of Zelda*?"

"Kind of. I'm actually named after the same person the video game character was named after."

"*The Legend of Zelda* is named after a real person?"

"Yep. Zelda Fitzgerald. She was married to the writer F. Scott Fitzgerald way back in the 1920s."

"Wow, that's cool. My Dada's a writer too. And his middle name is Fitzgerald." Junior inhaled a stream of Shirley Temple through his straw.

"I know," Zelda said. "I've read all of his books. He's one of my favorites."

"Not your *very* favorite?" Whit said.

"Shut up." Zelda smiled and swatted Whit's chest with the flat of her hand. "And not that I'm complaining, but aren't you boys here a bit early?"

"Yeah." Whit took a slug of whisky and rubbed his chin with the palm of his hand. "We left early."

"Really?"

"I don't wanna talk about it."

"You know Jim's just gonna tell me the minute he gets here, so why don't you beat that juvenile Wookiee to the punch?"

"I don't know."

Junior placed both hands against the bar and leaned forward. "My Dada told a funny joke at the funeral and made Bob and Sarah and Jim and Dave laugh, and then he yelled *the f-word* at my Uncle Adam so we got to leave early."

"Wow," Zelda said and raised her eyebrows. "There's got to be a good story behind that."

"Yeah," Junior said.

"Thanks, Agent Paige," Whit said to Junior. "Way to blow my cover."

"What?" Junior said.

"Hey, Junior," Zelda said. "Do you like classic video games?"

"Yeah," Junior said. "They're super fun."

"Damn right," Zelda said. "And it just so happens, we've got the original *Mortal Kombat* arcade game right over there." She gestured toward a line of arcade machines along the back wall.

"Cool, really?"

"Yep," Zelda said. "And..." She reached into her front jeans pocket and fished out the rigged quarter she used for the jukebox. "This," she swung the quarter from its string like a hypnotist, "is a magic quarter. I drilled a tiny hole through it and tied a string around it, so as long as you don't let the string slide into the coin slot, you can keep playing the same quarter over and over." She dangled the quarter out to Junior. "So you can borrow it and play all the games you want. Just remember to keep the string outside the slot and bring it back to me when you're done, okay?"

"Okay," Junior said and took the quarter. "Thanks."

Zelda nodded and winked at Junior.

Junior suspended the coin in front of his eyes and examined it like a holy icon, then slurped down the rest of his Shirley Temple. "Wanna play me, Dada?" he said.

"As soon as I finish this drink," Whit said. "Besides, you better get *warmed up* if you're gonna take on Sub-Zero. See what I did there?"

Junior smiled and shook his head. "Ha, ha, Dada." He pointed at Whit's glass of whisky and said, "Finish him!" then scampered around the corner to the *Mortal Kombat* game.

Whit grinned at his son and downed his whisky.

"Got time for another round, Sub-Zero?" Zelda said.

"Well, maybe just one."

Zelda poured two glasses of Bushmills and slid one to Whit. "Slainte," she said.

"Slainte," Whit said and they swigged their drinks.

"So, you okay?" Zelda said.

"About today?" Whit shrugged. "I'm fine. Just a lot of bullshit. It's just—you ever know someone who's such an asshole that they always make you look like an asshole too?"

"Yeah," Zelda said, "but my dad left when I was five, so…"

"Sorry," Whit said.

"Don't be. There's some people we're just better off without."

"That's true."

"And," Zelda said, raising her glass, "there's some people we're better off with."

Whit raised his glass in return. "That's true too," he said.

Whit and Zelda clinked glasses and drank.

"So," Zelda said, "now that all the fun, fun funeral business is over, how much longer will you be in town?"

"Can't wait to get me out of your hair?"

"Shut up," Zelda said. "You know I'll miss you. And I know that sounds really weird and stupid because we've only met twice, but—"

"Shut up," Whit said. "It's not weird or stupid. And if it is, then I'm weird and stupid too."

"Because you'll miss me?"

"It was implied."

"Okay, grumpy kitty," Zelda said. "We can be weirdos together."

Whit raised his glass. "Here's to that," he said.

They took a dram.

"So to answer your question," Whit said, "I'm not sure how long I'm gonna be weird and stupid in Rockwell with you. There's something very important I have to do before I leave. But I don't know if I'll be able to do it."

"Is it anything I can help with?"

Whit dropped his gaze. "No," he said. "Thank you, Zelda. I appreciate it. But this is something I have to do alone."

"Whitman Coe," Zelda said. "You silly kitty. Don't you know you're not alone? You've got a basket-case bartender and a juvenile

Wookiee and what seems like a pretty nice son over there. So just remember that you're not alone." She placed her hand on top of Whit's and squeezed. "I mean it."

"Anybody want a peanut?" Jim bellowed in his best Andre the Giant from *The Princess Bride* as he bulldozed through the kitchen doors. "See, Whit, I am the Dread Pirate Roberts, and I'm a poet too." He chortled and waggled his head as he approached the bar. "Whitman the wit man. The man who puts F-U-N in funeral."

Zelda narrowed her eyes. "My kitty," she said. "And don't make fun of him."

"I wasn't gonna make fun of him," Jim said. "I was just gonna say that was the best funeral I've ever been to in my life. Whit was totally awesome. That 'Moses invests' line. Good stuff. Hey, let's have a round before everybody else gets here."

Whit and Zelda polished off their glasses of whisky and Jim poured three more.

"Slainte," Jim said.

"Slainte," Whit and Zelda said.

They slammed the round.

"Raiden wins!" the *Mortal Kombat* game blared.

"Hey, Dada, I won!" Junior peeked over his shoulder at Whit and beamed.

"That's great, buddy," Whit called back. "But now I'm gonna kick your ass with Sub-Zero."

"Nuh-uh."

"Yeah-huh." Whit stood up and looked at Jim and Zelda. "Alright, kids," he said. "I'll be back," he turned toward Junior and raised his voice, "right after I kick Raiden's ass."

"You better," Zelda said.

"Kick Raiden's ass?"

"No, asshole. You better come back."

"I will."

"Besides, drinks are on Jim."

"They are?" Jim said.

"They are," Zelda said.

"Okay," Jim said. "You're the boss. I just work here."

"Well, in that case," Whit said, "set up a couple rounds for me. I'll be back after a couple rounds." He held up his fists in a boxer's pose. "See what I did there?"

"Come on, Dada!" Junior called. "I already picked Sub-Zero for you. I'm gonna hit you with lightning in five seconds."

"Ladies and gentlemen," Whit said, "I am being summoned." He bowed and backed toward the *Mortal Kombat* game.

"Raiden wins! Flawless victory!" the game greeted Whit.

"Hey, you cheater," Whit said, elbowing Junior.

Junior giggled. "I told you I was gonna hit you with lightning."

"Yeah, well now I'm gonna freeze your ass."

"Nuh-uh."

"Yeah-huh."

Zelda and Jim watched Whit and Junior's backs as they laughed, nudged each other, and slapped the video game controls.

"That's so sweet," Zelda said.

"Yeah," Jim said. "Kinda warms your heart, man. You know I remember when Whit was the same age his son is now. Time sure flies when you're drinkin whisky."

"Sub-Zero wins," the game grunted.

"You cheated, Dada," Junior said.

"How?"

"You froze me, then kept hitting me."

"That's what Sub-Zero does. He freezes his opponents. Hence the name Sub-Zero."

"Round three! Fight!" the game boomed.

"Okay, buddy," Whit said. "Final round. For the title."

"You're going down, Dada!"

"Nuh-uh."

"Yeah-huh."

The arcade game cabinet rocked violently as if it were caught in the shock of an earthquake. Static crackled behind the speakers, then the clipped flickering of music. A heavy guitar riff and a voice singing, "Paranoia the destroyer," wormholed through the speaker grates. The game screen went black.

Junior let go of the controls.

A faceless man stared at Junior through the black game screen. The same fallow husk Junior had seen the first time he'd looked into Adam's face.

The creature's mouth opened wide. It seemed to be screaming, but no sound came out. Just the refrain, "Paranoia the destroyer," churning through the speakers. The creature raised a gnarled claw and reached through the horizon of the black screen.

Junior jumped back and squeezed his eyes shut. When he opened them, the creature was gone. The song was gone. His father was tapping the game buttons and chuckling.

"Finish him," the video game rumbled.

"Here it comes," Whit said, toggling the game controls. He looked at Junior and his smile faded. "Junior, you okay?"

"It's too late," Junior said.

"Too late for what?" Whit said.

"Fatality," the video game growled.

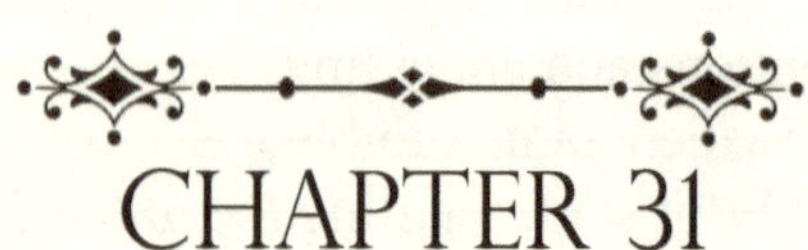

CHAPTER 31

"Paranoia will destroy yaaaaa!" Adam bleated along to "Destroyer" by the Kinks in a jerky, off-key drawl. He was two hits of meth and two lines of Oxy in, and the whole world was burning like an atomic torch. Everything was popping and rocking. Every object, shape, sound, and color. And, man, those African sick-letts were poppin like sons of bitches. Blue, blue, neon blue with blue trails shooting from their blue tails. They darted and flickered around the tank. Adam could hear the water. They were too real to be real.

Adam twitched like he'd just smoked a lightbulb charged with a thousand volts of uncut lightning. He bobbed his head in vehement and erratic parabolas to the music. He felt good and alive. More good and alive than he'd felt in years.

He eyeballed the pills and powder inside the translucent Ziplocs. *Take 'em all. Kill 'em all, let God sort 'em out. When you're feelin tits, why not feel even better? The most is best, and he who dies with the most toys wins.*

Adam picked up the modified light bulb, packed it with crystal, and stoked the glass bulb with a Bic flame. He inhaled deep and coughed in convulsive spurts.

"You don't cough, you don't get off," Adam said out loud and brayed to himself. His eyes felt dry, red, and bugged out. That felt good too.

"Yay-ah!" Adam shouted and bobbed his head with renewed vigor. Now he was flying like a little green fuckin space man.

He decided to go a little sideways. He fished two more Oxy out of the Ziploc and set them on the kitchen counter. Crushed the pills into a fine powder with the ass end of an empty Budweiser bottle. Shaped the powder into four parallel lines with his driver's license and snorted them through a rolled-up dollar bill.

Now he was really partying. He felt groovy. He was floating away from the world, watching it fade as he drifted through the aether.

It's better to burn out than to fade away.

But that feeling of ethereal zen didn't last long. The jagged jangles and jerky twitches began to sway through Adam's body and brain.

Something was watching him. Something was out to get him.

Adam's heart cranked. He could hear the blood in his head rushing through his ears. His mouth felt like it was filled with cotton and his skin prickled. His right eyelid spasmed. He couldn't stop twitching, and that goddamn voice wouldn't shut the fuck up.

Get your shit together, man. You just ain't been high in a real long time. Buck up, buttercup. You just gotta bring yourself down a bit.

He chugged a beer but didn't feel any better. He wasn't sure if his prescription meds did anything but decided to pop a couple just in case. He juddered across the shag carpet and turned down the hall to the head. Opened the medicine cabinet and unscrewed his medication bottle. Swallowed two pills with a handful of tap water. He shut the cabinet door and splashed some cold water on his face. He rubbed the water on his skin and against his eyelids and looked into the bathroom mirror.

It was there again. That stranger's face churning in the primordial tides. Its burning black eyes leered at Adam from behind the medicine cabinet mirror...

"Paranoia will destroy ya," Ray Davies sang over the radio. But it was too late.

CHAPTER 32

Whit snapped awake in the dark, heart and lungs rushing together in violent rhythm. The nightmare was fading. All that remained was its shadow.

He slid upright against the headboard and reached for the bottle of whisky he kept on the floor beside the bed. Something grazed his hand. Something rough and dry. He jerked his hand away from the tingling touch and drew into a crouch at the center of the bed, straining to see in the darkness. Listening for the nightmare shadow.

K-tchikitikitik. K-tchikitikitik. The scratching trailed beneath the bed and stopped below Whit.

Silence stretched across the room, taking form and intertwining with the dark, warping and extending like a corridor into the void. Then the scratching sound skirred like an insect, frenetic and erratic to the foot of the bed. *K-tchik. K-tchik. K-tchikitik...*

Whit felt the blankets move as something brushed against the comforter at the foot of the bed. The comforter rustled, then flopped downward.

The scratching sound came again. Slow this time. Deliberate.

A shape emerged from the blackness like a pale rift in the fabric of night. First the circle of a white, hairless head. Then the withered furrows of a brow. And beneath the brow there was nothing. Nothing but shriveled skin stretched and contorted over the empty hollows where the creature's eyes should have been.

Knurled fingers gripped the foot of the bed, pulling the misshapen creature to its full height. The creature towered over the bed and looked down at Whit through its empty eyes. There was recognition in its hollow gaze.

"Adam?" Whit said.

The creature stared at Whit, almost sadly, then bowed its bony shoulders and brought its claws, point down, on the foot of the bed. It gaped its mouth wide. Uneven, hooklike teeth peeled back from its lips. The creature threw back its head and bellowed. Then it sprang.

The shadow spread over Whit like a shroud.

***

Whit snapped awake in the dark, heart and lungs rushing together in violent rhythm. The nightmare was fading. All that remained was its shadow.

He rolled out from under the covers, planted his feet on the floor, and slumped forward. "Gotta stop having these fucked up dreams," he said, closing his eyes and burying his face in his hands.

When he opened his eyes, he saw a tiny pair of ruby slippers twinkling like red stars in the night.

He looked up and saw Astrid's face peering down at him. She pressed a finger to her lips, then walked to the door. She turned and motioned Whit to follow her.

Astrid led Whit back into their childhood home. To their mother's mirror, hanging on the living room wall again. Where it was meant to be. She looked at Whit and pointed at the mirror.

Whit took his place before the mirror and gazed into its depths. He saw himself standing in the attic, pulling a small piece of paper from a box. It was a miniature envelope. The name 'Whitman' was written on the face of the envelope in his mother's handwriting.

He watched himself open the envelope. He drew out something dark. It was the sun. The black sun burned. It grew and spread like a disease. It washed over Whit. And then over the world.

CHAPTER 33

Two days until the end of the world

"Hey, Adam, it's Whit," Whit said into his cell phone. His boots echoed off the wooden planks of Bob and Sarah's porch as he paced. "Just checking in to make sure you're okay. Maybe we can sort through some more stuff at Dad's place later today if you're up to it. Anyway, hit me back and let me know you're alright, bro. Bye."

He dialed again and got three beeps, then silence.

He slipped the cell into his jeans pocket and walked into the living room. Bob and Sarah were sipping coffee. The boys were wolfing down their third helping of waffles.

"I think I should swing by Adam's place and check up on him," Whit said.

"You think he's using again?" Bob asked.

"I dunno. Maybe. Maybe something worse."

***

Whit hustled up the walk to Adam's house. The front door was wide open and hanging askew where the top hinges had been ripped away from the frame.

He sprinted up the porch steps and into the house. The living room looked like it had been battered by the gale force of a tornado. Broken fragments of furniture spread across the floor like the silent remnants of a bomb blast. The aquarium was shattered. Adam's prized African cichlids lay dead on a soaked patch of orange shag carpet next to a tiny toy pirate's chest. A broken lightbulb, a folded wedge of tinfoil, and two Ziploc bags sat on the floor next to the overturned coffee table. One bag was empty, the other caked on the inside with dull white powder.

Whit stepped over the overturned coffee table. "Adam!" he called. "Adam, it's Whit!"

He crossed the hallway to the bedroom. Nothing there but a single bed, a bedside table with a clock radio, and a few centerfolds and Harley Davidson posters on the walls.

He checked the bathroom. The medicine cabinet had been ripped off the wall. Shards of the mirror were splayed out in a cascade on the moldy tile floor. Ragged gouges trailed down the sides of the sink in four parallel lines.

A prescription bottle peeked through the mirror shards on the floor. Whit bent down and picked up the bottle. He held it up in the morning half-light and read the label. The prescription was under Adam's name. He didn't recognize the name of the drug. But he recognized the name of the doctor who had prescribed it.

***

"I knew something was wrong," Whit said to Bob. "Sometimes I hate it when I'm right."

Bob surveyed the wreckage of Adam's living room, then looked at Whit. "I'm sorry, Whit," he said. "I know it looks bad, but let's not jump to any conclusions beyond what we can infer from the scene. Unfortunately, the drug paraphernalia means…"

"Yeah, I know," Whit said. "And all this other shit?"

"Like I said, let's not jump to any conclusions. I'll file a missing persons report on Adam just in case, but nine times out of ten in a situation like this, you're just looking for a meth head on a bender. I've seen this kinda thing before with tweakers. They get all strung out, lose their shit, go berserk. They break the furniture. The TV. Tear up anything that isn't nailed down. Shit, there was one guy just within city limits by the creek who actually did nail down his furniture. Said it was getting up and following him around the house. And this other guy on the same block got all tweaked out and knocked down all the walls to his house with a sledgehammer."

"Have you ever seen this kinda thing before?" Whit said and motioned Bob to follow him to the bathroom. Whit looked at Bob and pointed at the claw marks running down the side of the sink.

"What the—" Bob said.

"And get this," Whit said. "You know how I said I had a bad feeling about Adam when I got up this morning?"

109

"Yeah."

"Well, I had this dream last night. Really vivid. Felt real. I mean *real*. Anyway, in the dream Adam looked just like the faceless monster Stephen dreamed about on the night my old man died—pale, no eyes, bald, fangs, claws, the whole nine. Claws," Whit gestured to the scratches on the side of the sink again, "just like this."

"Okay, now you're freaking me out," Bob said. "How is that even possible?"

"I think we're past all that," Whit said.

"Fair enough," Bob said.

"Here's the other thing," Whit said. "Yesterday was the seventeenth. If Adam went missing yesterday—"

"That connects him to the other missing persons," Bob said. "A kid's gone missing on the seventeenth of every month like clockwork." He ran his fingers over his chin. "But Adam doesn't fit the pattern. All the other missing persons were in their late teens to mid-twenties. Adam's in his thirties."

"Which means that whoever or whatever is taking the kids from Rockwell made an exception for Adam. It chose him specifically."

"Why would it do that?" Bob said.

"There's only one explanation," Whit said. "One piece that's connected to all of it. Alice. My old man. Adam. The faceless creature. The missing kids." He looked Bob in the eye. "I don't know how, or why. But this thing is connected to me."

CHAPTER 34

Whit rapped on Mike Forester's decaying screen door. The chintzy aluminum frame rattled, and a cloud of dust particles wafted into the air like a miniature nuclear fallout.

Mike sputtered a jerky string of unintelligible words and skittered to the door. "Whachyall want?" he said, prying the door half open with one hand and peeking out at Whit through one dilated eye.

"Mike, my name is Whitman Coe. I'm Adam Coe's brother. You seen him lately?"

"Naw, dog. I ain't seen him in a coon's age. Why?"

"He's missing."

"Missin what?"

"No, he's missing. Like nobody knows where he is."

"Oh. Damn, dog. Well, I wish I could hep ya, but, like I said, he ain't been by in a stretch. But tell ya what. When ya do find him, tell him ol' MF said what's up, an he oughta stop by. Gets kinda borin out here without no comp'ny don'tcha know?"

"Uh, huh," Whit said. "Look, Mike, I'm not a narc or anything. I don't give two shits what you do in here. None of my business. I'm just trying to find my brother. That's it. Now have you seen him in the past couple of days?"

"What is you deaf? I already tol ya I ain't seen him. Now git the fuck off my property."

"Cut the shit, Mike. I know you're Adam's dealer and I know he came by here yesterday."

"Then whatcha axin me about it for, asshole? And don't say that shit about dealin out loud. They can hear ya. Oh, fuckdammit, now they heard me! You gotta get the fuck outa here, man!"

"Look, man," Whit said. "I'm not trying to get you into any trouble. I just want to know if Adam said anything to you. Like if he was planning on going somewhere or seeing anybody."

"Nope, but I'm plannin on blowin a hole in your chest if you don't git the fuck off my property." Mike pushed the screen door open with a bony shoulder and leveled a pump shotgun at Whit's chest.

***

"This should be good, Thomas," Jesus said as he watched Whit and Mike through the window of Tails Only Tommy's trailer. He peeled back the stained tobacco-yellow curtains to get a better look.

The curtains were not an anomaly within the universe of Tommy's trailer. Everything contained within its expanse was stained and grimy. Everything, that is, but Jesus and his robes. Jesus' robes were as crisp and white as a dentist's office in Heaven. His skin gleamed an unblemished alabaster. A golden aura encircled him, radiating like the sun. Even the blood dripping from the wounds beneath his crown of thorns seemed to sparkle a pure and brilliant sanguine.

"Yay, my son," Jesus said to Tommy. "Lo and behold."

"What, Lord?" Tommy said.

"Yo, peep this, sucka," Jesus said, waving Tails Only Tommy to join him at the window.

Tommy got off the couch and stood beside Jesus. He looked out the window and saw the demon Whitman Coe standing on the cinderblock porch of the dealer Mike Forester. Mike was aiming a scatter gun at Whit's chest.

Tommy jerked his neck and shoulders backward like a rooster with a cattle prod up its ass. "Jesus!" he said and recoiled a step back from the window.

"Yes, my son," Jesus said.

"No, I mean—shit—sorry, Lord. I didn't mean to take your name in vain and then to profane."

"It's cool. Ain't no thang but a chicken wang. Now check this shit out." Jesus winked at Tommy, then looked back out the window. "So who ya got, Thomas?"

"What?"

"Who do you think shall prevail in battle, the tweaker with the shotgun, or the big angry drunk? I've got twenty glasses of wine on the big fella. But then again, twenty glasses of wine is no big trick for me." Jesus leaned forward as Whit and Mike squared off. "Aaaaand... Go!"

Mike gesticulated at Whit with the shotgun and took a step closer. A step too close.

Whit snatched the shotgun by the barrel and wrenched it from Mike's grasp. He drove the butt of the gun into the center of Mike's face.

Mike screamed and hunched into a ball, face buried in his hands.

Jesus applauded and slapped Tommy on the back. "See, Thomas, I told you. I win. I mean, I always win. Well, except for that one time."

"But Jesus," Tommy said, "Whit Coe is a demon. He's the Adversary. I seen it with my own eyes. You gotta smite him like you smoted all them leopards 'cause they was stalagmites."

"What?" Jesus said.

"You know, like in the Bible."

"That's not in the Bible, Thomas."

"You sure?"

"Pretty sure."

"Oh. But can you still smite him?"

"Nay, my son."

"But you can do anything. All things through Christ. Ain't that in the Bible?"

"It is written again, thou shalt not tempt the Lord thy God." Jesus spread his palms and looked up to the heavens, or more accurately, at a stain on the ceiling of Tommy's trailer.

"Where's that wrote?" Tommy said.

"In the Bible."

"You sure?"

"Pretty sure. Thomas, there are rules that even I must abide by. I cannot take physical action in this world. You, Thomas, shall be my proxy. You shall be my right hand and my wrath. It is you who shall slay the demon Whitman Coe."

"Whoa, whoa, whoa!" Tommy did his rooster dance again. "I can't slay no demon."

"Do you doubt me, Thomas?"

"No, Lord."

"Then have faith, my son. I shall give you the strength and the means to slay the demon Whitman Coe. But only when the time is ripe. Only when he strays from the path."

"What path?" Tommy itched his head like a dog with a bad case of fleas.

"The path of fate, Thomas. As I said, there are rules that even I must abide by. And one of the rules is that I cannot strike down a man who is following the path of his destiny. But once he strays from the path of fate, his fate may be changed. That is when we catch him. It's like a loophole inside a wormhole."

"So we just gotta get him off the path," Tommy said.

"Word up."

"So how we gonna get him ta do that?"

"Whitman Coe is an angry and impulsive man. He shall walk off the cliff of his own free will. And then we shall destroy him. Just look at him now."

Across the street, Whit loomed over Mike with the captured scatter gun slung over one shoulder.

"Mike," Whit said. "Mike, you with me?"

"You broke my nose," Mike gurgled.

"Yeah, I've been known to do that. And worse. You don't wanna make me do worse, do you, Mike?"

"No."

"Good. Glad to see we're on the same page. Now, Mike, I'm gonna ask you something. Tell me the truth, and I'll go away and never darken your doorstep again. But—and this is very important, Mike— if you clam up or lie to me, your nose will be the least of your problems. Like I said, I've been known to do worse. And here's the other thing: if you lie, I'll know it. I always know a lie when I hear one. I guess I just have a sense for those kinds of things. Call it a gift. So why don't you make it easy on both of us and tell me the truth, okay?"

"Okay, I will. I will." Mike straightened his back and wiped blood from his upper lip.

"Alright then," Whit said. "So now that we understand each other I'll ask again: when my brother was here yesterday, did he say he was planning on going anywhere or seeing anybody?"

"Naw, dog. He just come by to score, then left. He didn't say nothin 'bout where he was goin."

"You sure?"

"Yeah, I'm sure, man. Swear to God. I ain't lyin, dawg."

Whit leaned in close to Mike and stared into his eyes without blinking. "You know what, dawg?" he said. "I believe you."

"You're next, Tommy," Jesus said, still peering through the window. He suppressed a giggle.

"What's that s'posed to mean, Lord?" Tommy said.

"Oh, Whitman Coe is going trailer-door-to-trailer-door killing all the firstborn sons. You're a firstborn son, aren't you, Thomas?"

"Yeah."

"Better spread some lamb's blood on your screen door. That's what keeps him out."

"For reals?"

"Yay, my son. It is my word and my word is the truth and the truth is the way."

Tommy clasped his head in his hands. "Oh, Jesus," he said. "I mean—shit. I mean—"

"Don't start that shit again, Thomas," Jesus said.

CHAPTER 35

"Hiya, Bob," Lucy said as Bob bellied up to the Rockwell PD reception desk. Today she was wearing a buttercream-yellow sweater with red and gray geometric patterns. "What can I do ya for?"

"Got another missing persons case, Lucy. I'm gonna need the keys to the evidence room."

"Oh, Jeez," Lucy said. "Another one?"

"Yep," Bob said.

"Who is it this time?"

"Adam Coe."

"Gosh, that poor family," Lucy said, shaking her head. "You send my best to Whitman."

"Will do."

Lucy shook her head again, fidgeted with her ballpoint pen, and stared at Bob like she was waiting for him to sing a song or perform a magic trick.

"Lucy?" Bob said.

"Yeah, Bob."

"I still need the evidence room keys."

"Oh, of course." Lucy tapped her head with the palm of her hand. "I tell ya, I'd forget my head if it wasn't attached." She fished a keyring out of the top desk drawer and handed it to Bob.

"Thanks, Lucy," Bob said. "Well, I better get cracking on this file. Seeya later, Lucy."

"Seeya, Bob. Have a good one."

"You too," Bob said, swinging open the opaque glass door to the PD office.

"Hey, Bob-O," Dave said. He was sitting at his desk thumbing through a copy of *Weekly World News* and fiddling with a letter opener engraved with Celtic knotwork. He tapped the paper and said, "So what'll it be today? The one about planet Niburu colliding with

Earth, how to tell if you're in a cult, or the one about why Bat Baby's band had to cancel their world tour?"

"No time for the funny papers today, Agent Mulder," Bob said. "Got another missing person. This time it's Adam Coe."

"Jesus," Dave said. "What happened?"

"Well, after Adam didn't show for his folks' wake yesterday, Whit got a bad gut feeling. So he tried to call Adam this morning, but Adam's cell was dead. So then Whit goes over to Adam's place to check up on him and the place is all smashed up. Drug paraphernalia all over the floor. The door's off the hinges and wide open, and Adam's just gone."

"Sounds like he's on a tweak bender. He'll probably turn up after he comes down."

"I hope you're right," Bob said, plopping into his desk chair.

"My gut's always right, Bob-O," Dave said. "And my gut says give it a day. Maybe two. Adam'll turn up and probably end up in one of our cells just like old times. My gut also says it wants a bear claw." He reached into a pink donut box on his desk and shoved a bite of bear claw into his mouth. "But keep me in the loop and let me know if I can do anything to help. I'm here for ya, buddy. And let Whit know I'm here for him too."

"Thanks, Dave. Will do." Bob loaded a sheet of paper in a black Smith-Corona typewriter and punched up Adam's missing persons report. He picked an empty file folder off his desk, slipped Adam's file into the folder, and ducked into the evidence room.

The evidence room was cramped and musty. Crammed with rows of stacked metal shelves, which were in turn crammed with cardboard boxes. The cardboard boxes were, in turn, crammed with myriad items of case evidence, all tagged and bagged. Two metal file cabinets—one labeled A-N, the other O-Z—pressed against the near wall on Bob's right.

Bob slid open the A-N cabinet, flipped to the letter C, and slid Adam's file into the appropriate slot. He started to slide the drawer shut, then stopped. He shuffled to the letter M and pulled the file for Jimmie Macomber.

He cracked open the file. Page one was a photo of Jimmie. Thin and frail. Pale pink skin. Tawny freckles. Strawberry-blond hair. Blank blue eyes. The facing page listed Adam's date of birth, height, weight, address. When and where he was last seen. A description of the clothes he was last seen wearing. Standard fare.

He turned the page and studied the report. The last-known person to see Jimmie was his father Horace, a retired mechanic who now spent most of his days on his front porch working the Miller-time shift. Jimmie's mother had died when he was six years old.

Bob thumbed through to Horace's witness statement. Read the first few pages and stopped. Scanned a few more pages and stopped again. Turned to the final page and pursed his lips in a tight line.

He pulled Paul Harris' file. The second kid to go missing. He leafed through the pages. Stopped. Riffled back and forth through the file. Stopped again. Landed on the last page.

"Son of a bitch," he said.

***

Twenty minutes later, Bob meerkated his head out of the evidence room.

"Dave," he said low and waved Dave into the room.

Dave followed Bob into the evidence room and gawped at the pile of files fanned out on the floor like a hand of cards.

"What are you doing, dude?" Dave said.

"These are all the missing persons files for the last three years, starting with Jimmie Macomber and ending with Adam Coe."

"You know Chip doesn't want us reading those files. You better put them away before he gets back."

"I know," Bob said. "And I think I just found out why he doesn't want us reading them."

"What do you mean?" Dave said.

Bob picked Jimmie's file off the floor and handed it to Dave. "Give it a look," he said. "See if anything jumps out at you."

Dave perused the file, then paused and squinted. He turned one page over, peeked under the reverse side like he was looking for a snake under a rock, then rummaged through the rest of the file. "There's pages missing," he said.

"Right."

Bob handed Dave another file. Dave skimmed the documents. He snapped the folder shut and looked at Bob. "It's missing pages too," he said.

Bob pointed at the spread of files on the floor. "Same thing with every single file in the bunch. They've all been redacted."

"But why?" Dave said. "Who would want to redact a bunch of missing persons files?"

Bob opened one of the files to the last page. "I don't know why," he said. "But I do know who." He handed the file to Dave.

Dave read the signature line aloud: "Investigating officer: Sheriff Merril Gustafsson."

CHAPTER 36

Whit stood in the shadow of the yellow Victorian house and gazed up at the widow's walk. In his mind's eye, he could almost see her—the weeping widow in her high-collared black mourning dress. Her haunted eyes watched the horizon, forever searching for a lover who would never return. Her form translucent as if she were slowly fading away from existence, while her memory refused to ebb.

Whit watched the widow evanesce into nothingness, then climbed the steps. He read the sign painted in stencil on the opaque glass door: 'Dr. Alfred Moore, Cognitive-Behavioral Psychiatric Therapy.' He gripped the brass doorknob and let himself in.

A prim and pasty little man greeted Whit from behind Dr. Moore's reception desk. "Good afternoon," the man said in an accent that made Whit think of manservants, mid-ranking civil servants, and underlings at the BBC. "Do you have an appointment to see Dr. Moore this afternoon, sir? I don't believe he has any appointments on the books." A note of condescension entered the man's voice, subtle yet palpable beneath its trained façade of servility.

"No, I'm afraid I don't," Whit said, "but I was hoping I would be able to speak to him briefly. I was one of Dr. Moore's patients a long time ago, and I believe my brother was seeing him before he went missing. I just wanted to find out if Dr. Moore might have any information that could help me find him."

The manservant raised an eyebrow. "Your brother is missing, you say?"

"Yes."

"And how long, may I ask, has he been missing?"

"He didn't show up for our father's wake yesterday, and when I went to his house to check up in him this morning his place was trashed, the front door was wide open, and he was gone."

"Hmm." The manservant tapped his index finger on the desk three times. "That does sound irregular. However, I am not legally permitted to provide any information about Dr. Moore's patients, nor am I permitted to disclose whether or not an individual is in fact one of Dr. Moore's patients at all."

Whit fished Adam's prescription bottle out of his front jeans pocket and slapped it on the reception desk. "I think this covers the question of whether or not my brother was one of Dr. Moore's patients."

The manservant picked up the prescription bottle and read the label. He looked up at Whit and sheepish recognition dawned on his face. "Coe," he said. "Then you must be Whitman Coe."

"I presume," Whit said.

"I do apologize, sir." The manservant placed a hand over his heart and gave Whit a slight bow of the head. "I can't believe I didn't recognize you. I feel so foolish. Please excuse my curtness earlier. It's just that I frequently have to turn away patients who wish to see Dr. Moore without an appointment. They can be quite insistent to say the least, but the rules must be upheld, otherwise Dr. Moore's home and practice would turn into—"

"Bedlam?"

"Yes, quite," the manservant chuckled. He stood up and extended his right hand. "I'm Dr. Moore's assistant Mr. Hooker. At your service, sir."

Whit shook Mr. Hooker's hand. "Whitman Coe. How do you do?"

"How do you do?" Mr. Hooker said. "It's a pleasure, sir." He released his grip on Whit's hand, straightened his trout shoulders, and said, "Well, sir, if you'll excuse me for just a moment, I'll inform Dr. Moore that you're here. I'm sure he would very much like to see you. He often speaks of you quite fondly."

"Thank you, Mr. Hooker. I would appreciate that."

"Splendid, Mr. Coe. Feel free to have a seat and peruse the periodicals. I won't be but a moment." Mr. Hooker pursed his lips in a smile, then turned and exited through a door behind the reception desk.

Whit circled the waiting room, then sat down and riffed through a stack of magazines on a clear glass coffee table. He selected an archaeological magazine with a picture of the Battersea Shield on the cover and leafed through its pages.

Mr. Hooker swung open a door leading to a narrow hallway and sashayed back into the waiting room. "Mr. Coe," he said. "Dr. Moore will see you now. Please follow me." He tented his fingers and smiled, then spun on his heel and led Whit down the hallway to Dr. Moore's office. He rapped on the door three times. "Whitman Coe here to see you, sir."

"Enter," came a refined but warm English voice from the other side of the door.

Mr. Hooker opened the office door and extended an arm, palm open, in invitation. "Right this way please, Mr. Coe."

"Thank you, Mr. Hooker," Whit said and entered the room.

"Of course, sir," Mr. Hooker said. He gave Whit another quick bow and shut the door behind him.

Dr. Moore sat in a red wingback chair holding a weathered copy of *the Complete Works of William Shakespeare*. Without looking up he read aloud, "Tomorrow, and tomorrow, and tomorrow, creeps in this petty pace from day to day, to the last syllable of recorded time; and all our yesterdays have lighted fools the way to dusty death." He paused, removed his reading glasses, and looked up at Whit.

"Out, out, brief candle," Whit continued. "Life's but a walking shadow, a poor player, that struts and frets his hour upon the stage, and then is heard no more. It is a tale told by an idiot, full of sound and fury, signifying nothing."

"Well done, Whitman," Dr. Moore said, smiling. "You always did have a flair for the Scottish play." He set his book and reading glasses on the side table, stood, and buttoned his gray tweed suit. He shook Whit's hand with a firm grip, which was as good as a hug from an old waspish Anglo-Saxon academic like Dr. Moore. "It's wonderful to see you again, my boy. It's been far too long."

"It's good to see you too, Doc," Whit said. He cast about the familiar room, scarcely changed in the decades since he had last seen it. Still Dr. Moore's red wingback chair and the green patient's sofa. Still the bookshelves brimming with volumes by Freud, Jung, Nietzsche, and Hesse; books by and about Winston Churchill; heavy tomes on Roman, Celtic, and World War II history. Still the Hindu and Buddhist icons lining the walls and shelves. Still the pastoral paintings of the rolling English countryside and a framed print of Queen Elizabeth II.

"You haven't changed the office a bit," Whit said. "Except for over there." He gestured at a wall adorned with an octagonal Himalayan mirror and a painted wooden mask of Ganesh. "I remember that space being bigger or something." He narrowed his eyes and stared hard at the wall as though he were trying to see through to the other side.

"You don't remember, then?" Dr. Moore said.

"Not really. It's like it's somewhere in my memory, but it's blurry."

"Memory is like a locked box, Whitman. It requires a key to open it. That key is somewhere within your mind. If you search hard enough, you'll find it."

"Actually, Doc, right now I'm just searching for my brother. I understand he was a patient of yours. He went missing yesterday after our dad's funeral, and I was wondering if you might have any insight as to where he might have gone."

"Ah, yes," Dr. Moore said. "Mr. Hooker apprised me of your situation, Whitman. I'm sorry to hear about Adam. But as far as your brother's whereabouts, your guess is as good as mine. He seemed to be making progress. Staying away from temptation, if you will. But the hungry ghost never fully vanishes, does it? And who knows where it leads."

Whit slumped his head, then gave Dr. Moore a weary smile. "Well, Doc," he said, "I should get going. It was nice seeing you. Thanks for your time."

"You're welcome, Whitman. It's been a pleasure seeing you again, my boy. I'm sorry I couldn't be of more help with your brother. And on a personal note, I'm deeply sorry I wasn't there for you after your mother passed away. I wanted to be there to help you through that trauma, but after your mother passed, your father wouldn't allow me to continue your therapy. I even offered to treat you for free, but he declined. I regret that to this day."

"That's okay, Doc. There's nothing you could've done about it. Any of it. That's not on you."

"Thank you, Whitman. That said, I am free for the rest of the afternoon if you'd like to chat. I know you're dealing with a great deal of psychic trauma. And although I know better than to think that I can heal those wounds, I do still think it might be helpful for you to talk to someone who understands."

"I appreciate the offer, Doc. And no offense, but I lost the closest person in my life three years ago. I lost my best friend and the only woman I ever loved. So how could you possibly understand something like that?"

"Because, Whitman," Dr. Moore said, "I lost the only woman I ever loved."

"I'm sorry, Doc," Whit said. "I never knew."

"It was a long time ago, Whitman."

"Time doesn't matter. Has it healed your wounds? Because it hasn't done a goddamn thing for mine."

"I'm afraid it hasn't, my boy. That time heals all wounds is one of the great misnomers of this world. All we can do is to carry on as best we can for those whom we love. Those still left in this world, as well as those gone from it."

Whit glanced away from Dr. Moore and caught a flash of his own face in the octagonal mirror. It looked like the face of a stranger.

Dr. Moore followed Whit's eyes to the mirror. "Perhaps I can take you back to a fonder memory, Whitman," he said. "Would you care to see the room?"

***

Dr. Moore opened the door and led Whit inside the room. It was exactly as Whit remembered it. His childhood museum of awe and memory. He walked through the room admiring the items hung on walls or displayed inside clear glass cases: a British Army uniform and cap, a British Army compass, a captured Nazi flag, a collection of confiscated Nazi silverware, a shadowbox filled with war medals, a bayonet, an Enfield revolver, and a liberated German Luger.

Whit drew to a halt in front of the display case with the Luger inside.

"That Luger always was your favorite," Dr. Moore said.

"It's amazing all the memorabilia your father brought home from the war," Whit said. "I can't even begin to imagine all the things he must have seen and experienced."

"Nor can I. My father was a stoic man. Stiff upper lip and all that. He rarely spoke of the war. But I know that it changed him. My father suffered grave physical wounds in the war, but his emotional wounds were far worse. They called it shellshock back then, before the term PTSD had been coined. I think it was my father's condition that led me to become a psychologist. I saw firsthand the deep psychological, physical, and spiritual damage that man inflicts upon his fellow man, and I devoted my life to healing that damage, and preventing it any way I could."

"That's admirable," Whit said.

"It's only logical, Whitman. One of the things I learned from my father's example is that we must stand up and fight against the tide of corruption and evil, no matter the cost. The fight against the Nazis cost my father the use of his right arm and a lifetime of emotional turmoil. It cost the lives of sixty million people. That was the price of stopping the evil of man. But we didn't learn from that tragedy. We continue to kill each other, to wage unjust war, to forge weapons, to destroy the very world—" Dr. Moore lowered his head and smiled to himself. "I apologize, Whitman," he said. "I'm afraid I've taken to rambling in my old age."

"That's okay, Doc. I know what you mean."

Dr. Moore started to say something else, but Whit's cell phone ring cut him off.

Whit looked at the caller ID and answered. "Hey, Bob. What's up?"

"Whit, where are you right now?" Bob said.

"At the old town center, why?"

"Perfect," Bob said. "I'm about to leave the station. I was digging in the missing persons files and I think I might have found something. Can you meet me at O'Malley's in about twenty minutes?"

"Sure thing," Whit said. "Seeya then."

"Seeya, Whit. Oh, and could you order me a double bacon cheeseburger?"

"Will do, Bob. Gotta maintain that girlish figure."

"Exactly," Bob said and ended the call.

Whit slipped his cell phone into his pocket. "Sorry, Doc," he said. "I've gotta run. Thanks for everything."

"The pleasure was all mine, Whitman," Dr. Moore said. "Oh, I nearly forgot." He reached into the pocket of his tweed coat and handed Whit a bottle of pills. "Take two of these before bed. They may help you sleep better."

"Thanks, Doc, but I think I'll stick to killing my liver the old-fashioned way."

"They're all natural, Whitman. My own proprietary herbal blend."

"So mostly peyote?"

Dr. Moore chuckled. "No, Whitman," he said. "Although they do contain psylocibin. And trace amounts of ayahuasca."

"So am I gonna wake up at the zoo in the morning gnawing on an antelope or something?"

"Not unless that's part of your usual routine."

Whit laughed and took the bottle. "Seeya, Doc," he said.

"Goodbye, Whitman," Dr. Moore said and shook Whit's hand.

Whit nodded a farewell to Dr. Moore, then turned and walked downstairs.

"Thank you, Mr. Hooker," Whit said as he passed the check-in desk. "Good afternoon."

"Good afternoon, Mr. Coe," Mr. Hooker said. "See you tomorrow."

"Oh, no, I didn't make an appointment."

"Of course, sir. My mistake."

The door swung shut behind Whit. Mr. Hooker picked up a pencil and Dr. Moore's appointment log. He turned to the next day's schedule and wrote, *Whitman Coe. 10.25 a.m.*

CHAPTER 37

Zelda clapped her hands, bounced on her toes, and said, "Kitty!" when Whit stepped through the front door of O'Malley's.

"There he is," Jim said. "I was hoping you'd show up today."

"Why?" Whit said. "What's going on?"

"Nothing. I was just hoping you'd show up."

"And here I am." Whit spread his hands and sidled up to the bar.

"Power of positive thinking," Jim said and shook Whit's hand.

Zelda scratched the new stubble on Whit's chin. "Your scruffles are growing back, kitty."

"They tend to do that."

Jim reached for the bottle of Bushmills, but Zelda swatted his hand away. "Nih," she grunted. "I pour for the kitty. You can has too, if you behave."

"O-kay," Jim said, backing away from the bottle.

Zelda poured three glasses of whisky and they drank. She looked at Whit. "Have you been sleeping?"

"Not much."

"Have you been eating?"

"I think I might have grabbed a pancake on the way out the door this morning. I had a lot of shit to do today."

"Have you been drinking?" Jim said and smiled. "You gotta eat, man. You're a growing boy. And you gotta drink milk, get eight hours of sleep, don't do drugs, stay in school, fool. Mr. T says so."

"What?" Zelda said and squinted at Jim. "Anyway," she said to Whit, "I was thinking of getting a pizza for my shift meal, but I can never finish one by myself. So you'd be doing me a favor if you'd share one with me. And I'm pretty sure Jim will accidentally add another pizza and some pub grub to go. You and your boy like Hawaiian, right?"

"I will now?" Jim said.

Zelda nodded once and raised her chin. "Yes."

"Okay," Jim said, "but only accidentally. Not because you told me to." He gulped down his whisky, tossed his bar rag onto the bar, and backed toward the kitchen.

"Hey, Jim," Whit said. "Can you add a double bacon cheeseburger for Bob? He's on the way from the station."

"Two days in a row? You're a bad influence, Whit." He winked at Whit, then scooted behind the double doors into the kitchen.

"Ahh," Whit said. "That adolescent Wookiee is priceless."

"I guess that leaves you and me," Zelda said.

"And the whisky makes three."

"Slainte," Zelda said.

"Slainte," Whit said.

They drank.

Whit stared at nothing in particular and smiled to himself.

"What's that look about?" Zelda said.

"Oh, nothing," Whit said. "It's just sitting at the bar like this. For some reason it made me think of Alice."

Whit downed his whisky. Zelda polished hers off and poured another round.

"What was she like?" Zelda said. "If you don't mind me asking."

Whit took a dram of whisky. "Alice was," he said, "like no one I'd ever met. She had the biggest, brightest personality I'd ever seen. It's like what Bukowski said about the free soul: it's rare, but you know it when you see it because you feel very good when you're near or with them. That's what she was—a free soul. And that's how you felt around her. Very good.

"She was also the most spontaneous person I ever met. Like I'd be asleep in bed, and she'd bust into the room and say, 'Wake up, Giant! We're driving to L.A. to see a baseball game!' Or this one time she says, 'Wake up, Giant, we're getting a cat!' So I got up and we got a cat." He grinned and took another drink.

"And she was so fucking stubborn. Man, you couldn't make her do anything she didn't want to do, even if she knew it was for her own good. And if she wanted to do something, it was just gonna happen. No use arguing. But if she loved you, she'd do anything for you. And she always had a soft spot for the underdog and the outsider. When we first met, Alice's mom asked her what I was like, and Alice said, 'He's green.' She meant like Kermit the frog. It's not easy being green. We were two people who didn't quite fit in the world, but we fit together in our own world. She got that. She got me. She was the only person who ever really knew me. And she loved me anyway. She lived life like a big adventure, and I was lucky enough that she decided to drag me along for the ride. That's what she was like. That's what I remember about her."

"I think I would have liked her," Zelda said.

"I think so too. You know you remind me a little of her."

"Really? How?"

Jim shouldered his way through the kitchen doors balancing a red plastic serving basket packed with a stacked burger and a heap of chili cheese fries. "Accidental double bacon cheeseburger and chili cheese fries up for—oh, hey Bob. Good to see ya."

Whit spun in his barstool and saw Bob stepping through the front door. "Goddamn, boys," he said. "Did you rehearse your entrances?"

"Nope," Jim said. "I'm just a master of timing."

"By that," Zelda said, "do you mean you hid in the kitchen with Bob's food, peeked out the window, and waited until you saw him come in?"

"I didn't *not* do that."

Bob shook Jim's hand and bellied up to the bar beside Whit. "Hey, Jimbo," he said. "Good to see you too."

"Officer Bob," Jim said. "Back in the saddle on the barstool again."

"Out where a friend is a friend," Bob said. "Guess I've fallen off the wagon since Whisky McPizza Slice rolled into town." He jerked his thumb at Whit.

"Well," Jim said, "a bad influence is a good thing to find. Cheers, Whit."

"Happy to be of service," Whit said.

Bob leered at the sloppy cheeseburger. "Oh, baby," he said to the burger. "I've missed you. Don't tell my wife." He took a big bite and groaned. "Mmm, Jim, this burger is awesome. It's just missing one thing."

"What's that?" Jim said.

"A beer."

"You got it." Jim pulled the suds and set a pint in front of Bob. "So to what do I owe this rare pleasure?"

Bob glanced at Whit. Whit lifted a shoulder and gave Bob a nod.

"Well," Bob said, "Whit and I are trying to piece together a puzzle."

"I like puzzles," Jim said. "I once put one together that was a picture of a bunch of pooping puppies."

"Not that kind of puzzle," Bob said. "And thanks for that image while I'm eating chili cheese fries."

Jim tilted his head and winked at Bob.

"Anyway," Bob said. "So you know about that string of missing persons we've had in town over the past couple years?"

"I read about it in the paper," Jim said. "I knew most of the kids. Small town."

"Yeah," Zelda said. "I went to high school with some of them. One of them, this kid named Jimmie Macomber, used to live down the street from me. Sometimes I see his dad sitting on the porch when I pass by, just drinking beer and staring at the woods."

"Okay," Bob said. "Now what they haven't said in the paper is that the disappearances aren't random. They fit into a pattern. Every month, three kids go missing. One on the thirteenth, one on the seventeenth, and one on the twentieth."

"Sounds like some sort of lunar cycle," Zelda said.

"Could be," Bob said. "Anyway, yesterday was the seventeenth, and we got another missing person. But this time it was Whit's brother Adam."

"Jesus," Jim said.

Zelda opened her mouth but didn't say anything.

"And it gets even weirder," Bob said. "I went to the evidence room at the station today to file Adam's report, and while I was there I pulled the rest of the missing persons files. See if I could piece anything else together. Maybe find another connection between the cases. Turns out all the files have been tampered with. Pages missing. Witness statements removed."

"So that's what you found," Whit said. "But who the hell would want to tamper with those files?"

"Well, Chip was the investigating officer in all the cases. Maybe he was trying to cover up some shit that could make him look bad if it got leaked to the press. But I don't know. It feels bigger than that. Either way, it makes it a hell of a lot harder to find another connection between the missing kids."

"I got one," Jim said.

"One what?" Bob said.

"A connection between the missing kids."

"What's that?" Bob said.

"Well, except for Adam and the ones who were underage, they were all regulars here."

"Did you notice anything else?" Whit said. "Like did any of them seem to know each other, or talk to each other? Was there any kind of pattern to their visits?"

"You know," Jim said, "now that I think of it, there's a couple of things that seem kinda odd."

"Like what?" Whit said.

"Well, for one thing," Jim said, "even though they were all regulars, I never saw any of them at the bar at the same time. And they all came in on a pretty specific schedule. Like once or twice a week and always at about the same time of day. You think that means something?"

"It might," Bob said.

"So what do you think it means?" Jim said.

Whit and Bob looked at each other and shrugged.

"No idea," Whit said.

CHAPTER 38

After dinner, Junior and Stephen decided to take a walk along the trails that cut through the woods behind the house. The sun was reddening as it grazed the line of treetops on the horizon. Soon it would sink into the forest.

They followed the trail into the clearing where they had eaten their lunches the other day. Junior reached into the Ziploc bag he was carrying and munched on a chicken tender.

"How can you still be hungry after all you ate at dinner?" Stephen said.

"I don't know. I'm just not full," Junior said and stuffed the rest of the chicken tender into his mouth.

"Dude, you're gonna shit the air mattress tonight." Stephen made a fart sound with his mouth and the boys giggled.

The path curved through a stand of trees that lined the trail like terracotta soldiers guarding the secret shadows of the forest. As the boys drew near to the next clearing, a putrid, sickly-sweet stench wafted to their nostrils. It smelled like old meat and garbage rotting in a dumpster.

"Oh, gross," Junior said, pulling his T-shirt over his nose.

Stephen followed suit. "Dude, I think something died," he said.

"Let's go back," Junior said as they entered the clearing.

"Wait." Stephen pointed at a brownish clump sticking out of a patch of withered grass.

The boys edged toward the small brown clump, noses buried in their hands and T-shirts.

"Oh, shit," Junior said. "It's a cat."

"Oh, man, that sucks," Stephen said. "I wonder what happened to it."

The boys peered down at the cat. It was brown with dark brown stripes. A long, jagged slice ran the length of the cat's stomach. Its entrails were spread out on the ground beside it like a bloodeagle. Its teeth protruded from its mouth in a grimace of agony. Its lifeless eyes were squeezed shut. A small, rectangular bit of paper lay nestled in the blood-matted fur on the cat's chest. A playing card: the Deuce of Spades.

"That son of a bitch," Junior said. "I knew it."

"Knew what?" Stephen said.

"Remember when I said I can sense bad things about people, and that I sensed something really bad about Deuce?"

"Yeah."

"It was this."

"What do you mean?"

"I sensed *this*." Junior pointed at the cat. "Almost like I saw it."

"You mean like in a vision or something?"

"I don't know. It was like little flashes. Almost like pictures. And this feeling of darkness around him. Like it was something you could almost touch. And in these pictures, I saw that Deuce had hurt other animals like this one. Cats, dogs, rabbits, possums, lizards—any animal he can catch. He likes to hurt them as much as he can. He likes to cut them open with his pocketknife. And one of the animals I saw him hurt and cut open was a brown striped cat. This cat, I think."

Stephen studied the brown cat. "The smell is pretty bad," he said. "But this blood hasn't completely dried, which means—"

"I saw him kill this cat before it happened," Junior said.

"Whoa. That's freaky."

"This whole thing is freaky." Junior couldn't stand to look at the cat anymore, so he let his eyes wander across the brushy clearing.

"Oh, shit," he said.

"What?" Stephen said.

Junior raised his arm and pointed toward a patch of weeds deeper in the clearing. His hand trembled.

Stephen's eyes followed in a straight line to where Junior was pointing. He squinted at the weed patch, trying to make out what Junior was pointing at. Then he saw it. A pale shape lying in the brush. Withered and lifeless, rotting in the dirt and brambles.

"No fucking way," Stephen said.

CHAPTER 39

The letter was in the envelope. The envelope was in the box. The box was in the attic.

The moment Whit stepped through the door he felt the cold and the dark. He felt the presence. He flipped the switches on the foyer light plate. The lights clicked on, and Whit's face stared back at him through the looking glass. His mother's mirror hung on the living room wall again. Just as it had all those years ago. Just as it had in the dream. In the dream…

The letter was in the envelope. The envelope was in the box. The box was in the attic.

Whit stalked up to the mirror. He looked at his reflection in the glass. Ran a finger across its icy surface. The mirror was encircled by an oval of bronze. The bronze frame was inscribed with three conjoined spirals. The same spirals as the tattoo on Whit's right shoulder. But he had forgotten all about the triskeles on the mirror frame by the time he had taken his ink.

When he touched the mirror, Whit felt a ripple run through the glass. A hum beneath the surface. A whisper in the back of his consciousness. The presence summoning him to the attic.

In the attic was the box. In the box was the envelope. In the envelope was the letter.

Whit followed the presence into the hallway. Outside, the sun was setting. In the cramped tunnel of the corridor, it was pure night. The corridor walls were the darkness itself, pressing in, slithering in a coil against Whit's skin. Pressing down. The borders of the corridor wavered and stretched. The whisper grew louder. And beneath the whisper, a low wailing drone, rising and falling like a hypnotic tide. The echoes of fathomless souls crying from the depths of the black hole sun.

Whit drifted down the hallway until he stood below the attic trapdoor. He pulled the cord to extend the ladder. The door groaned and trembled, but refused to descend.

Above Whit's head, one of the attic floorboards moaned. Something scuttled across the trapdoor. *K-tchikitikitik. K-tchikitikitikitik.* Then silence.

An ominous thud rattled the trapdoor. Again the silence descended. And waited.

Whit glared at the trapdoor. He yanked the cord again. Hard. The cord snapped off in his hand, but the door remained sealed.

Whit felt the rage building inside him. His head burned in a white fog. He closed his eyes. In his mind's eye, he saw himself as a child. He was standing in the dark. He could feel walls pressing around him on all sides like he was trapped in a box. On the wall in front of him was a mirror. An ancient mirror with *ogham* inscriptions carved around its oval frame.

Whit stood in two places at the same time. In the darkness of the hallway beneath the attic. And in the darkness within the walls before the ancient mirror.

The Whit trapped inside the dark walls stared through the looking glass. He focused his rage to a point of singularity. Let the white mist consume him. He reached out his hand and pulled.

The attic door plunged open.

***

Whit heaved himself over the top and into the attic. He cast about the room. Nothing there. Nothing but a no-man's-land of old memories covered in a thick layer of dust. Memories that woke and stirred and shook off the dust as Whit's gaze fell upon them. His mother's piano. Her grandfather clock. Her sewing machine and sewing dummy. Her favorite cobalt blue vase. Her music box ballerina.

Whit had always loved the little ballerina and her music box. The black lacquer box emblazoned with sakura blossoms and a red-orange firebird. The chimes that sounded their bittersweet tune when he wound the key.

But most of all he had loved the tiny ballerina herself. Graceful, emotive, and enchantingly beautiful. As child, Whit had imagined that when he turned the key to the music box, he opened the door to the ballerina's secret world. This world stretched far beyond the confines of the music box. It transcended time and space. And so did she.

Whit's first published short story had been about her.

He walked to the music box ballerina and lovingly picked her up. He turned the key to the music box and the melancholy chimes drifted into the air, driving away the darkness, if only for a spell. The ballerina pirouetted in a lithe spiral.

And then he saw it. The ballerina looked exactly like Alice. The same dark hair and fair skin. The same full red lips. The same proud jut of her chin.

Whit felt the sinking emptiness again. His body slumped.

Perhaps he had always been looking for Alice. In this world and in others.

He listened to the chimes of the music box, lost in memory. At last, the twinkling chimes wound down, slowed, and faded. A final note lingered in the air, then dissolved into the aether.

Whit gently set the music box ballerina back in her place on the dresser. He pressed his fingers against the corners of his eyes and traced them down his cheeks, smearing his tears across his face. He took in a drag of air and set his shoulders. Let it out and returned to the task at hand.

The letter was in the envelope. The envelope was in the box.

What damn box? The attic was full of boxes. Boxes on top of boxes. Boxes behind boxes. The attic was so crammed with boxes he hardly knew where to begin. And he only had a vague idea of what the box looked like in the first place. The image in his dream had been hazy and had grown hazier still after he returned to the waking world and the dream ebbed away.

"Fuck it," he said, grabbing the cardboard box from the top of the stack next to him. He pulled off the lid and sifted through its contents: photo albums, loose photos stuffed into unsealed envelopes like afterthoughts, random documents and letters—but not *the* letter. He rummaged through more cardboard boxes and chests and desks and drawers. He uncovered a few trinket and jewelry boxes, but not *the* box.

"Goddammit!" Whit said and swatted a cardboard box across the room. The box's contents spilled onto the floor like a cascade of dominos.

He ran a hand through his hair.

I looked everywhere. What am I missing? I know it's here. I know I'm supposed to find it. So why haven't I found it yet?

He looked at the grandfather clock pressed against the far wall.

Because it is not yet time, a voice whispered in Whit's head.

Time for what?

Time to unleac.

Unleac? What does that mean? Unleash? Unlatch? Unlock?

Unleac. Not yet time to unleac the Dom.

Whit still wasn't entirely sure what *unleac* meant, but he recognized the word *Dom*. It was the Old English word for Doom. Judgment with a capital 'J'. The end of the world.

CHAPTER 40

"Dada! Dada!" Whit whipped his neck toward the sound of his son's shouts. Junior's feet peppered the hardwood floor downstairs. Then the shouts and footsteps stopped.

Whit scurried down the ladder and shot to the living room. He found Junior standing in front of the mirror, face blank and eyes glazed.

"Junior," Whit said.

Junior didn't answer. He didn't move. He kept staring into the mirror.

Whit put a hand on Junior's shoulder. "Junior," he said, turning the boy away from the mirror's gaze.

"Dada!" Junior snapped back as if he hadn't missed a beat. "Me and Stephen found it!"

"Stephen and *I*, and what did you find?"

"The monster. The one Stephen saw before. It was dead, but it's real."

"Where did you find it?"

"In a clearing in the woods out back."

"Are you okay?"

"Yeah, Dada, I'm fine."

"Where's Stephen?"

"With his parents."

"Okay, let's go."

Whit ushered Junior out the door. Bob, Sarah, and Stephen were standing on their porch. Sarah had an arm around Stephen's shoulder. Bob clopped down the steps and jogged across the lawn to meet Whit.

"Junior told you what they found?" Bob said.

"Yep," Whit said. "Let's go get this son of a bitch."

"Whit, I'm sorry buddy, but you're gonna have to ride the bench on this one. It's a crime scene and you're a civilian."

"Of course," Whit said, shaking his head. "I don't know what I was thinking."

"You were thinking you wanna solve this thing," Bob said. "And we're gonna. Together, buddy. Just hang back here for now. I gotta call this thing in, then cut through the woods before anyone else arrives on scene. I'll fill you in when I get back. On everything, okay?"

"Yeah," Whit said.

Bob tipped his head at Whit, then hustled to his squad car. He leaned against the car, pulled out his cell, and called Dr. Ellicott at the medical examiner's office. Then leaned into the cab and torqued himself over the dash to call in the body on the police radio. He clapped the door shut and chugged down the trail as fast as he could. By the time he reached the first clearing, his legs were burning and his lungs were sucking wind.

About halfway through the canopy of the woods, the smell of the rotting cat hit him. He stifled a gag and slung his forearm across his nose. He slowed to a jog. When he reached the clearing, he stopped and put his hands on his hips. He hoovered in a gulp of air, and a second wave of nausea wrenched his stomach. He turned and vomited into a bush at the edge of the clearing.

Bob steadied himself against a pine trunk, then staggered into the clearing with his hand over his nose. He looked down at the dead brown cat. Noted the sadistic way it had been eviscerated. Noted the Deuce of Spades left on its chest like a calling card.

He stepped back from the cat and searched the clearing for the creature. He spotted its pale shape in a clump of weeds, partially covered. He walked toward the shape. Unlike the cat, the creature didn't emit any smell. Bob hunched down, hands on knees, to examine the creature, taking care not to touch the body or trample the weeds next to it.

The creature was an exact match for the monster Stephen had described on the night of the Coe killings: pale and hairless. Humanlike, but with an impossibly elongated body and facial structure. Long, ragged claws. No eyes. The mouth was closed, but where the lip was peeled back, Bob could see the point of a fang peeking out. The creature's skin was dry and leathery like it had been preserved in an arid climate for some time.

"Hoo-lee shit," Bob said. He glanced over his shoulder, then watched the dirt road that cut through the woods and hollows up ahead. He slipped his cell phone out of his pants pocket and snapped some photos of the body from different angles.

Tires ground over dirt and gravel behind the cover of the trees. Bob slipped his phone back into his pocket, stepped away from the body, and ambled toward the turnout at the side of the road.

Dave's patrol car emerged from the woods and pulled into the turnout next to the clearing. Dave hopped out of the car, waved at Bob, and hobble-jogged across the clearing to join him. He saw the creature and pulled up mid-stride. "Hoo-lee shit," he said.

"That's exactly what I said," Bob said.

Dr. Ellicott and the forensics team rolled into the clearing five minutes later. The forensic zoologist Dr. Planck was with them. Chip showed up twenty minutes after that. The clearing was a seven-minute drive from the station.

By the time Chip arrived on scene, forensics had already planted stakes in the ground and cordoned off the scene with yellow tape. Swept the area for evidence. Dusted the body for prints. Photographed the body.

Chip parked his squad car, set the brake, took a big gulp from a paper soda cup, and chocked the last bite of his Jumbo Jack into his mouth. He got out of the car, looped his thumbs behind his belt buckle, and said, "Alright boys. cavalry's here." Then the stench of the rotting cat hit him full-on. He coughed and contorted his face like he'd just sucked on a lemon and said, "What the fuck is that smell? One of you ladies have that not so fresh feelin today?"

"It's a dead cat," Bob said, looking square at Chip. "Somebody cut it open with a knife."

Chip tensed at the mention of the dead cat.

"You okay, Chief?" Dave said.

"Shut the fuck up, Dave," Chip said. "Bob, you wanna show me why you dragged my ass out here?"

Bob led Chip to the creature.

Chip looped his thumbs behind his belt buckle again and glared down at the body. "What the hell's that supposed to be?" he said.

"We don't know yet," Bob said. "Forensics and the ME said they've never seen anything like it. That forensic zoologist Planck says he thinks it might be a match for the thing that killed Allan and Barbara Coe."

"Fuck's that egghead still doin here?"

Bob lifted his shoulders. "But look at the body, Chief. It matches Stephen's description of the thing he saw on the night of the Coe killings. To a tee."

"Oh, Jesus Christ, Bob. Really? We're back on your kid's monster story?" Chip widened his stance and looked down his nose at Bob. "You know what I think?" he said. "I think this body's a fake. Ain't no animal or person looks like that. It's a fuckin hoax like crop circles, or bigfoot, or those little green alien autopsy fuckers. When somethin like this thing," he flicked his head at the body, "turns up, you know who's always behind it? Kids. So when I hear a kid make up a crazy story about a monster, then I get called out into the woods to look at a fake monster that looks just like the one the kid says he saw, you know what I start to think?"

"I can assure you that this body, whatever it is, is not fake," Dr. Planck said as he stepped into the clearing. He ducked under the crime scene tape and hunched next to the body. "The tissue—skin, muscles, tendons—is all real. As are the teeth, bones, and claws. The morphology is highly unusual—unprecedented in fact—but this creature is a genuine biological entity. The specimen appears to be hominid, but not *homo sapiens*. Judging by the teeth and claws, I would say it's carnivorous. The teeth and claws also lead me to suspect that a member of this species—though not this particular individual—may be responsible for the mauling deaths of Allan and Barbara Coe. I'll have to conduct a thorough autopsy and a DNA analysis, but I believe this specimen represents an undiscovered species." He clasped his hands together. "I feel like Darwin in the Galapagos."

"Yeah, that's great," Chip said. "Whatever that means."

"Doctor," Bob said. "Why do you think this particular creature isn't responsible for the Coe killings?"

"This specimen has been dead for far too long," Dr. Plank said. He hunkered down and pointed at the back of the creature's head. A circular hole gaped in the back of its skull. "The cause of death appears to be a single gunshot wound to the back of the head. Likely from a pistol or other handgun. By the level of decomposition, I would say that the specimen has been dead for approximately three years in a relatively dry climate. There are also traces of dirt and soil on the skin and under the claws, which leads me to believe it was buried, then exhumed and placed here."

"Why would someone do that?" Dave said.

"Your guess is as good as mine," Planck said. "But I believe someone meant for this body to be found. Also, the fact that the body was placed in a clearing near a ritualistically slaughtered cat leads me to suspect that there may be a nexus between the killing of this creature and the killing of the cat."

"Why don't you leave the police work to me, Doc?" Chip said.

"Yes, of course, Sheriff," Planck said. "Now unless there's anything else I can do for you, I would like take the specimen to Dr. Ellicott's office for examination now."

"Knock yourself out," Chip said.

The creature's body wouldn't fit into a body bag, so the morgue attendants draped it in plastic sheeting and rolled it on a gurney over the bumpy ground to the coroner's van. They grunted as they heaved the creature into the back of the van, then clanged the door shut and drove away.

"Fuckin weirdo," Chip said. "Well, boys, you might as well take off too. I'll walk the perimeter to make sure nobody missed anything."

Bob and Dave said their goodbyes, then Dave pulled his cruiser away from the turnout while Bob hiked the trail back home.

When he was satisfied he was alone, Chip stood over the dead brown-striped cat. He looked at the Deuce of Spades card on its chest for a long time.

CHAPTER 41

Deuce was sitting on the living room couch drinking a Schlitz and playing a POV shooter video game when Chip shoved the front door open.

"Son, we need to have a little talk," Chip said when he entered the living room. He stood at an angle beside the couch, looking down at Deuce over the boy's shoulder.

"Yeah, yeah, whatever," Deuce said. "What'd I do now, old man?"

"You know what you did." Chip's voice was quiet, almost calm.

"I dunno what the fuck you're talkin about," Deuce said. He paused the video game and leaned back on the couch.

Chip picked the can of Schlitz off the coffee table and chugged it down in four gulps. He crushed the aluminum can in one hand and tossed it back on the table. He crossed his arms over his chest and stared at Deuce without saying a word.

Something about his father's uncharacteristic silence unnerved Deuce. *Why ain't he hollerin at me about stealin his beer?*

Chip reached into his back pocket, pulled out the gore-stained Deuce of Spades card he'd found on the dead cat, and flipped it onto the couch next to Deuce. Still he didn't speak.

Why ain't he hollerin? Why ain't he talkin? "Daddy, I—" Deuce started then stopped.

The silence stretched in the room. Between father and son. Then Chip said, "Son, I've tried. I know you might not think so, but I have tried. But I just don't know what to do with you no more. You're bent and you need some straightening out. You need some discipline. That's why tomorrow morning at zero four hundred hours you are getting into the back of my squad car, and I'm taking you to Bunker Hill Military Academy."

Deuce jumped to his feet. "You can't do that, you old prick! I ain't goin, and you can't make me!"

"Oh, but I can, boy," Chip said, still not raising his voice. "I'm your father. I call the shots. Now go to your room. You're confined to quarters until further notice."

"I'll run away, and you can't stop me!"

"Try it." Chip hooked his thumbs behind his belt buckle and bowed up on Deuce.

Deuce looked past Chip's shoulder at the front door. He twitched his legs like he had caffeine jitters, then made a break for the door.

Chip reached out one hand and snagged Deuce by the shirt collar. Deuce struggled and writhed like a wild animal caught in a snare, but Chip dragged him back and slammed him against the wall, pinning the boy with a meaty hand. Deuce writhed again and hit his father on the forearms with his fists. Chip didn't budge.

"Fuck you, you one-eyed cocksucker!" Deuce screamed. "I'll kill you!"

One-eyed. That's it. The old bastard's blind on his left side. Deuce knew he had just one shot. If he fucked it up, the old man would tan him worse than he'd ever done before.

Deuce slipped his hand into his jeans pocket. He slid the pocketknife out, careful not to move too fast, not to show any sign of what he had in mind. Just like hunting animals.

He measured the old man. Let him think he had won. Had him trapped and helpless. He waited for the right instant to strike. Then, as if cued by instinct, Deuce flipped open his pocketknife and slashed across his father's forearm in a red arc. Chip lost his grip on Deuce as his arm recoiled.

Deuce blitzed past the foyer and out the heavy oak door into the night. He nashed across the lawn, yanked his bike off the turf, and pedaled off.

Chip staggered onto the porch, panting. His blood-smeared right hand clasping his wounded forearm. He watched Deuce pedal past the murky yellow light of the streetlamp, framed in the halo of the spotlight like a falling angel or a cavorting devil. He watched Deuce pedal out of the light and into the darkness, drawing further and further away until the darkness swallowed him whole.

That was the last time Chip Gustafsson would ever see his son.

CHAPTER 42

After the boys went upstairs to Stephen's room, Bob grabbed three beers from the refrigerator and led Whit and Sarah into his office. He shot a glance down the hall to make sure the boys weren't heading downstairs for snacks, then closed the door. He pulled his cell phone from his pocket and took a gulp of beer. "Well," he said. "That thing Stephen said he saw on the night Whit's dad was killed. It wasn't a dream. It's real."

"Oh my God," Sarah said.

"This is way outside procedure," Bob said, "but I took some pictures of it on my phone." He waved Whit and Sarah to stand beside him and opened the camera icon on his cell. A picture of the creature—ashen pale, hairless, and faceless as advertised—popped up on the screen.

"Jesus, Bob," Sarah said. "You mean that thing was outside our house? Outside our son's window? And the boys found the body in the clearing just up the trail?"

"Well, yes and no," Bob said. "Here's where it gets weird."

"Because up until now, this whole situation has been so normal," Sarah said.

"Right," Bob said. "So anyway, after the boys found that thing, I called the ME. And the ME brings that forensic zoologist Planck with him to the scene. Planck examines the body and says that based on the level of decomposition, it's probably been dead for about three years. Then he shows me a hole in the back of its skull and says the COD was a gunshot wound to the back of the head. Small arms like a pistol or other type of handgun. And then he says there are traces of dirt on the thing's skin and under its claws. Says he thinks someone shot it, buried it, then dug it up and planted it in the clearing to be found."

"Who the hell would wanna do that?" Whit said.

"You got me," Bob said.

"So if this thing was killed three years ago," Sarah said, "then that means a different one of these creatures killed Whit's dad. And it could still be out there."

"Yep," Bob said.

"You know what else it means," Whit said. He reached out his arm and raised his thumb and index finger in the shape of a pistol. "We can kill it."

CHAPTER 43

Junior knocked on Whit's door. "Hey, Dada," he said.

"Hey, buddy," Whit said. He put a bookmark in his copy of *Kafka on the Shore,* set the book on the desk, and shifted in his chair to face Junior. "You heading off to bed now?"

"Yep. Hey, Dada, Stephen and I played Dungeons and Dragons for like five hours."

"You have fun?"

"Yeah, it's super fun. You can create your own characters, and monsters to fight, and you can make up your own quests and stories. Stephen's character is a cleric because he's really smart, and my character is a clairvoyant mage so I can see things far away like Yoda."

"Pretty cool that is, young padawan," Whit said in a Yoda grumble.

Junior giggled.

"And what character should I be?" Whit said.

"Hmm. Well, you could be an evocation mage because they have super powerful magic…" Junior paused and squinted. "But I think you're a knight." He nodded to himself. "Yeah, you're definitely a knight."

"Really?" Whit said. "Why a knight?"

"Well, knights are really good at melee fighting. They're really strong fighters. And you're big and strong. But mostly because knights still believe in chivalry. They believe in honor and loyalty and they protect their kingdom and the people they love. No matter what."

"Sounds like a good character," Whit said.

"Yeah," Junior said. "Oh, and I created a new monster and a whole story for the quest. Wanna hear it?"

"Sure, buddy. You can tell me a bedtime story for a change."

"Okay, cool," Junior said. "So, long ago there was an ancient universe floating in the void of space. One day a new universe grew out of the first universe like when a tiny tree grows out of a big tree, or like when you're playing with bubbles and a little bubble pops out of a big bubble. Anyway, the two universes stayed connected for billions of years, but over time they drifted apart. The first universe got really cold because it kept growing and all its planets drifted farther and farther away from the sun. Meanwhile, the people who lived in that universe fought big wars for like hundreds of years. Some of them were powerful evocation mages. And one of them was the most powerful sorcerer in the universe. He destroyed his enemies with his magic, but he also destroyed most of his universe, so now he wants to make a portal into the newer universe and take it over. The heroes Stephen and I created are from the new universe and their quest is to stop the evil mage from destroying their world like he destroyed his own."

"That's some detailed worldbuilding and storytelling, kiddo. Looks like your heroes need an evocation mage of their own to join the quest."

"Nope," Junior said. "The big boss monster is too powerful and trained at magic. Only a knight can stop him."

"Why's that?"

"I dunno. I think maybe because the knight is the protector and because he fights for love. Oh, wanna see the bad guy? I made a card of him."

"Yeah, let's see this sucker," Whit said.

Junior pulled a hand-drawn playing card out of his Hello Kitty notebook and placed it on the desk in front of Whit. The character on the card was crudely scribbled in black-and-white crayon. Its face was a white blur framed by a black halo. Black eyes stared back at Whit above a gaping black mouth. Beneath the drawing, the character's name was scrawled in crimson:

'The Other.'

CHAPTER 44

After about ninety minutes of picking at his blankets, shuffling his feet under the covers, and glaring at the blackness behind his eyelids, Whit gave up on sleep. He got out of bed, sat at the desk, and tugged the chain on the green reading lamp.

Sleep. Good luck with that. Wish I had something—

He reached into his duffel bag and pulled out the bottle of pills Dr. Moore had given him. He popped two pills with a dram of Bushmills and swallowed. He didn't feel any different. *All natural. Herbal. What did I expect?*

"Ayahuasca my ass," he said to the empty room and went back to reading *Kafka on the Shore*. After a few minutes, the words in the book started to blur. They drifted across the page, then lifted into the air like they were part of a 3D movie. The letters floated around like alphabet soup and began to rearrange themselves. They formed the sentence: *'Down the rabbit hole.'*

"Down this whisky," Whit said and took a pull on his Bushmills bottle.

Down the rabbit hole, a voice inside his head said.

He looked around the room. "No bunny," he said. "No waistcoat-pocket watch, tick-tock. I'm late. Where's the hedge? Orange marmalade." He took another slug of whisky.

Concentrate, the voice said. *Focus on the door.*

Whit focused on the door. He still didn't see any rabbit hole. He closed his eyes, breathed in from his gut to his chest, and pictured himself in a dim room, walls on all sides like a box. Standing in front of a mirror.

He heard a wailing drone rising and falling like the cries of the infinite souls of the damned. The same unearthly moan he had heard in the corridor beneath the attic.

He opened his eyes.

A dark disk hovered in the center of the door. Incandescent red-orange tendrils rotated in a burning ring around the disk.

The black hole sun pulled Whit to his feet.

As he drew nearer to the shadow of the horizon, Whit felt the pull of the black hole sun grow stronger. Its gaping maw spun faster. He could feel the abyss tugging at his clothes and whipping his hair. The maw opened wide.

With a final crushing lurch, the maw pulled Whit into its gullet. He felt his feet leave the ground as a vacuum of cold air plunged him into the darkness. He felt the heavy grip of gravity. And then he felt nothing.

***

Upstairs in Stephen's bathroom, Junior gripped the sides of the porcelain sink and stared into the looking glass. The Other stared back at him.

CHAPTER 45

One day until the end of the world

Bob pressed the button to end the call and slipped his cell into the pants pocket of his police tans. He left his office and peeked down the hall at the guest room. The door was still closed. He crossed the hall and knocked on the door. "Hey, Whit," he said. "Wakey, wakey, eggs 'n' bakey. I've got some news."

Behind the door, the room was silent.

Bob knocked again. "Whit, you up, buddy?" He waited a few seconds, then opened the door. The room was empty.

Bob shuffled to the living room. Sarah was sitting at the table with the morning paper and a cup of coffee. The boys were beating pancake batter and jabbering in the kitchen.

"Hey, Sarah," Bob said. "You see Whit this morning?"

"Nope," Sarah said, "but the front door's open next door. He probably got up early to clean up his dad's house."

"All work, no sleep," Bob said. "I got some news for him. I think I'll take him a beer for his troubles. And maybe bring one along for my own."

"A nice refreshing breakfast beer before a long day on the police beat, eh Bob?"

"I wouldn't want to be unsociable."

"Right. Have a nice chat. And tell Whit breakfast's almost ready."

"Will do."

Bob dodged the boys and the pancake batter, grabbed two beers from the fridge, and trotted over to the Coe house. When he walked through the door, he saw Whit standing in front of the living room mirror, not moving. Bob set the beers on the foyer floor and eased up to Whit's side. He looked at Whit's reflection in the mirror. Whit's eyes were wide open, fixed on nothing.

"Whit," Bob said, low and even. "You alright, buddy? Whit!" He waved his hand in front of Whit's face and snapped his fingers. Whit didn't blink. He just kept staring into the mirror. Bob grabbed Whit by the shoulders and shook him. "Whit. It's Bob. Come on, pal. Snap out of it." No response. Still gripping Whit by the shoulders, Bob spun Whit around, away from the gaze of the mirror.

"Bob?" Whit said. "What's going on? How did we get here?"

"I dunno, Whit. I was looking for you and saw the door open, so I came in. When I got here, you were standing in front of that mirror, just spacing out like you were hypnotized or something. Had a hell of a time snapping you out of it."

"Where's Junior?" Whit said.

"He's fine. He's making breakfast with Stephen."

"Okay," Whit said, blinking and rubbing his temple.

"You alright, man?" Bob said. "You looked like you were seriously contemplating the immortality of the crab."

"I'd rather contemplate the immortality of the lobster, but, yeah, I'm good. I couldn't sleep again, so I took some experimental sleeping pills. Must've had a bad trip or something."

"Like bat country and giant lizards in golf shoes?"

"Something like that," Whit said.

Bob grinned and swatted Whit on the shoulder. "Anyway," he said. "Dr. Ellicott at the ME's office called a few minutes ago. He and Planck finished examining that thing Stephen and Junior found in the woods yesterday. They compared its teeth and claws to the bite indentations and claw marks on your old man and Barbara. He says they're a near match, but not an exact match, meaning they're the same species, but not the same individual creature. Which we already figured. They also analyzed the creature's DNA. It doesn't match any species known to man. No big surprise there either." Bob cocked an eyebrow and held up one finger like Socrates. "Now here's the twist: they pulled a metal rod out of the thing's leg. Turns out it's the type of rod surgeons implant in patients whose bones have been shattered and need a replacement, usually in car and motorcycle accidents. They got a serial number off the rod and they're using the number to trace the rod's manufacturer and see if it was used in an operation."

"An operation on one of those things?" Whit said. "So like if old Mr. killer monster got hip replacement surgery?"

"I guess even carnivorous cryptids want to play golf in their twilight years. Anyway, we should have something on the metal rod this afternoon. Oh, but wait there's more," Bob said in an infomercial voiceover impression. "Ellicott and Planck recovered the bullet that killed the creature. It was lodged behind its cheekbone. So they extracted it and ran it for a match. They couldn't match it to a particular gun, but get this. Turns out the bullet's from a fucking Luger. Like from World War Two. I mean how many people you know have one of those old blasters?"

"I can think of one," Whit said.

CHAPTER 46

"Ah, good morning, Mr. Coe," Mr. Hooker said. He glanced at the clock on the wall. It read 10:25 a.m. He smiled to himself and said, "Right on time for your appointment. May I escort you—"

"No, I got this, Jeeves," Whit said and stalked down the hall to Dr. Moore's office. He knocked on the door and entered without waiting for a response.

Dr. Moore sat in his red wingback chair reading William Manchester's biography of Winston Churchill. When he saw Whit, he smiled, placed a bookmark in the hefty tome, and set it on the coffee table. He removed his reading glasses and placed them on top of the book.

"Good morning, Whitman," he said. "I've been expecting you."

"Why would you be expecting me?"

"Because of the Luger, of course."

"Then it was you who killed that creature."

"Indeed it was, my boy," Dr. Moore said, rising to his feet.

"Why?" Whit said. "And what the hell was that thing in the first place?"

"I killed the creature because it is my job. My true evocation. And I did it for you, Whitman."

"What do you mean you did it for me?"

"What I mean, my boy," Dr. Moore said, "is that creature is what killed your wife three years ago."

Whit felt a sickening wave of emptiness jolt through his body. His breath caught in his lungs. "What?" he said.

"I'm so sorry, Whitman," Dr. Moore said. "Truly. I know this is terribly painful for you. But I also know you came here to find out what happened to your wife. I know you didn't come for Allan Coe. You came for Alice. Only for Alice. You came for an answer, and now you have it. At least part of it."

"What's the rest of it?"

"The creature that killed your wife was not always as it is. It was once human—a patient of mine called Jimmie Macomber. Jimmie was a very disturbed young man. He told me a malevolent being had been watching him from behind the mirror. He said the creature had a blurred face, burning black eyes, and a swirling pit of a mouth that whispered inside his head, telling Jimmie what to do. He called this pit the maw mouth. And he called the dark entity—"

"The Other," Whit said.

"Yes." Dr. Moore raised his left eyebrow. "The Other. Jimmie said that the Other had promised him the answers to all his questions. An end to all his pain and fear. He only had to listen to the words of the maw mouth and give himself over to those words. Then and only then would Jimmie become his true self."

"The creature he became," Whit said.

"Yes," Dr. Moore said. "The Other preyed on Jimmie's fear and anxiety. It took advantage of his illness. That's what the Other does. It is drawn to psychic trauma. That is where it manifests and takes hold. Emotional trauma creates wounds in a person's psyche like cracks in a suit of armor. The Other creeps in through the vulnerable spots in a person's psychic armor and latches onto the trauma of its host—the fear, the pain, the grief. It twists that trauma as it twists the mind of the host. And in Jimmie's case, it twisted him into something inhuman. A beast. A mindless servant with no will or purpose but the will and purpose of the Other."

"So this entity—the Other. Is that what I started seeing after Astrid died?"

Dr. Moore raised his eyebrow again. "Then you remember?" he said.

"I didn't," Whit said. "Not for a long time. I'd forgotten all about it. I guess I forgot about a lot of things after I left town. I moved on. Lived my life. And all those old memories faded away like they'd been swallowed in a fog. Then I came back to town and that fog started to lift. Most of the memories are still blurry. They're more like disjointed images without context, but they're starting to come back. The Other's starting to come back. I think I'm starting to see it again. Christ, Doc, I think my son's starting to see it. What does that mean? Does the Other want to turn me and my son into monsters like it did to that Macomber kid?"

"No, Whitman," Dr. Moore said. "You and your son have certain... gifts. The Other couldn't transform either of you into one of its beasts even if it did want to. But that is not the Other's plan. It has much bigger plans for you, Whitman."

"Great," Whit said. "That's not cryptically ominous or anything."

"As I said, you and your son have certain gifts. Powers, if you will. These powers can be used to protect yourselves and others. They can also be used to destroy. Hypothetically, if your powers manifest completely, they could destroy entire armies. Entire nations in a single stroke."

"So, what, my son and I are like Fat Man and Little Boy walking around, going to baseball games, sharing a pizza?"

"I actually can't be sure what your son's particular gifts are without seeing him. They manifest differently in different individuals. But in reference to the power of your particular gifts, Whitman, nuclear fission would be an apt comparison."

"And the Other wants to use me as some kind of superweapon? Like drop me on Hiroshima?"

"I don't believe that's the Other's end game," Dr. Moore said. "You see, the Other and its race used their powers to fight devastating wars that lasted centuries. At full force, their powers constituted mutually assured destruction. But one of the Other's race pushed the button, so to speak. Consumed by the desire for victory at all costs, he unleashed the full force of his destructive powers on his enemies. And on their world. Those who survived drifted in a dying, unlivable world. The plants and trees withered and died. The animals starved. The only creatures that survived were hideous, misshapen predatory beasts. The Other is the last of its people, alone in a dead and desolate world. It wants to conquer our world because it is still alive and green—in places anyway. And the Other wants to keep it that way. I believe the Other is turning the weak and the vulnerable like Jimmie into drone soldiers in its invading army. And you, Whitman, are to be the Other's general."

"Why me?" Whit said. "Why doesn't the Other just lead its own army?"

"That I don't know, my boy," Dr. Moore said.

"Well, that's comforting," Whit said. "Hey Doc, how do you know all this stuff in the first place?"

"I told you about my father. About how he fought against the Nazis but returned home from the war broken in body and spirit. What I didn't tell you was that when I was in my first year at

Cambridge, my father hanged himself in the attic of my family home."

"Jesus," Whit said. "I'm sorry, Doc."

"Thank you, Whitman. It was a very long time ago, but the memory never fades." He gave Whit a melancholy half-smile. "Anyway, When I returned to school from my father's funeral, two men in trench coats and Fedoras were standing in front of my dorm room. They asked me what I knew about my father's war service, my family history, political leanings and affiliations, religious beliefs, et cetera. At first I thought they were trying to recruit me into a spy ring, but it turned out to be something much bigger.

"The men said they were members of an ancient order of philosophers, scientists, and mystics who had been trying to stop a malevolent being called the Other from entering our world for centuries. They said that if the Other unlocked the door to our world, it would mean the end of our world. The doom of all mankind.

"Naturally, I thought the men were completely mad, but then one of them removed a photograph from his coat pocket. The photograph showed the two men standing beneath a tall ash tree with my father. It was before the war. My father was young and smiling. The men told me that my father had been the head of their order, that membership in the secret order was passed down from father to son, and that I was the last of an ancient line of mystical scientists sworn to protect our world. It was therefore incumbent upon me to take my father's place in the order and to prevent the Other from destroying our world.

"I still had my doubts about the two men. I had never seen them before in my life. My father had never spoken of anything they had just told me. But I couldn't walk away from the smiling image of my father in that picture. I couldn't let him go.

"The men led me to a black Studebaker. I got in and they drove me to a clearing on the edge of an ash grove. We got out of the car just as the sun sank behind the tree line and we walked into the grove. At the center of the grove, a great, gnarled ash tree rose into the gloaming. I remember thinking the tree must have been centuries old. One of the men instructed me to clear my thoughts and stare at the tree, to breathe in deeply and to exhale slowly. The second man pulled a makeup mirror from his coat and told me to close my eyes. He told me to keep breathing and to think of my father, to concentrate on the pain and the anger. Then he told me to open my eyes and look in the mirror. When I did, I saw a fathomless face wavering beneath the surface of the glass. In that face, black eyes burned like collapsing stars and a gaping maw groaned like the pit of Charybdis. The men told me this was the face of the Other. This was the malevolent spirit that would end our world. In that moment, I vowed to learn all I could about the Other and its world in order to save our own."

Dr. Moore glanced at the octagonal mirror on the wall, let out a breath, then looked back at Whit. "I've already told you a great deal of what I have learned about the Other," he said, "but there are three more things you must know. First, even as we speak, the Other is entering our world. And second, it is entering our world right here in Rockwell."

"Why here?" Whit said.

"Because this is where the portal to the Other's world is. Where it has been since the creation of our universe. Are you familiar with multiverse theory by any chance?"

"Only what I learned from Dr. Strange."

"I don't believe I'm familiar with his work."

"Never mind. You were saying?"

"Where was I?" Dr. Moore said, scratching his chin. "Ah, yes, multiverse theory. One tenet of multiverse theory posits that there are several, perhaps infinite universes. As one universe expands, it forces forth a second universe—an offshoot like a plant bud. Or think of it like a bubble expanding and creating a second bubble. That second bubble is an entirely new universe which expands and expands until it buds yet another universe. Do you follow?"

"I think so," Whit said. "It's like saying the universe is turtles all the way down, except here it's Mr. Bubble all the way down."

Dr. Moore furrowed his forehead. "Well, yes, actually," he said and grinned at Whit. "Now as I was saying, Rockwell sits on the precise location where our universe sprouted from the Other's universe. It stands to reason that Rockwell is where the veil between the Other's world and ours is the thinnest."

"Veil?" Whit said.

"Think of it this way, Whitman. If multiverse theory is the science behind the Other and its world, the veil is the magic. Our ancient ancestors knew there was an Otherworld that could be reached and could reach us. They believed that on certain holidays—solstices equinoxes, Samhain for example—the veil between our world and the Otherworld disappeared. So the veil may be pierced at certain times and in certain places. Rockwell is that place for the Other to enter. And the time is—"

"Tomorrow," Whit said. "The summer solstice."

"Yes, Whitman," Dr. Moore said. "The cycle is already beginning. The young adults of Rockwell vanishing in regular lunar cycles. The Other shaping them into its twisted servants. Your return."

"What does my return have to do with all this?"

"That brings us to the third thing you must know about the Other: Whitman, you are the only one who can stop it."

"Why me?"

"Because it always had to be you, Whitman. You have stardust in your blood."

"What does that mean?"

"That's another long story, my boy," Dr. Moore said. "One we don't have time for. At this very moment, the Other is preparing to enter our world. We must prepare you to face it. We must unlock your powers, as we tried when you were a boy."

"No," Whit said. "Bad things happen when I use my powers. I hurt people."

"Whitman, my dear lad," Dr. Moore said. "You were not responsible for your mother's death. She died at home in childbirth. You were here with me. True, you were honing your powers in the moment she passed, but the two occurrences were unrelated. It's a simple correlation of events, but it is not causation. You did not cause your mother's death."

"But I saw it happen," Whit said. "I was staring deep into the mirror, past the mirror. I was pushing through the mirror with my mind. With my anger. Then I saw her. I felt her. She was standing in front of our living room mirror. She looked through the mirror back at me. And she smiled. So sadly. Then she hunched over in terrible pain. Her water broke. She screamed and—" Whit's voice broke off.

"Whitman," Dr. Moore said, "you did not cause her death with your powers. You merely saw it with your powers. I'm so sorry. I know it must have been terrible. Your powers are not limited to telekinesis. You saw your mother through the power of clairvoyance. The power of clairvoyance is enhanced in the presence of reflective surfaces such as water or mirrors. That is why we used mirrors in our exercises: to see far and wide. Our ancient ancestors believed that scrying in mirrors allowed them to see things that were happening far away, things that had happened in the past, things that had not yet happened. They even believed that if you gazed into a mirror and thought of love, the face of your beloved would appear to you. But they also believed that mirrors provided a gateway into other worlds. That is why the Other manifests in mirrors. They act as portals into our world. So far he has only been able to peek through and to whisper into our world. But soon he will tear the rift wide open. He and his army will conquer our world and annihilate the human race. They will sweep even the memory of humanity away. Unless you embrace your powers and stop him."

"Okay," Whit said. He straightened his back and rolled his shoulders like a boxer limbering up. "What's the plan, Doc?"

"We must make your unconscious conscious. We must accelerate your training to make up for three decades of lost time."

"Sounds like we're gonna need a montage," Whit said.

"The film editing technique?" Dr. Moore said.

"It's a joke, Doc. You know like *Rocky* or the puppet movie the *South Park* guys made? No? Nothing?" Whit shrugged. "Anyway, I'm ready. Let's do it. What do I have to do first?"

"First you have to die, Whitman," Dr. Moore said.

CHAPTER 47

"**I** would prefer not to," Whit said.

"Ah, Bartleby. Ah, humanity," Dr. Moore said. "My favorite Melville short story." He placed a hand on Whit's shoulder. "You'll be fine, Whitman. You will only be dead for a few minutes. I'll bring you right back."

"Sure, just a few minutes. What could go wrong? Doc, have you ever seen *Flatliners*?"

"You're referring to another movie, I assume."

"*Flatliners* isn't just a movie, Doc. It's Joel Schumacher and Kiefer Sutherland's follow-up to *The Lost Boys*."

"I'm not familiar."

"You're killin me, Doc. And then you're killin me."

"Whitman," Dr. Moore said, "you need to make the subconscious conscious. Your powers are buried deep in your subconscious mind where you cannot harness them. You may tap into them instinctively, or even accidentally under certain circumstances, but you must gain complete control over your powers if you are to defeat the Other. And you must do so now. Had I been able to continue your training when you were a boy, I could have gradually taught you to bring your powers from your unconscious to your conscious mind. But without the luxury of all those years, the only way to merge your conscious and unconscious minds is through death. Think of it as something of a hard reboot on a computer."

"You think of it," Whit said.

"First," Dr. Moore said, "I will inject you with an herbal serum of my own concoction to stop your heart. After you are clinically dead, I will wait ninety seconds and inject you with another of my serums that will restart your heart. You will remain in a deep sleep for several hours, floating through the universe of your subconscious until your conscious and subconscious minds have melded. Theoretically, anyway."

"Theoretically? Tell me, Timothy Leary, have you ever performed this procedure before?"

"Once," Dr. Moore said.

"Once? What happened to the guinea pig?"

"He survived."

"And where is he now?" Whit said.

"Right here, my boy. I performed the experiment on myself."

***

Whit laid on Dr. Moore's reclining therapy chair.

"Whitman," Dr. Moore said, "could you please extend your arm?"

Whit held out his left arm. Dr. Moore removed the belt from his slacks and used it to tie off Whit's arm.

"Doing this thing the trainspotty way, huh, Doc?"

"I'm not familiar with that reference, Whitman."

"It's another movie thing. Forget it. Let's get this road on the show."

"Very well, my boy." Dr. Moore pulled two serum jars from a drawer and held them up so Whit could see them. He tapped one jar with his finger. "This one makes you larger," he said. He tapped the second vial. "And this one makes you small. In other words, the first serum will stop your heart, and the second will start it again."

"Got it," Whit said. "Okay, Morpheus. Down the rabbit hole."

"Ah," Dr. Moore smiled. "The Greek god of sleep and dreams. Very apt analogy, Whitman."

"No, I meant like in *the Matrix*."

"The matrix of what?"

"Doc, if the world doesn't end, I'm mailing you a whole box of DVDs."

"I look forward to it. Are you ready, Whitman?"

Whit took a long drag of air. Let it out. Let his arm go limp. "Shoot," he said.

Dr. Moore stuck a needle into the first jar and drew a dose of serum into the syringe. He held the needle upright and pressed the plunger until a few drops of serum dribbled down the tip of the needle like beads of blood. He found a good vein on Whit's arm and slapped it. "Just a little pinprick," he said and spiked Whit's vein.

Whit felt the cold fluid slide into his veins. The cold spread upward through his arm, then through the rest of his body. He felt his heart and his breath slow. He started to drift. Out of this world. Out of warmth and light. Into the cold. Into the abyss. Into the outer dark, reflecting the inner dark. And then beyond the outer dark and into the nothing, where even the darkness ceased to exist. Where Whit ceased to exist.

Then from the depths of the nothing, the darkness rose. Whit could feel it growing, expanding exponentially across the face of the deep. He could feel a soft, rolling rise and fall like the waves of a calm sea. A muffled sloshing gurgled in rhythm with the waves, faraway like the sounds beneath a deep ocean. And then he heard a wailing drone, ringing high and low like a chorus of tormented souls howling in time with the waves of the deep. A monstrous black hole spiraled in the dark, red-orange arms spinning as it churned. Whit felt the black hole pulling him forward. Felt his consciousness judder and snap into the arms of the black hole, through the event horizon, through the singularity, through the looking glass.

He emerged in a misty wasteland. He stood at the head of the Other's army of twisted beasts. Their hollow, skin-covered eye sockets stared at Whit, awaiting his command. He raised an arm. The creatures tensed. He lowered his arm and a gale of snow lashed across the wasteland. The creatures stormed through the mist. Human voices screamed in the distance.

The Other turned toward Whit. He lowered his cowl to reveal his face, but the darkness swallowed the world.

Now Whit was in the attic of his old house. The glow of the sunset pierced the slats high on the wall, carving narrow rectangles of red-orange light in the darkening room. The chimes of the ballerina's music box and the grandfather clock came to life as one. *Sunset. The time. The box. The letter. The darkness.*

Whit was in the darkness again. A tiny flickering light darted back and forth ahead. It flitted forward, dancing in front of Whit's face.

"Think happy thoughts," she said, then beckoned Whit to follow her.

Whit followed and the darkness was gone. In its place was a radiant white light, yearned for and yearning, rotating in an infinite circle. He drifted into the embrace of the spiral's white arms. Into her arms.

Whit opened his eyes. He was back in Dr. Moore's office, lying in the reclining chair. The needle was no longer in his arm, but an angry red mark marred his skin where it had pierced his vein.

"Welcome back, Whitman," Dr. Moore said and patted Whit on the shoulder. "How do you feel?"

"I know what I have to do," Whit said. "What time is it?"

"Almost half past seven," Dr. Moore said.

"Almost sunset," Whit said. "I have to go."

"Whitman, you need to rest a moment."

"No time. The sun's setting. Thanks, Doc. I'll see you."

Whit sprang to his feet and rushed out of the office, passing Mr. Hooker without a word.

Mr. Hooker glanced at the clock. "See you tomorrow, Mr. Coe," he said to Whit's back as the door swung shut.

CHAPTER 48

Whit jumped out of the Audi and bolted for his old house.

"Whit, wait up!" Bob called from his front porch and ran to Whit's side. "Jesus Christ, you scared the shit out of us. I called you like a dozen times."

"Shit, I'm sorry, man," Whit said. "I had to go somewhere that doesn't have cell service. Is Junior okay?"

"Yeah, he's fine. Sarah and I told him you had to tie up some loose ends with the house and the funeral. He's been watching Godzilla movies with Stephen all day."

"Okay, good."

"Oh, hey. The reason I called in the first place is because we got a match on that steel rod Ellicott and Planck took out of that creature's leg—"

"Jimmie Macomber," Whit said in a monotone.

"Yeah. How did you—"

"I'll explain later." Whit looked up at the red-orange disk of the sun as it sank below the tree line. "But right now there's something I have to take care of next door."

Whit turned and dashed into his old house.

"You gotta go, you gotta go," Bob said, scratching his head.

***

Whit burst through the trapdoor to the attic. Just as in his vision, the room was sinking into darkness, sliced by rectangular shards of the setting sun piercing the slats in the wall. He stood and waited. The red-orange light faded, and the shadows of night stalked into the corners of the room.

When the final coal ember of sunlight faded from the attic, the chimes of the ballerina's music box and the grandfather clock rang in chorus. Whit pulled the chain dangling next to his head, and a dust-coated bulb buzzed to life, casting a dim yellow halo in the center of the cramped attic. The corners of the room remained in shadow.

The grandfather clock chimed twelve times, then fell silent. Its hands wound to twelve o'clock. The music box continued to chime a few moments longer, then it too quietened. A hidden drawer inside the music box slid open.

Whit peeked into the drawer. There was an envelope inside. Whit's name was written on the envelope in his mother's handwriting.

Of course. It had to be the ballerina's box.

He took the envelope from the drawer and opened it. Inside were two sheets of paper, folded and refolded to fit the tiny envelope. He unfolded the paper.

It was a letter from his mother, dated the day Whit was born. It read:

My Dearest Whitman,

Today is the happiest day of my life. The day you came into this world. You already mean so much to me, and I know that you will mean even more to the world you have just entered. I know that by the time you read this, you will have suffered horribly. I am sorry, my son. I know that you have endured many losses. I know that you lost your sister far too early, and that you still carry the weight of that loss. I know that by the time you read these words, I will be gone. Leaving you behind is the greatest regret of my life. I dream of another world where you and I walked a different path, a path together. But our world is not so kind. And, Whitman, I am so sorry about your wife Alice. I know you loved her with all your heart, and that your heart is forever broken. I wish things could have been different for you. I wish you could have had the chance to live a simpler life. A long life of peace. I would have given anything to keep you from enduring the pain I know you are feeling. But it had to be this way. It always had to be this way. You have a great fate, my son. And great fate is tied to tragedy. My dearest boy, it is at last time for you to know who you are and what your fate is.

Our ancient ancestors believed in gods and magic, in the sanctity of nature, in mythic creatures and otherworlds, in fate and prophecy. The conquest of our people by foreign armies and religions did not fully drive our faith from the earth. Some of the faithful survived, practicing our religion in secret and taking it with us to new lands.

Our family, along with other members of our order, were among the founders of the town of Rockwell. They sailed across the treacherous sea and crossed the wilds of this continent following a portal and a prophecy, following the whispers of the Other. The prophecy told of the beginning of our world, the end of our world, and its glorious rebirth.

Our world was born of the ashes and dying embers of a far older universe. We were a sapling universe, sprung from the great tree of the older world. Life in death. And our world remained attached to its mother universe through a hidden veil, too weak to pass through physically, but strong enough for the Other to reach out to some. To whisper his truth. The truth of his world and the truth of ours.

Once the Other's world had been a realm of nature and beauty. A universe of stardust and magic. But its inhabitants warred against each other for power and glory. In the process, they destroyed their world, just as we humans are now destroying our own.

The Other was the last survivor of his world. He had seen its tragic fate, wrought by the greed and hubris of his people. And in our young world, he saw a second chance. A world of green grass, blue lakes, and majestic trees. An Eden, unspoiled by the ravages of man. And in the groves and lakes, he whispered to our ancestors.

But mankind ignored the whispers of nature. We tamed nature to suit our whims, and in the process began the destruction of nature itself. We drove animals and plants to extinction. We covered the green earth in concrete, then blew up that concrete with bombs and artillery. Our bootprint on the earth has so marred the planet that our footprints must be erased completely in order to restore the balance of nature, to restore the earth to her sacred form, green and blue and beautiful, a pure and thriving garden of life. This manmade castle of asphalt, concrete, Spanish tile, and silicon chips must fall. The corrupted world of mankind must come to an end. The Other must purify it in ice and mist. He must erase all memory that this world ever was. And you, my son, must stand beside him. That was always your destiny. That is the reason you were born. To reap the weeds and to sow the seeds of a new paradise. To rule over a new Eden with your son beside you. That is the prophecy you were born unto.

It is you, Whitman, who were the final piece in the prophecy. It is no mere coincidence that our ancestors settled here in Rockwell. We came here because the woods near town are the strongest point of connection between our universe and that of the Other, the site from which our sapling world sprouted. It is here that the portal will open, and the

Other will enter. And it is here, the prophecy tells, that the man who shall open the door will be born. That man shall have the powers of the Other, for he shall have stardust in his blood. But that man must endure great suffering before the door shall open. Four tragedies shall befall him. Four sacrifices to open the door. The first sacrifice shall be the man's twin. The second sacrifice shall be the man's mother. The third sacrifice shall be the man's wife. And the fourth sacrifice shall be the man's father, for the blood of the ancestors shall be the final key that opens the door to the Other. And the door shall be fully opened upon the setting of the summer solstice sun. Then shall the old world end and the new world begin.

My dearest Whitman, I am so sorry for these sacrifices you have suffered through, that you still suffer through. And I wish I could have been there to raise you and watch you grow into the fine man you have become. That is the sacrifice I must make. But our sacrifices are for a greater good.

The sunset tomorrow brings a new dawn, my son. The portal lies hidden in Dr. Moore's house. You must be there with him tomorrow when it opens. He knows the way and will lead you where you need to go. I know you are an impatient and curious man. A man who always wants the answer immediately. But please, Whitman, you must not seek Dr. Moore until sunset. It is not part of the plan. If you deviate from the plan, you make yourself vulnerable to your enemies. So please stay far from the old center of town. Far from the door. And you must not tell a soul about the contents of this letter. If you tell anyone, you put their life at risk. There are cosmic forces at play, and they will wipe any pieces off the board that were not meant to enter the game.

My dearest Whitman, I want you to know how proud of you I am. I want you to know how much I love you. That love is eternal. It exists in all worlds. So, my son, do not weep for the end of this world. Smile for the new world about to begin.

With eternal love,
Mother

Whit refolded the letter, carefully following the seams his mother had smoothed into the paper over four decades ago. Then he crumpled it in his hand and squeezed. He opened his hand and a scattering of ash fell to the attic floor. He extended a finger and the music box drawer closed.

The room was still except for the ticking of the grandfather clock. Whit looked at its face. The hands were ticking backward.

CHAPTER 49

23 hours 52 minutes until the end of the world

Bob flashed a glance out his study door. The boys were sprawled on the living room couch munching cheesy poofs, zoned out on another Godzilla movie. He eased the door shut and turned to face Whit and Sarah.

"Okay, Whit," Bob said, "do you want to tell me what the hell's going on? You vanish all day, come back looking like death warmed over, then somehow know the steel rod the ME dug out of that creature belonged to Jimmie Macomber. How do you even know something like that?"

"I can't tell you," Whit said.

"What do you mean you can't tell us?" Bob said. "We're supposed to be in this together."

"Why can't you tell us, Whit?" Sarah said, her tone patient.

"Because if I tell anyone, I put them in danger. I'm not going to risk that any more than I already have by coming here in the first place. Although I guess I have to be here to stop it."

"Stop what?" Bob said.

"Can't tell you that either, Bob. It just has to be me. It always had to be me. And I have to do it alone."

"Whit, buddy," Bob said. "You're not making a lick of sense."

"Why does it have to be you?" Sarah said.

"Believe me," Whit said, "I've been asking myself that same question all day."

"Whit," Sarah said, "we've all been friends since we were kids. Friends for life. We're your family and we love you. You don't have to carry the entire burden yourself. Please let me and Bob help."

Whit shook his head. "I can't," he said. "I'm not putting you or the kids in the line of fire. I know none of this makes sense. I wish I could explain it to you. I really do. But this is my fight. Alone."

"God love you, Whit," Bob said. "You are one stubborn son of a bitch. Why do I get the feeling you're about to walk into a meat grinder?"

"Because I probably am. But I have to. And I'm tired. I just want all of this to be over." He drooped his shoulders and looked down at the floor, then raised his head and looked Bob and Sarah in the eyes. "Listen, Bob, Sarah. Junior's been having a great time here with you guys and Stephen. I think he feels at home here. So if anything happens to me, would you take him in? I know it's a lot to ask, but…"

Bob and Sarah looked at each other and nodded. "Of course, Whitman," Sarah said.

"We're honored that you asked us, brother," Bob said. "But it won't be necessary. You're gonna raise that boy yourself. And the two of you can visit us any time you want. Whatever it is you're up against, you're gonna beat it. Know how I know?"

"How?"

"Because you're Whitman fucking Coe, that's how I know." Bob smiled and gripped Whit's shoulder.

"Okay," Whit said, slapping Bob on the back. "Now let's put a moratorium on the subjects of monsters and imminent death for the evening. If it's okay with you guys, I'd just like to watch a movie with the kids and maybe knock back a few beers with you."

"Sounds good to me," Bob said.

"We wouldn't miss it for the world," Sarah said.

Outside the study, Junior and Stephen huddled together and listened at the door.

CHAPTER 50

22 hours 3 minutes until the end of the world

"This is major," Stephen said. "I mean really, really major." He looked at his Einstein poster, but old Albert had no words of wisdom to impart.

"I think my dada is in trouble," Junior said. "I know he's trying to protect everybody, but I think he's walking into a trap."

"What kind of a trap?"

"I don't know, but it's something big. It has something to do with that monster we found, but it's way bigger. Did your dad say anything about it today?"

"The monster?" Stephen said, shaking his head. "No. I think he's trying to protect us too."

"Maybe it's time for us to protect them," Junior said.

"How?" Stephen said.

"We find out what those eyeless freaks are ourselves. We find out everything we can about them. We need to know what they are, where they come from, why they're here, how to stop them. Maybe we'll find out something that can help my dada."

"Okay," Stephen said. "What are nerds for?" He flipped open his laptop and turned on the power. "So we'll start with a basic internet search and see where that leads us. Just let me type in our description." Stephen spoke as he typed. "Okay, let's try pale hairless long eyeless monster claws fangs." He hit the search icon. "And we've got fangs and claws for costumes. Fangs and claws for costumes. More fangs and claws for costumes—wait here's one: the wendigo. Oh, shit! I've read about them before. I don't know why I didn't think of it. Let me click on the website." Stephen rolled his eyes. "*Tales from the Cryptid?* Webmaster: Dr. Hieronymus Planck, forensic zoologist and cryptid hunter?"

"What a dork," Junior said.

"Yeah," Stephen said and giggled. "Anyway, the entry on the website says they have sharp fangs, razor-like talons on their hands and feet. They're humanoid. Antlers. Nothing about the eyes."

"What else does it say?"

"Just the general folklore about wendigos. They're cannibal monsters. But that's not the important part. The important part is that I once read a book that said when the first settlers came to Rockwell, the indigenous population had already abandoned the area because they thought there were wendigos in the woods. Only the settlers thought they were something else. Something connected to some old pagan religion. Damn, why didn't I remember all this crap until just now?" Stephen slapped himself on the side of the head.

"Do you have the book here?"

"No, it's a library book. In fifth grade, I wrote a paper about the history of Rockwell, and it was one of the books I looked at. It wasn't really useful for my paper, so I just skimmed it. But I remember where it is. It's in the Local History section in the back of the library."

"Looks like we're going on a field trip tomorrow," Junior said.

CHAPTER 51

21 hours 54 minutes until the end of the world

"That's a pretty big question," Whit said, sitting in a wicker chair on the porch. He took a long pull on his beer bottle. "I don't know. What do you guys think?"

"Come on," Bob said. "That's an easy one. You're Emilio Estevez. He's the jock."

"Yeah," Sarah said, "but Emilio Estevez is a bully and a follower. He's got no backbone. No, I think Whit's Judd Nelson. He's got that rebellious bad boy thing going on."

"But Judd Nelson was a dick," Bob said. "And even though he ends up with Molly Ringwald at the end, he pretty much browbeats and sexually harasses her throughout the whole movie."

"That's true," Sarah said.

"Alright," Bob said. "So which *Breakfast Club* character are you, Whit?"

"Isn't it obvious? Take off your gender goggles."

"Well, you're not Molly Ringwald," Sarah said.

"I don't know," Bob said. "He is kind of a princess. And weren't you prom queen, Whit?"

Whit flipped Bob the bird.

"Oh my God," Sarah said, looking at Whit. "You're a total Ally Sheedy. A big old mopey, neurotic goth basket case."

"Plus you have dandruff and wear too much eyeliner," Bob said.

"Fuck you," Whit said and swigged his beer.

Four footsteps buzzed across the living room carpet. Stephen and Junior swung open the front door and hopped onto the porch. "Mom, Dad," Stephen said. "Can Junior and I go to the library tomorrow?"

"On two conditions," Sarah said. "First, Junior's dad has to say it's okay. And second, I'm dropping you boys off and picking you up."

"Can I, Dada?" Junior said.

"Well," Whit said. "I was thinking of taking you out to breakfast tomorrow."

"Can I go after breakfast?"

"I don't know. I don't want to make you go to breakfast if you don't really want to."

Junior giggled. "I know what you're doing, Dada," he said.

"Alright." Whit grinned at his son.

"Can I have waffles?" Junior said.

"Why not? I don't think you've had enough waffles this week. Now go get ready for bed. I'll be in to say goodnight in a minute."

"Okay, Dada."

The boys scampered for the stairs.

"Hey, no running in the—" Bob waved his arm in defeat.

Whit, Bob, and Sarah sat in silence, sipping their beers. When Whit drained his bottle he said, "I think I'm going to say goodnight to Junior and wind down with a book. Goodnight, all."

"Goodnight," Bob and Sarah said.

Whit stepped inside the house, and Bob got up to watch the night.

"I know that look," Sarah said. "What are you thinking?"

"I'm thinking Whit's about to walk into a meat grinder. And I'm thinking I'm not going to let him do it blind and alone."

"What are you going to do?"

"I'm going to fill in the blanks from those doctored missing persons files," Bob said. "Every last one of 'em."

CHAPTER 52

9 hours 56 minutes until the end of the world

The waitress set Junior's stack of waffles and Whit's scrambled eggs and bacon on the table.

"Thank you," Whit said.

"Thank you, Mary," Junior said, reading the waitress' name tag.

"You're welcome," Mary said. She looked at Whit. "Your boy is so polite."

"Yeah," Whit said as Junior drowned his waffle stack in an egregious outpouring of maple syrup. "But his table manners leave something to be desired."

Mary topped off Whit's coffee and laughed. "Can I get you boys anything else?" she said. "Another beer or orange juice?"

"Sure," Whit said. "But for this round I'll have the beer, and he'll have the orange juice."

Mary laughed again. "Coming right up," she said, then sidled over to check on a neighboring table.

Whit sipped his black coffee and watched Junior cram a huge and dripping pile of waffles into his gob.

"Junior," Whit said. "I wanted to talk to you about something. Actually, a lot of things. Probably more things than you can fit into one conversation. I guess that's just the way it is. You always want to say more. Do more. But there's never enough time. And you always forget to say or do something important. You know what I mean?"

"I think so," Junior said. "What's up, Dada?"

"You've had a fun week, right? Playing with Stephen and stuff?"

"Oh, yeah, Dada. Stephen is like my best friend now."

"Cool. And you like his parents?"

"Yeah, they're really nice. And Uncle Bob's really funny. Especially when he's pretending to be Kong."

175

"Right," Whit said. "That's good. Listen, I'm sorry I haven't been around a lot this week. Just sort of popping in and out. I've been crazy busy, but I should've tried harder to make more time for you."

"Dada, you've always made time for me," Junior said. "Even when you were in the middle of writing a book, you'd take me to the zoo and baseball games and watch movies with me and read me bedtime stories. You're the best dada in the world. I know you've been super busy this week. And I know it's because you're trying to do something for Mommy. I know you'd do anything for her, and so would I. Is there anything I can do?"

"Thank you, son, but no. I'm almost done with what I came here to do. Then we'll go home, and things will go back to normal."

"Can I still stay friends with Stephen?"

"Of course."

"Can he come visit us in the city?"

"Sure."

"Can we come back and visit here?"

"We'll see."

Junior poured more syrup on his waffles and took another mastodonic bite.

"I'm glad you made a good friend," Whit said. "You'll make a lot of friends in your life. Some good. Some will turn out to be bad. Some will just be people you know for a while, then they drift out of your life. Cut the bad ones loose and let the drifters drift, but hang on to the good ones. That's something I forgot for a long time. I don't want you to forget it. So I think it's a good thing that you want to keep in touch with Stephen. Good friends are important. But family means more than the whole world. That's what you and your mom mean to me. I've gotten a lot wrong in my life, but I got it right in choosing your mom. She was so smart and creative and funny and kind and beautiful. And she loved us both so much. Always remember how much she loved you, Junior. We were really lucky to have her as our family, even if it was for far too short a time. I hope you're as lucky as I was if you decide to get married or have a partner. Look for someone who's kind and interesting and loves you more than anything. And don't settle for anything less. Okay?"

"Okay, Dada. And I'm lucky I have you too."

"Thanks, kid. I love you."

"I love you too, Dada."

Mary set Whit's beer and Junior's orange juice on the table and topped off Whit's coffee. "Any room for dessert?" she said.

"Dada, can I have a chocolate ice cream?" Junior said.

"Sure," Whit said. He turned to Mary. "One chocolate ice cream, a pitcher of maple syrup, a pitcher of hot fudge, and another beer to wash down the carnage."

CHAPTER 53

8 hours 13 minutes until the end of the world

After Sarah and the boys left for the library, Whit found himself drawn into the attic again. He paced the floor. He gazed at the music box ballerina. He glowered at the grandfather clock, tracking its hands as they ticked backward, counting down to the apocalypse. The tick, tick, tick pulsed in his brain like the beating of a heart. And as the ticking beat louder in Whit's head, his impatience grew. He was sick of waiting to confront Dr. Moore. Sick of waiting for the answers to questions he wanted to know now. He felt anger flood his mind, pulsing in time with the ticking of the clock.

"Fuck this," he said.

Whit stormed out of the house and slid into Alice's car. He peeled out of the drive and gunned the engine to Dr. Moore's office. He cleared the steps in one leap, grabbed the shiny brass doorknob, and let himself in.

"Mr. Coe, you can't be here," Mr. Hooker said from behind the reception desk. His eyes were wide and his face was even paler than usual. "You're not safe here. You must leave at once."

"Save it, Jeeves," Whit said. "Where is he?"

"I'm afraid Dr. Moore is out, sir. I assure you, he will be here for your appointment this evening."

"Out where?"

"He's out."

"Uh, huh. We'll see about that." Whit prowled past the reception desk down the hall.

"Mr. Coe, please," Mr. Hooker said, chasing after Whit. "I assure you Dr. Moore is not here. Please, Mr. Coe. You're early. It's not safe." He placed a hand on Whit's shoulder.

Whit grabbed Mr. Hooker's wrist and twisted. Mr. Hooker winced and let out a squeak of pain. Whit shoved him against the wall with a dry thud.

"You're damn right it's not safe," Whit said and stalked down the hallway. He turned the knob to Dr. Moore's office door. It was locked. Whit kicked it open and stepped inside. Empty. He searched every room in the house, Mr. Hooker trailing at his heels like a nervous chihuahua. He didn't find Dr. Moore.

"As I said, Mr. Coe," Mr. Hooker said, "Dr. Moore is out. Now please go somewhere safe. Go home. Dr. Moore will give you the answers you seek at sundown. It's almost time, Mr. Coe. Just be patient. And stay indoors far from here."

"Why?" Whit said.

"Because we have enemies, Mr. Coe. Powerful enemies. And we must not reveal ourselves to them until the time is right."

CHAPTER 54

7 hours 31 minutes until the end of the world

Jesus took a massive bong rip as the Backstreet Boys belted "I Want it That Way" through Tails Only Tommy's paint-and-ash-encrusted transistor radio. He sat upright on Tommy's grimy sofa and held the smoke in his lungs, feeling them fill with searing smoke like dragon fire until they erupted in a spasm of coughing.

"Yay, verily I say unto thee my son," Jesus said: "if thou dost not cough, thou dost not get off." He offered the bong to Tails Only Tommy. "Here, my son. I shall not bogart mine weed. I pass thee the bong in my mercy."

Tommy took the bong, lit the bowl with a Bic, and sucked a deep draw. The bongwater gurgled and the pungent smoke flooded Tommy's lungs. He fought to hold in the smoke. He sputtered a series of convulsive coughs, then hacked out a spew of skunk mist.

As Tommy hunched over coughing, Jesus stood up and stared off into space as if he were looking through the wall at something far away. A beatific yet predatory smile spread across his glowing visage. He giggled, then coughed.

"I see you," Jesus said. His smile widened, exposing his gleaming white teeth. "Whitman Coe, you have just fucked up royally. Patience is a virtue, and you are not a virtuous man. You have wandered off the path of the beam. And now your ass is mine."

"What beam?" Tails only Tommy said.

"Read a book, my son. Never mind, you're illiterate. It's a metaphor."

"What's a metaphor?"

"Oh, Jesus Christ," Jesus said. "Now see what you've done, Thomas? You made me take my name in vain. Anyway, as I told you, all of this business with Whitman Coe is a game. A game with very high stakes—it is the apocalypse after all—but a game nonetheless. And all games have rules. Whitman Coe just broke one of the rules.

180

He just stepped out of bounds, so to speak. All players must be in their correct places on the board at the correct time. Whitman Coe was in the wrong place at the wrong time. Now I can see him. I know where he is. And you, my son, shall destroy the demon Whitman Coe in my name."

"Why me, Jesus?" Tommy said. "Why don't you just smite him like you smited them Filipinos in the Bible?"

"Philistines, you imbecile. And we've already been over this, Thomas. Now, as I said, it's against the rules for me to interfere through direct action. I must act through a chosen intermediary, poor though that intermediary may be. You, Thomas, shall act in my stead. And ye shall be mine champion. I shall anoint thee and grant thee my blessing, and thou shalt kill the demon Whitman Coe in my name."

"Aright, then," Tommy said. "I better call my bro. Imma need some backup."

"Nay, my son," Jesus said. "Lewie is lukewarm for the Lord. Only the man who is on fire for the Lord can truly serve the Lord. Only the man who is on fire for the Lord shall have the power to destroy the Adversary. Now, Thomas, Are you on fire for the Lord?"

"Yes, Lord," Tommy said.

"I don't think I heard you, Thomas. Are you on *fire* for the *Lord*?"

"Yes, Lord! I'm on fire! You are my fire! My one desire!"

"Good, Thomas. Now bow to me."

Tails Only Tommy got down on his knees, extended his arms, and touched his palms to the ground, pressing his face to the floor.

Jesus breathed in deep, his nostrils flaring. He licked his lips. "Very good, my son," he said. "I love the smell of supplication in the morning. It smells like power. And the taste. Just like Gummy Bears." He breathed in once more, splayed his arms and said, "Arise, my son."

Tommy got to his feet and peered into Jesus' eyes.

"Wilt thou be mine faithful servant, Thomas?" Jesus said.

"Yes, my Lord," Tommy said. He felt the Holy Spirit rushing through his body like fifteen bucks worth of crank.

"Wilt thou doubt me, Thomas?"

"No, my Lord."

"Wilt thou act like that little pecker Peter and cock-a-doodle thrice deny me?"

"Hell no! I mean, no, my Lord."

"Then by the power vested in me by my dad and the State of California, I name thee my champion, Sir Thomas of the Tails Only." Jesus spread his hands again and beamed at Tommy.

"Thank you, Jesus," Tommy said. "I ain't gonna let you down. Imma smite that demon good. Do I need a magic sword or somethin?"

"Nay, my son," Jesus said. "I'll hook you up with something. But first I must change this bitch-ass radio station." He held his hand above Tommy's radio and the knob spun. The signal hummed through static, ads, and a country-western caterwaul until Jesus found the song he wanted and lowered his hand. He whooshed his arms like an orchestra conductor as "Saturday Night Special" by Lynyrd Skynyrd cranked off Tommy's wood-chip walls.

"Now that's more like it," Jesus said. He bopped his head, hair flowing behind him like a lion's mane or the luxurious locks of a shampoo model.

As if from thin air, Jesus pulled out a .38 Special and flourished it in front of Tommy's face. "And now, Thomas," he said. "I present thee with thy holy sword, which thou shalt use to strike down the Adversary."

"But Jesus," Tommy said, "that ain't no sword. It's a gun."

"It's another meta—Never mind. Just take the goddamn gun, Tommy." Jesus placed the gun in Tommy's hand.

"And now, my son," Jesus said, "ye shall gird thyself for the trial ahead of you." He closed his hand, then opened it. Two pills of Oxy rested in his palm. "Verily I say unto thee: this is my body. Crush it up and snort it, my son."

Tommy swept a pile of crumpled Schlitz cans off the coffee table. He placed the pills on the table, crushed them into a fine powder with the butt of the .38, and shaped the powder into four lines with a stolen credit card. He rolled up a dollar bill and snorted one of the lines. A million-watt buzz shot through Tommy's brain. He snorted another line. Now he had become comfortably numb.

"Hey, Jesus," Tommy said. "You want a bump?"

"Nay, my son," Jesus said. "That shit will fuck you up."

Tommy tooted the other two lines, licked his gums, and stood up.

"It is time, my son," Jesus said. "I know where the demon Whitman Coe lurks. I shall now send thee forth to fulfill thy destiny."

"Aright then," Tommy said. His words vibrated in his head like he was speaking underwater. "Oh, hey, Jesus. I just got one question."

"Ask, my son."

"Where'd you get that gun and the Oxy from? I didn't see 'em on you before you pulled 'em out."

"They were up my sleeve, Thomas. Right next to the loaves and fishes."

CHAPTER 55

6 hours 57 minutes until the end of the world

"I know it's somewhere around here," Stephen said to Junior as he ran his fingers across the spines of the library stacks.

"What's the title of the book?" Junior said.

"It doesn't have a title. It just has a symbol."

"Okay, then what does the symbol look like?"

"Like… this." Stephen pulled a tan leather-bound book from a low shelf. He tapped the Celto-Pictish spiral calligraphed in red-black ink on the book's spine with his finger. He turned the book upright. The same spiral was mirrored on the book's cover.

"Whoa," Junior said. "That spiral kinda looks like one of my dada's tattoos." He traced the spiral on the book cover with his index finger. "So this is the book?"

"Yep," Stephen said. "Come on. Let's dive in."

The boys sat at a table in the back corner of the room, and Stephen flipped open the book. He muttered to Junior as he perused the table of contents. "Let's see," he said. "We've got a section called 'The Great Prophecy' and—here it is: 'The Founding of Rockwell.' Just give me a minute to find the part I'm looking for."

Stephen scanned the pages and drummed his fingers on the desk. "Here it is," he said. "It says, 'When the American settlers arrived in Rockwell, the local Indians had already abandoned the land. They believed that a dark spirit haunted the woods, consuming human souls and transforming people into wendigos, a mythical cannibal creature. The American settlers, however, primarily of Celtic ancestry, believed that the woods were the sacred domain of an ancient pagan god of the grove whom they called 'the Other.' Their great prophecy held that a portal to the Otherworld lay hidden in the heart of the woods, and that one day the chosen one, a man with stardust in his blood, would open the portal and let the Other into our world. This act, they believed, would lead to the end of our world, and the beginning of a new world made in the image of the Other.'"

"So what does it mean?" Junior said.

"I don't know," Stephen said. He turned the page and studied an intricate quill-and-ink drawing. In the drawing, a cloaked figure, face covered in shadow, was crawling from the mouth of a swirling black vortex. The cloaked figure was emerging into a forest. A forest Stephen knew well. It was a grove of pines on the outskirts of Ross Wood near the creek. In the grove stood a man, hand extended toward the swirling void, a look of fierce concentration on his face. Beneath the drawing, an inscription read, 'The Chosen One Opens the Door of Doom.'

"Holy shit," Stephen said. "Junior, you've got to see this."

Junior leaned over Stephen's shoulder and looked at the drawing. "That's my dada," he said, springing to his feet. "We've got to find him. Now."

"But my mom isn't picking us up for like hours," Stephen said.

"Then we go on foot," Junior said. "We cut through the forest."

CHAPTER 56

6 hours 49 minutes until the end of the world

"You're leaving, aren't you," Zelda said.

Whit took a swig of whisky. "I am," he said. "There's one last thing I have to do today. If it works out, I'll swing by tomorrow and give you guys a proper goodbye. If it doesn't work out," he splayed his hands, "this is it."

"Then here's hoping for the best," Jim said. He raised his glass of whisky. Whit and Zelda raised their glasses and joined Jim in a slug. "So what're you gonna do when you get back to the city, Whit? Other than calling me first thing. You gonna to catch some ballgames, maybe write another book?"

"I haven't really thought about it," Whit said. "I'll take Junior to some baseball games for sure. But I don't write anymore."

"What would you like to do?" Zelda said. "I mean if you could do anything or go anywhere."

Whit rubbed his chin and looked at the baseball pennants on the wall. "You know," he said, "I think I'd like to go visit Japan again. It's been a long time. And I think Junior's old enough to appreciate it now."

"You've been to Japan?" Zelda said. "I've always wanted to go there. I'd like to walk through the streets in Tokyo with a camera slung over my neck like a big old tourist, just snapping off photos of random memories."

"Do it," Whit said. "I'm pretty sure your boss will give you the time off." He winked at Jim. "Don't wait. Do all the things you want to do in life before it's over. Life is short and it goes by so fast. We never get enough time to do the things we wish we could've done. We put it off, then it's too late. So my advice is to make the most of that time. Do the things you want to do now. Squeeze every last ounce out of this life."

"You hear that, Jim?" Zelda said. "You have to give me time off so I can go to Tokyo with a camera slung over my neck."

"As long as you bring me some prints of the pictures you take," Jim said.

"Deal. Can I get paid vacation time too?"

"Don't push it."

"So what's it like, Whit?" Zelda said. "Tokyo, I mean."

"Bright, beautiful, and bustling," Whit said. "Nighttime is the best time to see the city. The main drag in Shinjuku is alive and lit up in neon lights—red, yellow, blue, white, some green and purple. But my favorite parts of the city are the little side streets and alleyways. They're like this winding maze lined with neon lights and little carts selling trinkets. And police booths, and potted plants stacked on tables, and banners outside restaurants with the restaurant's name written in Kanji. And the restaurants are amazing. You duck in under drapes or slide open a patio door like the sliding doors to a tea garden. There are all these cool little bars called *izakayas* that serve beer and sake and Japanese-style pub grub. And if you want to take a break from the noise, you can catch a train out to Kyoto and visit the shrines for a day."

"It sounds beautiful," Zelda said.

"It is," Whit said.

"They have those fox shrines out in Kyoto, right?" Jim said.

"They do," Whit said.

"Sweet," Jim said. "That's it. You sold me on it, Whit. One day, I'm going to one of those fox shrines. I could go for some zen in my life. Oh, shit. Pub grub. I've gotta make those fries and wings for the table in the back corner. Whit, I'll be right back." He kanpied his whisky. "Don't go anywhere."

"I'll be here," Whit said and saluted Jim with his whisky glass.

Jim raised his right hand, touched his index finger to his brow, and backed into the kitchen.

Whit and Zelda polished off their whiskies. Zelda poured another round. She raised her glass and said, "Slainte."

"Slainte," Whit said. They clinked glasses and drank.

"I know it's selfish of me," Zelda said, "but I wish I could keep you here. I'm really going to miss you, you know."

"I'll miss you too," Whit said. "I'll miss sitting here drinking whisky and talking to you."

"Whit," Zelda said, "I've been meaning to ask you something."

"Shoot," Whit said.

"The other night you said I reminded you a little of Alice. How do I remind you of her?"

Whit took another belt of whisky. Bigger this time. "I guess," he said, "I meant that you have that same spark she did. That same big, wild energy. You live in the moment. And you do what you want in the moment. You follow that wild energy. You don't let doubt hold you back. And you're the only person besides Alice who could ever keep up with me in a conversation. That back-and-forth. It takes a certain sense of humor."

"Where did you meet, if you don't mind my asking?"

"You'll think this is funny, but Alice was a bartender too."

"Really?"

"Really. But she was off the night we met. One night I wandered into the bar where she worked, and the bartender thought my weird sense of humor was entertaining, so he gave me all my drinks for free. Naturally, I came back."

"Naturally."

"So one night I was sitting there drinking free wine, and she came in for a drink on her night off. The bartender introduced us, and Alice sat next to me, and we talked for the rest of the night. I don't even remember what we talked about, but that was our first conversation. And it was a conversation that lasted for years. And I really fucking miss that conversation." Whit took a long drag of whisky.

"I'm sorry, Whit," Zelda said. "I shouldn't have—"

"It's okay, Zelda. It's been a comfort talking to you. The truth is our conversations remind me a bit of that long conversation I had with Alice. I'm glad I've gotten to know you, Zelda Bell Sloan. I enjoy your company and I enjoy our conversations for exactly what they are. But I have to admit that some of that comfort is because our talks are the closest I can get to talking to Alice again. Well, unless I wrote another book and created characters based on her and myself so I could keep having that long conversation by proxy. But I'm not sure I could handle the Charlie Kaufman of it all. And besides, wouldn't that just be sad?"

"I'd call it romantic," Zelda said. "Loving someone so much you keep trying to find ways to talk to them even after they're gone."

"Sad, romantic. A distinction without a difference. Potato, poh-tah-to."

"I got some poh-tah-toes right here," Jim said, stepping through the kitchen doors carrying a basket of fries and wings. "Whit, you sure you don't want anything to eat? You look a little pale today."

"I can't," Whit said. "I should probably head out."

"Okay," Jim said. "Just let me drop off this food. Two seconds." He dashed to the table in the back, dropped off the fries and wings, then popped back behind the bar. "One for the road?" he said.

Whit and Zelda downed their whiskies and Jim poured three more.

Jim raised his glass. "To my dear friend Whitman Coe, the prodigal bastard son of Rockwell. May he be in Heaven a half hour before the Devil knows he's dead."

"To Whit," Zelda said, smiling a smile that didn't reach her eyes.

The three friends touched glasses and downed their drinks in a single draught. Whit set his glass on the bar and stood up. Zelda and Jim walked around the bar and stood beside him.

Jim wrapped Whit up in a bear hug. "I love you, brother," he said. "It was great seeing you again."

Whit clapped Jim on the back. "I love you too, Jimbo," he said.

Jim let go of Whit and slapped him on the shoulder. "Don't be a stranger."

"I won't."

"Jim, I'll be right back," Zelda said. "I want to walk Whit to his car."

"How chivalrous of you," Jim said.

Zelda flipped Jim the bird.

Jim laughed and said, "Go on, then."

Whit and Zelda walked across the parking lot and stood beside the Audi.

"I know I already said it," Zelda said, "but I'm really going to miss you, Whitman Fitzgerald Coe."

"And I know I've already said it back," Whit said, "but I'll miss you too, Zelda Bell Sloan. But I'll keep in touch. And like I said, if things work out today, I'll swing by the bar tomorrow. So maybe this is just a practice goodbye. Like a dry run."

"Yeah, a dry run," Zelda said. "Yes." She nodded her head once and raised her chin, then wiped her eyes with the heel of her hand. She looked up at Whit for a long moment, then wrapped her arms around him and buried her face in his chest.

"Whatever you're fighting," she said, "fight it with all you've got. Kick its ass."

"I will."

"Good. Then I'll see you tomorrow." Zelda clutched Whit's back and buried her face deeper into his chest.

"Step back from that demon, little girl," Tails Only Tommy said, creeping out from behind a dumpster. He raised his .38 Special and pointed it at Whit.

Whit sidestepped away from Zelda and stretched his arm out between her body and his. He raised his other arm toward Tommy, palm out, and continued to sidle away from Zelda. "Now hold up there, Tommy," he said. "Take it easy, man. What's going on?"

"You're a demon, Whitman Coe," Tommy said, "and I gotta kill you. I knowed you was a demon since that night by the water tower. I seen your black eyes and I knowed. And now Jesus said you was a demon too, and I was to shoot you with thishere gun."

"Tommy, are you on Oxy right now?" Whit said.

"That ain't the point, goddammit! Quit tryna trick me with your sorcerer's ways, Whit."

"Tommy, look at me," Whit said. "Look at my eyes. They're not black. I'm not a demon. See?"

"That's just what a demon would say."

"Look at me, Tommy. I'm human. You don't have to do this."

The gun shook in Tommy's hand. "But I do," he said. He leveled the gun at Whit's chest. "In the name of the Lord Jesus, demon be gone! The power of Christ compels you!"

Tommy squeezed the trigger.

Whit extended his arm toward the gun, splayed his fingers, and pushed with his mind the way he had pulled at the attic door. The gun exploded in Tommy's hand. Tommy screamed as chunks of mangled hand and mangled gun rained outward in a gory spray of shrapnel, spattering across the blacktop of the parking lot. Whit felt a wet lump of flesh carom off his shirt.

"You son of a bitch!" Tommy squealed as he hunched over cradling the mutilated stump of his hand. "You blew off my fuckin hand!"

"You tried to shoot me, you stupid asshole," Whit said.

"Oh, Lord Jesus," Tommy said. "Help me, Lord. Save thy servant." Jesus didn't show up. "Whit, you gotta help me. I'm bleedin to death. You gotta call an ambulance. Please, brother."

Whit turned to check on Zelda. He found her lying on the asphalt. Her eyes were closed, and blood was welling beneath her T-shirt on the left side of her belly. Whit thought of Alice lying in a pool of blood in the liquor store parking lot, dying alone.

The white rage blazed in Whit's mind. He emitted a feral growl and wheeled toward Tommy, glowering through the smaller man as he advanced.

"Whoa, whoa, whoa," Tommy said, backing up. "Just wait a minute now, Whit. I didn't mean to—"

Whit lashed his arm toward Tommy. He splayed his fingers and pushed again.

The last thing Tails Only Tommy saw in his life was Whitman Coe's black eyes burning with wrath and death. Tommy's neck snapped with a crack that rang through the parking lot like a second gunshot. The skin around his throat split open and peeled back in a gaping gash. The muscles and tendons of his neck shredded apart, and a dark arterial spray spurted from the stump of Tommy's neck like a macabre fountain. His head dangled limply down the back of his neck by a single flap of skin.

Whit ran to Zelda's side, knelt down, and rested her head in his lap. He placed two fingers against her neck. Her pulse beat hard and fast.

Jim bowled through the back doors of the pub. "I thought I heard a—oh shit!" he said.

Whit pressed his hands against Zelda's wound. "Jim," he said, "call an ambulance, then bring me a stack of clean bar rags."

Jim pulled out his cell phone and shot back into the bar.

"Come on, Zelda," Whit said. "Hang on. Stay with me. Please. Please."

Zelda remained limp and motionless, eyes closed as her blood washed over Whit's hands, staining them red.

***

Jesus wept, shimmered like a mirage, and faded into the aether.

CHAPTER 57

6 hours 28 minutes until the end of the world

Junior and Stephen raced along a winding dirt trail through the woods, Junior clutching the purloined library book under his arm like a running back. Both boys gasped for air, their legs and lungs burning with each step. They could hear the creek babbling from the depths of the forest.

The boys rounded a turn in the trail and shunted into a clearing. "Oh, shit," they said in unison and skidded to a halt. Next to a rusted-out car beside a patch of dry brush, Deuce and the McGee boys were huddled around a skin mag drinking cans of Schlitz.

The bullies looked up at the sound of Junior and Stephen's footsteps. They stood up and approached, chins raised, chests puffed out, shoulders swaying side-to-side with each step.

A wide predatory grin spread across Deuce's face. "Well, lookie what we got here, boys," he said. "A couple of trespassin faggots. Hey, faggots, don't you know you ain't supposed to cross the creek?"

"We didn't," Stephen said. "We're still on the Rockwell side."

"You callin me a liar, nerd?"

"No, Deuce," Stephen said. "I was just saying that—"

"Shut up, nerd," Deuce said. The McGee boys cackled.

"I say you two faggots are trespassin," Deuce said, stepping forward. "And the toll is one eyeball each." He pulled his pocketknife out of his jeans and unfolded it.

Stephen recoiled a step. Junior held his ground.

"We don't have time for this bullshit right now, Deuce," Junior said. "We have to get to the other side of the woods. Now."

"Oh," Deuce said. "Looks like little Satan Jr. grew a sack. Maybe I'll cut that off instead of your eye."

"Or maybe," Junior said, "I'll tell your buddies here about the problems you've got down around your sack. Specifically, your limp little dick." He held up his pinky finger and wiggled it back and forth. The McGee boys giggled.

"What the fuck are you talkin 'bout, kid?" Deuce said.

"You really want me to tell them? Okay, then. Boys, your big bad leader here can't get it up unless he's torturing and killing little animals."

The McGee boys chortled again.

"No, really, guys," Junior said. "Deuce here likes to catch a little animal like a cat or a dog or a rabbit. Then he likes to whip his pocketknife out of his pants and cut that poor little animal open. Real slow. Then he likes to pull out the animal's guts and run his fingers over the intestines. He likes the smooth, squishy way they feel between his fingers. He likes the way they shine all wet in the light. And then he comes in his pants."

The clearing was silent for a moment, then the McGee boys caterwauled with laughter.

"Oh, shit," Travis said, doubling over.

"Daayum," Billy said.

Skunk stopped laughing and looked at Deuce.

Deuce stumbled a step backward. His mouth hung open. "How the fuck did you know that?" he said. "You're a fuckin witch, that's what you are. You're a fuckin liar!" He pointed at Junior with the tip of his knife.

"So which is it, Deuce?" Junior said. "Am I a fucking liar, or am I a fucking witch who just told your buddies the truth about you being a limp-dick psycho perv?"

"I'm gonna fuckin kill you, kid," Deuce said. He raised his knife and stalked toward Junior.

Junior swept his hand in the air, and Deuce slipped on the gravel beneath his feet. He fell flat on his back. The McGee boys crowed.

Deuce sat up and held out a hand. "Help me up, boys," he said.

The McGee boys put their hands in their pockets and looked down at their shoes.

"So it's like that," Deuce said. He hobbled to his feet and glared at the McGee boys. "Then you boys can go fuck yourselves. Fuckin traitors."

Deuce took one last look at his former minions, then turned and scrambled through the brush into the woods. He left his pocketknife lying on the ground.

Junior and Stephen circled past the McGee boys, then scarpered down the trail. They cut through a tree grove and shot up beside the shoulder of one of the back roads.

A Rockwell Police cruiser rolled in from the back road and pulled up next to them. Junior and Stephen ground to a halt. The prowler door swung open.

"Get in, boys," the voice said.

CHAPTER 58

6 hours 11 minutes until the end of the world

Deuce skirred alongside the creek. He didn't know where he was going. He didn't have anywhere to go. He couldn't go home to his asshole dad. He hated the old fucker, and no way in hell was he going to that bullshit military school. His friends had backstabbed him. He was all alone in the woods. All alone in the world.

As Deuce ran, his head began to spin. He felt a searing pressure building in his skull. A whispering drone rose in his ears. He stopped and listened to the whisper. It was coming from the creek, its words blending with the babble of the trickling stream. It called his name.

Deuce clawed through the bracken and knelt by a shallow pool formed by the creek's runoff. He gazed into the water and saw a wavering face. Black eyes burned in the reflection of the sun's glare. A yawning whirlpool mouth spiraled downward into the darkness below. The wind surged, casting ripples across the surface of the water, blurring the face, then wiping it away.

Deuce looked at his own reflection. His own face. It wasn't there.

CHAPTER 59

5 hours 56 minutes until the end of the world

The EMTs lifted Zelda's gurney into the back of the ambulance. "She's stable, but unconscious," a young EMT with neatly groomed sideburns told Whit and Jim. "Fortunately, the shrapnel missed her internal organs, but she's lost a lot of blood. She may need a transfusion at the hospital."

"Can I ride with her?" Whit asked.

"Are you related to Ms. Sloan?" the EMT said.

"I'm a close friend."

"Then I'm sorry, sir, but you won't be able to ride with her in the ambulance. We're taking her to Rockwell Mercy Grace Hospital. You can enquire about Ms. Sloan's status at the reception desk."

"Okay," Whit said. "Thank you."

The EMT nodded to Whit. "We'll take good care of her, sir," he said. He climbed into the ambulance and shut the double doors behind him.

Forensics had arrived while the EMTs were stabilizing Zelda. Two evidence techs were stringing yellow crime scene tape between light posts, while another snapped off photos of what was left of Tails Only Tommy. A morgue attendant leaned against the back of the coroner's van, waiting for forensics to finish their job so he could start his.

The ambulance with Zelda inside flashed its lights, roared its siren, and peeled out of the parking lot. As the ambulance pulled out of the lot, Chip's squad car zoomed in, tires squealing as it skidded on the blacktop, narrowly missing the ambulance. Chip parked the car sideways across two parking spots and climbed out.

"Nice of you to show up, Sheriff," Jim said. "Where the hell have you been?"

"At your mama's house, lardass," Chip said.

"What about Bob and Dave?" Whit said. "Where are they?"

"They ain't comin," Chip said. "I told dispatch to keep them out of the loop."

"And why might that be?" Whit said, folding his arms across his chest.

"Fuck you, none of your fuckin business is why. Them two ain't been worth a stale dog turd since you rolled back into town. And I knew in my gut that whatever bullshit was going on here, you had somethin to do with it. Every time somethin really fucked up happens in my town, it's got somethin to do with you, Whit. Seems kinda suspicious, don't it? Now if you and your boyfriend'll excuse me, I've got some police work to tend to."

Chip turned to one of the evidence techs and said, "Got a report of shots fired here." He looked past the tech at the pile of mangled pulp that had once been Tails Only Tommy. "What in the jumped-up Christ happened here? Looks like this guy tried to do a keg stand on a fuckin landmine."

"We're still not sure," the evidence tech said. "From what we can gather, Mr. McGee accosted Mr. Coe and one Zelda Sloan brandishing a handgun—"

"Hold up," Chip said. "Did you say McGee?"

"Yes, Sheriff."

"Thomas or Lewis?"

"Thomas, Sheriff."

"So let me get this fuckin wrong," Chip said. "You're sayin that stain on the blacktop over there is Thomas McGee?"

"Yes, Sheriff," the tech said. "Mr. Coe and Mr. O'Malley identified Mr. McGee, and we found Mr. McGee's driver's license in his wallet."

"So what the fuck happened here?"

"As I said, we're still not sure. We're just starting to piece the evidence together. It appears that Mr. McGee accosted Mr. Coe and Ms. Sloan with a handgun. Mr. McGee was apparently under the influence of narcotics and suffering from the delusion that Mr. Coe was a demon. Mr. McGee attempted to shoot Mr. Coe, at which time Mr. McGee's firearm exploded in his hand. Ms. Sloan was wounded by shrapnel from the explosion and is on her way to Rockwell Mercy Grace Hospital."

"And what about Mr. McGee's head?" Chip said. "The explosion take off his whole fuckin head?"

"At this point I couldn't say, Sheriff. We still need to gather more evidence and wait for Mr. McGee's coroner's report."

Chip spread his feet wide and looped his thumbs through his belt loops. He shook his head. "No," he said. "No, that's bullshit." He pointed at Whit. "You did this, didn't you, you son of a bitch."

"That's not possible, Sheriff," the tech said. "Mr. McGee's head was nearly torn clean from his neck. His muscles, tendons, arteries, and neck vertebrae were all severed. No man, even one as large as Mr. Coe, could possibly exert that much force."

Chip shook his head again. "Nuh-uh," he said. He looked the tech in the eye and pointed at Whit. "You don't know this guy. I do." He pulled his handcuffs from his police duty belt.

"Whitman Coe," he said, walking toward Whit, "you're under arrest for the murder of Thomas McGee."

"Are you fucking kidding me?" Whit said.

"Fuck no, I ain't kiddin. I know you killed Tommy. Now you're coming with me to the station and you're gonna tell me how you did it."

"Sheriff," the evidence tech said. "I assure you that no human being could have killed Mr. McGee in this manner."

"I know," Chip said. "Come on, Whit. Hands over your head, lace your fingers."

Whit advanced a step toward Chip. Chip took a step back. His palm shot to the butt of his service revolver.

"No need to be so jumpy, Chip," Whit said, turning around and lacing his fingers over his head. "I'm just trying to comply."

Chip patted Whit down, cuffed him, and recited his Miranda rights.

"You can't do this, Chip," Jim said.

"I'm the sheriff," Chip said. "I can do whatever the fuck I want." He took Whit by the arm and led him to the squad car.

"Jim," Whit said. "Don't worry about me. Go to the hospital and take care of Zelda."

"I'll guard her with my life."

"Good man," Whit said. "Let's hope it doesn't come to that. Be careful, Jimbo."

"You too," Jim said, scratching the ladybug tattoo on his arm.

Whit winked at Jim as he slid into the back of Chip's squad car. "I'll see you on the other side, Jimbo," he said.

CHAPTER 60

"Okay," Chip said, watching Whit across the interrogation room table, "let's try this again. Did you, Whitman Coe, kill Thomas McGee?"

"How many times are you going to ask me the same questions?" Whit said.

"As many times as it takes to get the answers I want."

"You're wasting your time. And mine."

"Why, you got someplace to be?"

"You could say that."

"Where?"

"None of your fuckin business, that's where," Whit said.

"Oh, that's real cute, asshole," Chip said. "I know you killed Tommy. So why don't you just tell me how you did it so we can stop this whole song and dance?"

"Yeah, you don't look like much of a dancer, Sheriff. But I'm not gonna sing. So if we're just gonna keep jerking each other off all day, I want my lawyer."

"So that's how you're gonna play it, huh, Whit?"

"I just invoked my Sixth Amendment right to an attorney, Sheriff. That means this conversation is over."

"Alright, fine," Chip said. "But I know you killed Tommy. And I'm gonna nail your ass to the wall for it." He stood up. "Come on, Whit. Get up. You can cool your heels in a cell for a while. Maybe some time alone'll help it sink in just how much shit you're in."

Chip led Whit into an empty cell in a row of empty cells, unlocked Whit's handcuffs, and slid the cell door shut behind him.

"You know," Chip said. "I have a feelin the phone lines in the station are gonna be down for a stretch. I wouldn't expect to talk to a lawyer for a while there, Whit. Now if you'll excuse me, I'm gonna take a long lunch and a big dump. You have a nice afternoon, now."

He flipped a salute at Whit, then walked down the hall and out of the police station.

Whit stared past the bars of his cell into the detention mirror hanging on the hallway wall.

CHAPTER 61

4 hours 52 minutes until the end of the world

Bob had spent the past six-and-a-half hours interviewing the families of the young men who had vanished from Rockwell over the past three years, and he still wasn't any closer to finding a nexus between the cases. He was burnt. One more witness to interview.

When he stepped out of his squad car, Bob saw Horace Macomber sitting in a wooden rocker on his front porch, disheveled and unshaven, watching the woods across the way. Bob climbed the steps and saw old Horace was decked-out in his finest—blue boxer shorts, house slippers, and a once-white undershirt stained yellow brown at the chest and armpits. A can of Budweiser dangled from Horace's fingers beneath the chair. His nails were the same yellow brown as his pit stains.

"Can I help you, Officer?" Horace said.

"Good afternoon, Mr. Macomber," Bob said. "I'm following up on your son Jimmie's disappearance. I was wondering if I could ask you some questions."

"Alright, then," Horace said, getting up with a grunt. He opened the screen door, crossed the threshold, and looked back at Bob. "Well, don't just stand there on the porch like a Jehovah's Witness. C'mon inside, Officer."

Horace led Bob inside the house. Dirty clothes were strewn across the floors and piled up on furniture. Empty Budweiser cans, pizza boxes, and TV dinner trays littered the coffee table.

Horace gulped down the rest of his Budweiser and tossed the empty can on top of a pile of clothes. "You want a beer, Officer?" he said.

"I appreciate the offer," Bob said, "but I'm not allowed to drink on duty."

"Shit, Officer," Horace said. "Beer ain't real alcohol. Even them commies over in Russia know that." He shuffled into the kitchen and came back with two beers. He popped the tabs and handed one to Bob.

"Thank you, Mr. Macomber," Bob said. He took a swig of Bud.

Horace raised his can of Budweiser and chugged another gulp. "So what can I do ya for, Officer?" he said. "I don't suppose you got any news about my boy."

Bob shook his head. "I'm sorry, Mr. Macomber," he said. "But I am trying to find out what happened to Jimmie, and to the other young men who went missing. That's why I'm here. I'm reinterviewing family members of the missing young men and trying to piece together what happened to them."

"Shiiiit," Horace said. "All the old timers in town know what happened to them boys."

"And what's that?"

"They was taken out in the woods someplace by satanists or witches or somethin like. Part of some cult ritual. Human sacrifice or somethin."

"And why do you believe that?"

"Oh, we old timers know. We know the woods. Well enough to stay clear, anyhow." Horace took another slug of beer. "Officer, have you seen them crows flyin over Ross Wood on the old side of town?"

"Can't say I've noticed them."

"Well, take a peek at the sky next time you're around there. There's a pack of crows just circlin in the sky above the woods. They don't never land. They just keep circlin and circlin. That's a bad omen. See for yourself. But don't go into them woods. Don't ever go in there."

Bob sipped at his beer. "Mr. Macomber," he said, "did you notice anything strange about the way Jimmie was behaving before he disappeared?"

"You mean stranger than usual? You see, Officer, Jimmie was always a strange boy. He got that from his mama. She was diagnosed with paranoid schizophrenia shortly after we married. She kept seein things in mirrors. Hearin voices. I took her to a shrink for a while. Even took her to the city for electroshock therapy. It ain't like they show it in that *Cuckoo's Nest* movie, but it didn't help none either.

In the end, she had to be institutionalized back in the city. And that's where she died."

"I'm sorry to hear that, Mr. Macomber," Bob said.

"Thank you, Officer. I appreciate ya. Anyways, I think Jimmie took after his mama. Even when he was little, he just seemed kinda titched. Didn't play with other kids. Always talkin to himself. Then right before he disappeared, he started havin the same delusions as his mama. Seein things in the mirror, hearin voices. Hallucinations, you know? I took him to a shrink just like his mama, but it didn't help him none either."

"And what was the name of the psychiatrist he was seeing?"

"That fancy English one lives in that old Victorian house on the other side of town. Dr. Moore."

CHAPTER 62

4 hours 17 minutes until the end of the world

Bob flung open the police station doors and sprinted down the hallway, hard-soled shoes clacking on the polished linoleum floor. He squeaked to a halt at the reception desk. Lucy was slumped forward in her chair, eyes closed and snoring. Bob cast a glance toward the line of cells down the adjacent hallway. Empty as usual.

He stretched over the reception desk, back leg extending in the air like he was butchering a yoga pose, and eased the top drawer open. He lifted the evidence room keys, slid the drawer shut, and hustled into the main office.

Dave was sitting behind his desk zoning at a computer screen and rubbing his eyes. He looked up when Bob barreled into the room. "Yo, Bob-O," he said. "Where's the fire, buddy?"

"No time to explain now," Bob said. "I'll fill you in after I make some calls."

Bob slipped into the evidence room and reemerged a couple minutes later with the stack of missing persons files wedged under his arm. He scurried to his desk, opened one of the files, picked up his desk phone, and dialed.

"Mrs. Harris?" Bob said into the receiver. "Hello, this is Deputy Rockwell. We spoke earlier today. I'm sorry to bother you again, but I just had one more quick question. You said your son was seeing a psychiatrist before he went missing. By any chance do you remember the psychiatrist's name? Uh huh. Thank you, Mrs. Harris. Sorry again to bother you. You too." He pressed the hook switch, opened a new file, and dialed another number.

"Mr. O'Hearn?" Bob said. "Hello, this is Deputy Rockwell. We spoke this morning. I'm sorry to bother you again, but I had one quick follow-up question if it's not too much trouble. Great, thanks. Now, Mr. O'Hearn, you said your son was seeing a psychiatrist before his disappearance. Do you happen to recall the psychiatrist's name? Okay. Sorry again to disturb you. Thank you. Uh-huh. Goodbye, Mr. O'Hearn."

Bob made six more calls, then slammed down the receiver. "Hot damn, Dave," he said. "I've got it."

Dave shifted in his chair and looked at Bob. "Got what?" he said.

"A lead. A fucking lead in the missing persons cases."

"Alright, Sherlock, what's the lead?"

"So I followed up on those redacted witness statements from our missing persons cases. I interviewed the families of each missing person myself. And I found a nexus."

"Okay, so what's the nexus?" Dave said.

"It's not so much a what as a who," Bob said. "It turns out all the missing kids were suffering from mental health issues—stress, depression, anxiety. Some kind of emotional distress. Now, some of the families mentioned that their kid was seeing a psychiatrist. I didn't think much of it at the time. I mean, stands to reason kids struggling with mental health issues would be seeing a shrink. Then old Horace Macomber says his son Jimmie was seeing Dr. Moore. The same Dr. Moore Adam Whitman was seeing before he disappeared. The same Dr. Moore Whit used to see when he was a kid. And then it hit me. Some of these missing persons, the ones old enough to drink anyway, were regulars at O'Malley's. Jim said they tended to come in on a pretty regular schedule—you know, same day every week, about the same time of day. So I start thinking how Dr. Moore's office is right across the street from O'Malley's. And how psychiatric appointments tend to be at the same day and time every week. So I called up the families and asked who their kid's psychiatrist was. And you know who they said? Each and every last one of them?"

"Dr. Moore," Dave said.

"Yahtzee," Bob said.

"Goddamn," Dave said. "So now what?"

"I think it's time to pay the good doctor a house call."

"Right now?"

"No time like the present."

"We oughta wait for a search warrant," Dave said. "If we request one today, we should be able to search the entire premises first thing tomorrow. But if we go now, we can only enter with Dr. Moore's permission, and we can only use evidence that's in plain sight. And then he'll know we're sniffing around, and he'll have time to hide or destroy evidence before the warrant's issued."

"I know, I know," Bob said. "You're right. But something about this guy feels really hinky, and I know Whit's seen him at least once since he got back in town. With all the shit that's happened to people around this guy, I want to make sure I've got Whit's six covered. So I'm going to Moore's now and calling Whit on the way."

"Alright, then," Dave said. "If it's to protect Whit, screw the warrant. Let's check this guy out."

"Let's go then," Bob said, starting for the door.

"Bob," Dave said. "Better put those files back before we go. If Chip comes in and sees them on your desk he'll go apeshit."

"Oh, shit. I almost forgot. Thanks, Dave."

"No worries, Bob-O. I got your six too."

Bob scooped the files off his desk, tucked them under his arm, and made for the evidence room. Dave limped behind.

As Bob stepped into the evidence room, he heard Dave's feet skid behind him, followed by a clang as Dave tripped into a metal file cabinet. A loud bang like a firework reverberated through the room.

At first Bob didn't feel anything. Then he felt a searing sunburst of pain shoot through his back, followed by a warm, wet sensation blooming down his shirt. He fell to the floor.

Dave stood above Bob, service revolver in his hand. Smoke rising from the barrel like incense.

"I'm sorry, Bob," Dave said, tears in his eyes. "You have no idea how sorry I am. You're my best friend and I love you like a brother. But you can't interfere with destiny. Whit must face his fate alone."

Dave raised his revolver and pointed it at Bob's chest.

Another gunshot rang out in the stillness of the room.

CHAPTER 63

The sound rang out like a gun clap in the night. Grad night. Dave felt the sound in his bones. In his bones as they shattered to sharp fragments and tore through the flesh of his shin. Through his pantleg and into the moonlight. White on white. And red. White and red like the pain. The first wave in an excruciating microsecond. All at once. The following waves worse.

Dave saw stars. Stars of pain strangling his vision. And when his eyes cleared, the bright and tranquil night stars above. The night stars, where his fate was written. On the night he learned his fate.

***

Duncan Ross endured the two-month voyage across the tumultuous green waves of the Atlantic with his wife and three young sons in tow. He trekked across the wide and wild expanse of the untamed American continent, facing the perils of outlaws, *banditos*, and hostile native tribes. He trudged over wind-and-dust-swept plains. Over foothills and winding paths through gray and craggy, rock-hewn mountains.

Along fallow gulches and deep burnt-umber arroyos. Beneath the penumbra of primordial groves of pines where savage howls, human and inhuman, cried in the darkness. He marched through hunger and thirst and exhaustion on torn and tattered boots that wore thin at the soles. He pushed forward on blistered and bloody feet.

Duncan suffered these hardships with a light heart, for he knew he was following a bright and shining beacon to a new and better world. A world that he and his descendants would help bring to fruition. And when Duncan Ross staggered into the fertile woodlands that would become the heart of the town of Rockwell, he knew that his faith and perseverance had been rewarded.

While Duncan's dear friend Robert Rockwell rose to prominence as the new settlement's first mayor, constable, magistrate, and purveyor of dry goods, Duncan took a more humble role in the burgeoning township. He served as Robert's deputy constable and stood night watch, protecting the townsfolk from the dangers of the dark as they slept warm in their beds.

As generations passed, Robert's descendants forgot the true purpose of the settlement. They forgot the old gods and old ways. They forgot the prophecy. They forgot the face of the Other.

But the Ross family never forgot. They remained steadfast in their faith and devotion to the master. They passed the knowledge of the Other and his prophecy down the generations from father to son. It was a rite of passage in the Ross line that a father would take his son aside and say, "Son, you are a man now. It is time you learned who you are."

For Dave Ross, that fateful moment came on the night he graduated high school. The night Chip and the McGee boys pitched him from the water tower and shattered his leg. The night he knew he would never be whole again.

Dave was out of surgery. He was sitting up in bed. Despite the morphine drip tapped into his vein, his leg flamed in agony as it dangled in traction, wrapped in a plaster cast that would cocoon the ruined limb for the next ten weeks. He stared at the television mounted on the hospital room wall but didn't watch the actors or listen to their words. Stared unblinking at their black-and-white shapes flickering across the screen. Their voices a distant murmur beneath his shouting thoughts.

Dave's father knocked at the door and let himself in. Without a word, he walked across the room and sat in the chair beside Dave's bed. "Son," he said. "You are a man now. It is time you learned who you are."

***

Dave relived that conversation with his father in his mind as he cruised Third Avenue in his patrol car on the last day of the world. He gave side-eye to the smug hipsters and dudebrahs lounging in the outdoor seating in front of trendy brunch spots, wasting their final moments of existence sipping mimosas and double IPAs and clucking inauthentically over inauthentic Nashville hot chicken and waffles. By this time tomorrow, the street would be silent and empty, covered in purifying ice and mist. Ready to be reborn. Dave could barely hold in his elation. Spiritual agony and ecstasy ran through his body like a rapture of lightning.

But still a sense of dread shadowed his mind. He knew the prophecy. He believed the truth of it in his heart of hearts. His faith was unshakeable. He knew the time of the master's coming was at hand. He knew the master would prevail. And he knew that Whit would come through. Whit always came through in the clutch. But still… No. Dave understood his role. He had one duty. A duty he was born to perform: he had to make sure Whit met Dr. Moore at sunset. Alone.

He rolled past a crosswalk and checked his rearview mirror. The Other's face peered at him from beyond the glass. Its cavernous black eyes bored into his skull. Its maw mouth whispered in his mind.

"Yes, master," Dave said and turned onto the dirt road that cut through Ross Wood. The wood named after his ancestor. He followed the Other's voice down the road, flanking a grove of pines. He eased his cruiser onto the shoulder of the road as Junior and Stephen burst from the grove at a run. They ground to a halt.

Dave opened the door to his squad car. "Get in, boys," he said.

***

After he'd swept the boys from the chessboard, Dave hurried back to the station to make sure he had Bob in check. He shouldered open the plate-glass entrance door and limped inside. The station was cathedral silent, except for the faint sound of snoring coming from the reception desk. He gimped down the hall and found Lucy slumped forward at her desk, eyes shut and in a deep sleep. He ignored her and shuffled into the office. Empty.

He sat down at Bob's desk. Flipped through Bob's incoming and outgoing paperwork baskets. Riffed through the papers on his desk. Through the drawers. Nothing about Whit or Adam or the missing kids. He tapped his fingers on the desk.

He heard the metal hinges of the entrance door grind, and footsteps clack on the floor tiles down the hall. He leaned on Bob's desk, pulled himself to his feet, and scuttled back to his own desk. He rubbed his eyes and pretended to be on the computer when Bob came into the office. "Yo, Bob-O," he said. "Where's the fire, buddy?"

"No time to explain now," Bob said. "I'll fill you in after I make some calls."

Oh, no. Please don't let it be about that. Please don't let him figure it out. Not Bob. Please.

But Bob figured it out.

Dave tried to stop Bob from going to Dr. Moore's, if even for one day. Tomorrow would never arrive anyway. It was today that mattered. Only today. Whit must meet Dr. Moore today at sunset. Alone.

But Bob had made up his mind. He was heading to Dr. Moore's office and he was going to call Whit on the way. The die had been cast. Dave would fulfill his duty.

Dave trailed behind Bob as they stepped into the evidence room to return the missing persons files. He slid his service revolver from its holster and leveled it at Bob's back, center mass, pointing at his heart. Then Dave's leg gave on him. The leg that had been shattered on that fateful night so long ago. He slipped and jolted into a metal file cabinet as he pulled the trigger. The shot swung wide, hitting Bob on the right side beneath his scapula. Bob fell to the floor.

Dave righted himself and stood over Bob. "I'm sorry, Bob," he said. "You have no idea how sorry I am. You're my best friend and I love you like a brother. But you can't interfere with destiny. Whit must face his fate alone."

Dave raised his revolver and pointed it at Bob's chest.

Another gunshot rang out in the stillness of the room.

Dave's shoulders jerked back and his chest shocked forward. A red circle bloomed next to the badge on his Rockwell Police Department uniform. He looked down at Bob. Then Dave's eyes glassed over, and he crumpled to the ground beside his lifelong friend.

Chip stepped into the evidence room, smoking service revolver in hand. He holstered his gun, knelt down beside Bob, and placed a hand under Bob's head. "Bob," he said. "Come on, buddy. Hang in there. Lucy, call an ambulance!" he shouted over his shoulder. "Right fucking now!" He turned back to Bob. "Just hold on, buddy. The paramedics are on the way. You're gonna be okay. It's just a little scratch. You'll be fine. Bob? Stay with me, buddy."

But Bob's eyes were rolling into the back of his head. The world swam and grew cold. Then the world faded. The last thing his eyes saw before they closed were Chip's eyes mirroring his own fear.

CHAPTER 64

1 hour 49 minutes until the end of the world

Skunk, Billy, and Travis trudged through the woods, shoes and pantlegs caked in creek mud. Hands and arms and cheeks scratched by thicket brambles.

"Deuce, c'mon out man!" Skunk hollered. "We ain't believe that little city faggot what he said about you. And anyways, who gives a shit about a couple of cats and dogs?"

"Yeah, man," Billy shouted into the woods. "This one time I went out back to my daddy's coon-hound pen and I smeared peanut butter all over my—"

Skunk elbowed Billy's arm. "Man, shut the fuck up and quit fuckin around," he said. "We gotta find Deuce before it gets dark. Now keep followin the creek and keep hollerin for him."

The McGee boys marched up the creek into the heart of Ross Wood, calling Deuce's name. For a while, all they could hear were the sounds of their own footsteps, breath, and voices, and the babbling of the creek. Then the caw of crows, scores of them, rolled in like a fog from the far side of a nearby stand of trees.

"Follow them crows," Skunk said, hunching down and placing a finger over his lips. He slunk into the stand of trees. Billy and Travis tucked in behind him.

As the McGee boys strayed deeper into the woods, the cawing of the crows grew louder. The boys could hear the beating of wings above the trees. They looked up and saw flashes of dark shapes fluttering in the jagged shards of sky that pierced through the forest canopy. They followed the thrum of wings and the darting shadows above until they stood on the edge of a grassy ring-shaped clearing.

The McGees craned their necks to watch the black mass of crows spiraling in the sky above the clearing. Still gazing up at the crows, jaw slack, Travis drifted toward the clearing. Skunk horse-collared him by his T-shirt and yanked him back beneath the cover of the

211

trees. Skunk pressed a finger to his lips, then pointed to the clearing. What looked like about a dozen gaunt, cadaver-white creatures staggered in a circle beneath the crows, mirroring their course.

One of the creatures stepped out of the circle and stood facing the McGee boys. It watched them through hollowed-out eye sockets draped in withered shreds of skin. The monster looked no different from the other creatures. But it was different. It was Deuce. And it wasn't.

The creature looked at Skunk, Billy, and Travis for a long moment, then tuned and filed in beside its new brethren.

CHAPTER 65

Sarah pulled her silver Outback into the passenger pickup slot in front of the library. The same place she always picked Stephen up when he caught a jones to hit the stacks. She checked the dashboard clock. Five minutes early. She twisted around and snatched her *Father Brown* mystery off one of the back seats. She read a chapter. Checked the clock on her cell. The boys were ten minutes late.

She shook her head, stretched, and stuck a grocery store receipt inside the book. She set the book on the passenger seat, got out of the car, and headed for Stephen's favorite sections in the library. She started with science, but the boys weren't there. Next she scanned history. Not there either.

Sarah sped her pace. She trotted through biography. Jogged through the periodicals. By the time she reached the children's section, she was running.

Her head began to spin like it had when she was sixteen and Bob convinced her to ride the tilt-a-whirl at the Rockwell County Fair on the Fourth of July. The stacks churned in a disorienting spiral. The ceiling wavered and stretched.

She scurried to the librarian's desk, her breath coming quick and shallow. "Ma'am," she said to the librarian, "have you seen two boys? About eleven years old? One short and thin with glasses and light brown hair, the other taller with medium brown hair?"

The librarian leaned back in her seat. She pursed her lips and tapped the desk with her nail extensions. "As a matter of fact, ma'am, I have," she said. "They ran out of here a few hours ago with library property. When I called after them, they didn't even look in my direction."

"Did you see which way they went?" Sarah said.

The librarian pointed past the glass front doors at a dirt trail that cut through a stand of pines. "They went that way," she said. "Toward the woods."

***

Sarah plopped her purse onto the hood of her car and fished out her cell phone. She called Bob and got his voicemail. She paced in front of the car and called Bob again. Got his voicemail again. "Goddammit, Bob," she said. "Pick up the phone."

She redialed. Voicemail. She ran a hand through her hair and closed her eyes. She called Whit. Voicemail.

"Fuuuuuuck!" Sarah shouted into the sky.

Her cell phone rang in her hand. "Finally," she said. She let out a long breath and looked at the number of the incoming call. She didn't recognize it.

"Hello?" Sarah answered the phone.

"Hello," a woman's voice said. "Is this Mrs. Sarah Rockwell?"

"Yes."

"Mrs. Rockwell, this is Dr. Singh at Rockwell Mercy Grace Hospital. I'm afraid I have some bad news about your husband."

CHAPTER 66

One hour until the end of the world

"Your husband is right in here, Mrs. Rockwell," Dr. Singh said, leading Sarah into the hospital room. It was a white, salmon, and teal double suite. "He's going to be just fine."

Bob was lying in the bed closest to the door, eyes closed and heavy. Chip sat in the chair beside him. Zelda was propped up in the bed on the far side of the room watching the Padres game on the wall-mounted TV. Jim sat in a chair between the beds of his two friends. He stood up when Sarah entered the room.

"Hey, Sarah," Jim said.

"Hi, Sarah," Zelda said, toggling her hospital bed to an upright position.

Chip got to his to his feet, glanced at Sarah, and bowed his head.

"Oh my God," Sarah said. "What the hell happened?" She clapped a hand over her mouth.

"It was Dave," Chip said, his voice softer than Sarah had ever heard it. "I—I don't… Dave shot Bob in the evidence room. He was about to finish the job when I got there. So I shot him. Oh, Jesus, Sarah. I killed Dave."

Sarah's mouth slid open, her eyes wide and wild. "What?" she said. She flipped her gaze from Bob, lifeless-looking in his sleep, to Dr. Singh. "But my husband is going to be okay?"

"Yes," Dr. Singh said. "He's going to be just fine. Though your husband was shot, no vital organs were struck. The bullet struck your husband beneath the right scapula and broke three of his ribs. We performed surgery on your husband to remove the bullet, and he did quite well. We expect him to make a full recovery, though his ribs and back will take some time to heal. His anesthesia should be wearing off, so I expect he may be waking up any minute."

"Oh, thank God," Sarah said. "And thank you, Doctor."

"Of course, Mrs. Rockwell," Dr. Singh said. "Now if you have no further questions or concerns, I have to make my rounds, but I'll have a nurse come by to check on your husband shortly." She forced a quick smile and left the room.

Sarah watched Bob sleep for a handful of heartbeats, then looked across the room at Zelda. "Jesus Christ, Zelda," she said. "Did you get shot too?"

"Pretty close," Zelda said. "Tommy McGee tried to shoot Whit in the parking lot behind O'Malley's, but the gun exploded in his fool hand. I got hit in the stomach by a piece of shrapnel from the gun, but it didn't go in more than an inch or so. Didn't hit any organs. Ruined my Pixies T-shirt, though. And I lost a lot of blood. I had to get a transfusion and about eighty stitches, but they said I should be fine too. Looks like Bob and I picked the same four-leaf clover."

Jim scratched his ladybug tattoo.

"At least there's that," Sarah said. "I'm glad you're okay, Zelda."

"Yeah," Zelda said, "Bob and I are going to have matching warrior scars. Mighty!" She raised a fist in the air. "Ow." She winced and put a hand on her stitches.

"You said Tommy tried to shoot Whit?" Sarah said. "Where's Whit?"

"That's the first thing Zelda said when she woke up," Jim said. "I told her shitbird over there arrested him," he flicked his head at Chip, "but when he came back to the station Whit was gone. Like he vanished into thin air. Nobody knows where he is now."

"Shit," Sarah said. "This is bad." She looked at Bob. "Bob. Sweetie. I really need you to wake up now."

Bob opened his eyes. "Hey, beautiful," he said.

"Hey, babe," Sarah said. She smiled and a tear slipped down her cheek.

"Huh," Chip said, grinning. "He must like you better than me. I've been tryin to wake him up for over an hour now."

"Nobody likes you," Zelda said to Chip, narrowing her eyes.

"I caught that when you threw that flower vase at my head."

"Too bad you ducked."

"Bob," Sarah said. "Something terrible is happening. Stephen and Junior weren't at the library when I came to pick them up. The librarian said they ran out a few hours earlier carrying a book. She said they were running toward the woods. And Whit's missing too. Something is very wrong, Bob."

"Shit," Bob said. "I think I might know where to find Whit, but I've got no idea where the kids could be." He sat upright. Twisted his mouth and put a hand over his wound. "Chip, we've got to get a search party together and sweep the woods. Now."

Chip's phone rang. He picked it up and said, "Not now, Lucy. It's a bad time." He started to hang up, then stopped. "What? That doesn't make any sense. How long ago did they see him? And did they see Stephen Rockwell and another boy? Okay, thanks, Lucy." He hung up the phone and slipped it into his pocket.

"What's going on, Chief?" Bob said.

"Did someone find Stephen and Junior?" Sarah said.

"No," Chip said, "but I think I might have a lead. The story's ten kinds of crazy, but anyways, the McGee kids come runnin into the station and tell Lucy they had a run-in with Stephen and Whit's boy outside Ross Wood. Deuce gets upset about somethin and runs off into the woods. The McGee kids go lookin for him and find him in a clearing. Only now, they say, Whit's kid has somehow turned Deuce into a monster with no eyes. And he's walkin around the clearing with a bunch of other monsters look just like him. And there's a bunch of crows circlin in the sky overhead. It's nuttier than squirrel shit, but it does put all of the kids somewhere in the woods this afternoon."

"The McGee kids said there were crows circling overhead?" Bob said.

"That's what they told Lucy."

"I know where to go," Bob said, dragging himself out of the hospital bed.

CHAPTER 67

23 minutes until the end of the world

Chip rounded the corner onto Cedar Avenue. He glanced at the parking lot behind O'Malley's as he drove past. Yellow crime scene tape fastened to light posts flapped in the rising wind. Bob and Sarah sat in the back of Chip's squad car holding hands. Bob wore his hospital gown tucked into his police uniform pants.

Bob ducked his head to get a view of the widow's walk on top of Dr. Moore's house. "Take that dirt road on the left," he told Chip.

Chip turned the steering wheel, and they headed down the narrow, weed-smattered path. "How do you know this is the right way?" he said to Bob.

"You remember the first kid that went missing three years ago?"

"Jimmie Macomber, yeah, of course."

"I interviewed his old man today. He said there were some sort of pagan rites going on in the woods out here."

"Horace Macomber ain't nothin but a crazy old coot, Bob."

"Maybe, maybe not. But old Horace did say these rites were taking place in the woods near Dr. Moore's house, and that there were a bunch of crows circling overhead where it all was happening."

The road wended into the woods, cutting a path between two groves of pines. The shadows of the trees fell heavy on the trail, painting the way ahead in a false night. About a half mile on, the canopy began to thin. Fragments of orange and purple pre-sunset light dappled the gloom. The cawing of crows tolled above. Somewhere close.

Chip pressed the gas pedal and the squad car lurched forward. The cawing grew louder and now Bob, Sarah, and Chip could see the black swarm of crows circling ahead.

The road came to an end, and they emerged on the outskirts of a ring-shaped clearing. And there they were: a band of beasts just like the McGee boys had described. Just like the desiccated body Stephen and Junior had found. Pale, hairless creatures with grotesquely elongated bodies and ragged claws. The creatures were marching in a circle along the edge of the clearing as if under a spell.

Chip slammed the brakes. "No fuckin way," he said.

"I hate to say I told you so," Bob said.

Bob, Sarah, and Chip got out of the car and stood on the trail outside the clearing.

"The boys aren't here," Bob said. "We've got to go."

One of the creatures stepped out of the circle. It stared at Chip through eyes that were no longer human. That were no longer there at all.

The crows broke formation and spiraled off over the woods toward the high widow's walk peeking over the sea of trees.

"No, Bob," Chip said. "You and Sarah have to go." He handed Bob the keys to his squad car.

"Chief," Bob said.

"You're the chief now, Bob." Chip pulled the sheriff's badge off his chest and pinned it onto the front of Bob's hospital gown. "But go back to the station and get a new uniform. You look fuckin ridiculous like that."

"Chip—"

"You and your lady get out of Dodge, Chief," Chip said. "Go find your boy. I got a hunch you might want to follow them crows."

Bob tipped his head. He walked to the squad car and turned back to look at Chip one last time. He and Sarah held up their hands in farewell, then got into the car and drove back through the woods the way they had come, following the crows.

As they made their way through the heart of the woods, they heard a gunshot. A few seconds later, they heard a second shot.

CHAPTER 68

Whit spun around when he heard the first gunshot. He squinted at the reddening ring of the sun sinking into the forest. Another shot clapped through the woods. The first shot had killed one of the Other's servants. Whit could feel the creature die.

A massive murder of crows swarmed the horizon, approaching from the woods where the gunshots had sounded. They swept the sky, cloaking Whit in shadow as they passed overhead. When the shadow reached Dr. Moore's house, the crows began to circle. Whit could just make out the top of the widow's walk from where he stood.

It was time.

Whit's escape from jail had been easy enough. Wave a hand and slide the cell door open. Wave again and the woman at the reception desk takes a nice refreshing nap. He'd laid low in the woods near, but not too near, Dr. Moore's house until now.

He didn't dare go near Junior or his friends. There might still be forces out to destroy him, and he wasn't about to risk any more collateral damage to the people he cared about. Zelda had already been hurt, maybe killed, because of him. He wouldn't let something like that happen again. So he'd waited alone in the woods for sundown.

With the bloodred sun dipping below the horizon, Whit emerged from the woods, circled around to the front of Dr. Moore's house, and entered.

"Ah, Mr. Coe," Mr. Hooker said from behind the reception desk. "Perfect timing this time. I'm so relieved you arrived safely."

"Save it, Moneypenny," Whit said and stormed past the reception desk toward Dr. Moore's office.

"Of course, Mr. Coe. Dr. Moore is in his office. He's expecting you."

Whit ignored the manservant and barged into Dr. Moore's office without knocking.

Dr. Moore sat in his red wingback chair, hands tented in a mandala pose. A beatific smile spread across his face when Whit entered. He rose to his feet, still smiling. "Whitman, my boy," he said, "I am so elated that this moment has finally arrived. You can't imagine how long I have waited."

"I'm not your boy, Doc," Whit said. "I trusted you. All my life. And you lied to me. All my life. Enough bullshit. You're going to tell me exactly what's going on here. Right now."

"Yes, Whitman. You're right. It's time you knew the truth. It's time you knew who you really are. I apologize for the subterfuge. But it was the only way to get you here and now where you were always meant to be. It was the only way for you to fulfil your destiny. The hand of fate is greater than us both. Greater even than the love of a mother for her son. You've read your mother's letter. You must understand your destiny by now. And you must understand that everything your mother and I have done has been for love. Love of you, and love of the perfect world you will create."

"Oh, spare me the whole that which is done out of love is beyond good and evil bullshit. It's about power. You're an insane megalomaniac. And my mother was an insane martyr. Now tell me the truth. All of it. Or I'll snap your fucking neck, old man."

"Ah, that anger again, Whitman. That beautiful wrath. Very well. You want the truth. I shall give it to you. The truth is you were bred, born, and raised for one purpose, and one purpose alone: to serve the Other's will. You were created to fulfil his prophecy. To use your powers to open the gateway to his world. To lead his armies. To stand at his side as he sweeps away all memory of this corrupt world and establishes a new pure world in its place. A paradise for all eternity. That has always been your destiny, and every step you have taken in your life has led you to this moment when you shall fulfil that destiny."

"Bullshit," Whit said.

"Of course you required guidance to hone your powers. That's where I came in. Your mother brought you to me because she knew I could teach you to tap into your powers, to harness them, and ultimately to unleash them. But the prophecy required sacrifice. Great sacrifice. The four deaths of the chosen one's family: the twin, the mother, the wife, and the father. Your twin sister died of natural causes. Your mother died of natural and supernatural causes. True, she died giving premature birth. However, that premature birth occurred when you first touched the gateway to the Otherworld. When you first cracked the door. Your mother's death consecrated that gate and yielded the necessary second sacrifice. The third sacrifice, I know, was the cruelest, and for that I am truly sorry, Whitman. Truly. You said you wanted the whole truth. Well, here it is. The creature that was once Jimmie Macomber killed your wife. That is true. True, but incomplete. Whitman, the creature acted upon my orders. As much as it pained me to know how you would suffer, I knew that suffering was necessary. That sacrifice was necessary. So I carried it out. I'm sorry, Whitman."

"You?" Whit said, his voice flat, cold. A high-pitched drone screamed in his head, surging with the redlining tide of his pulse. Rising and accelerating with the burning white rage. The rage spiraled through Whit's entire body, shooting through his skull. He felt it flaming behind his eyes, blurring the world. He howled a visceral cry of pain and wrath and extended his arm. Dr. Moore rose off the ground, choking and clawing at his neck, feet kicking as he levitated in the air. Whit pushed. Dr. Moore hurtled across the room and cratered into the back wall, shattering the yellow octagonal mirror. He hovered above the floor, pinned to the wall, still clawing at his neck and kicking his feet in the air as his eyes bulged and his face turned purple.

For some reason Whit thought of the night he had left Rockwell all those years ago. He thought of choking his father against the wall. He thought of the words that ran through his mind as he squeezed Allan Coe's throat and watched his life draining away: *What kind of man kills his own father?*

Whit tensed his body. He clawed his hands and extended his thumbs. He pushed.

Dr. Moore wailed in agony as his eyes sank into their sockets and popped. Blood and gore ran down his cheeks like teardrops. Whit continued to push. The skull behind Dr. Moore's eye sockets caved and split apart in red and white clumps.

Whit released Dr. Moore's body. It dropped to the floor with a wet thud.

"Well done, sir," Mr. Hooker said from the doorway. He applauded as he entered the room.

"What the hell are you talking about, Jeeves?" Whit said, panting.

"You've made the fourth sacrifice, sir. You've opened the door."

"But the fourth sacrifice was my father. He's already dead."

"I'm afraid you're mistaken, sir. Allan Coe was not your father. Dr. Moore was your father. You have sacrificed him yourself, as the prophecy foretold."

The ground began to rumble, deep down like a cataclysmic earthquake. Dr. Moore's delicate glass and ceramic decorations toppled to the ground and shattered. Cracks shot through the plaster on the back wall like tree roots bursting through a sidewalk. A droning wail echoed from the depths behind the crumbling wall.

Mr. Hooker spread his arms and laughed. Whit waved a hand and snapped his neck.

A crushing force pulled at the wall from the other side, sucking its imploding splinters into the maw. Whit watched the wall fragment, collapse, and plummet into the chasm. The black hole sun spiraled its hypnotic tendrils, churning downward into the bottomless pit of the horizon.

When the wall fell away, Whit saw the secret alcove where he had honed his powers under Dr. Moore's tutelage. Inside the claustrophobic catacomb, Junior and Stephen stood, gagged and bound back-to-back, eyes wide and trembling. One of the Other's servants loomed above them, its claws clasping them by their shirt collars. The sightless creature stared almost sadly at Whit, then leapt into the void with the boys in its clutches.

"No!" Whit screamed. He charged toward the gateway at a dead sprint and flung himself into the abyss after the boys. Behind him, Dr. Moore's house snapped and rattled. It ripped apart into fractured particles and collapsed into the void behind Whit.

Then out climbed the creatures.

***

In the attic of the Coe house, the grandfather clock struck midnight.

223

CHAPTER 69

The end of the world

The hospital room roiled and trembled as the earth quaked its violent death throes. The TV rattled against the wall. The picture flickered, then the signal cut out and the screen went glass black. The remaining vase in the room teetered off the edge of the bedside table and mosaiced the linoleum floor in salmon pink ceramic.

"Earthquake," Jim said to Zelda. "A fucking big bastard." He gripped the arms of his chair.

Zelda sat rigid in her bed until the quake subsided. "Jesus," she said. "Biggest fucking bastard I've ever felt."

"I think it's over," Jim said, standing up. "You okay, Zelda?"

"Yeah."

The fluorescent ceiling lights crackled and the room went dark. A few seconds later a faint thrumming purred from a lower level in the building and the lights came back on.

"Looks like the generator just kicked in," Jim said.

For a while the thrumming purr was the only sound Zelda and Jim heard. Then a solitary scream from somewhere below. A scream of primordial fear extinguished midcry. More screams. A chorus of chaos rising. More screams. Different screams. Screams of excruciation and death. Screams choked and gurgled, then silenced. More screams. Screams louder. Screams closer. The click-boom reverb of the heavy stairwell doors battering open. Footsteps charging through the doors, up and down the stairs, frantic, echoing along the climbing narrow gullet.

A series of metallic thunderclaps erupted somewhere in the building.

"Gunshots," Zelda said.

Scuffling sounds clamoring up the stairwell. The stairwell door at the end of the corridor banging open. A frenzied patter racing along the hallway toward Zelda's hospital room. Scuttling, inhuman footsteps clacking in pursuit.

K-tchikitikitik. K-tchikikikitikitikitik. K-tchikitikitikitikitiktiktikitikitikit!

The hunt skirred along the hallway, almost to Zelda's room door now. Zelda slid out of bed, trailing her IV stand. She and Jim inched toward the door and peeked out through the viewing window at the top. They caught a flash of a middle-aged man in a hospital gown sprinting past, then a blur of something tall and white lunging after him.

A skidding thud juddered the ground outside the hospital room. The man screamed. The white shape howled. Then dead air.

Jim edged closer to the viewing window. He couldn't see anything outside but an empty patch of hallway and the door to the room directly across the hall. He leaned his face up to the glass and—

K-tchikitikitik!

A gnarled row of fangs snapped against the window, fracturing the glass and smearing its surface red. The gaping mouth drew back, and Zelda and Jim saw the creature's full hideous form. It bored its sightless stare through the broken window, peeled its cadaver lips around its fangs, and charged against the door. The door snapped off its hinges, knocking Jim to the floor.

The creature hunched into the room. It stepped over Jim and leered at Zelda. She drifted backward, eyes fixed on the pale creature, until her back pressed against the wall. The creature lurched across the room and loomed over Zelda, sniffing the air and rumbling in its throat. It bared its fangs and roared.

The creature's wail cut short as Jim hammered Bob's IV pole into its skull. The creature wobbled, then pitched to the floor. Jim straddled the creature and swung the pole again and again, pummeling the beast until it lay twitching on the floor. He turned the creature faceup with his boot. "You don't mess around with Jim," he said and drove the pole into the creature's face until it was nothing but wet pulp and splintered bone.

"Unhook your IV, Zelda," Jim said. "We've gotta get out of here. My truck's in the underground lot."

"Just a sec," Zelda said. She pushed the morphine button on her IV. "Aaand… Disco."

CHAPTER 70

Spirals. Circles. The eternal recurrence and the eternal hourglass of existence. Overturned and shattered. Ephemeral grains of the infinite scattered across the broken shards of space and time. The void of darkness. The abyss of light.

Whit slipped through the sunrise of the void following a white thread of light. Across the burning threshold of the horizon. Down into the depths of dream and dreamscape. Along the expanding expanse of corridors and labyrinthine walls. Through the heart of the dark disk to the far side of the black hole sun.

He emerged in a shadowland of night and fog. At first he felt nothing. Then the damp bite of the mist as it rolled over him on its way to the portal. On its way to his world. The desolate soil beneath his feet trembled in a storm of clattering claws. A churning chorus of *k-tchikitikitik, k-tchikitikitik, k-tchikitikitikitikitikitikitik* rising from the nebula.

The mist ahead of Whit began to thin, parting in a straight path like a long corridor. A gnarled black shape towered against the fading fog. A decaying tree, dead or dying. The outlines of four more shapes emerged from the mist beneath the tree. Junior and Stephen, still in the clutches of the eyeless creature. And another figure. A tall man shrouded in a black cloak, the cowl eclipsing his face. The man spread his arms in a welcoming gesture. Whit followed the path through the mist, feet crunching on hard black ground blanketed in drifts of ash until he stood before the cloaked figure. He flicked a glance at the boys, then watched the man in the cloak. "Who are you?" Whit said.

"Don't you know?" the figure said in a low echo. "But what's in a name?" The figure peeled back the dark corona of its cowl, revealing its face. Whit's face.

"That's impossible," Whit said.

"Your own eyes tell a different story, my boy," the Other said.

"Are you… me, somehow? Like some parallel universe version of me?"

"A reasonable question," the Other said. "But no. I am not you, and you are not me. I am I, and you are you."

"Then why do you look exactly like me?" Whit said.

"Because a mirror is a mirror. And there is stardust in your blood, my boy."

"What does that mean?"

"All in due time, lad. All in due time. And we've got eternity, you and I."

"Why me?"

"You know why."

Whit gestured with his head at Junior and Stephen. "I'm here," he said to the Other. "I opened the gate. I'm the one you want. Let them go."

"Done," the Other said and waved a hand. The creature let go of the boys, still staring at Whit through the hollowed pits of its eyes. The Other waved his hand again. The ropes fell from the boys' wrists and the gags popped out of their mouths.

"If they go through the portal, they'll be unharmed?" Whit said.

"You have my word," the Other said. "None of my servants will harm their prince or his friend."

The Other extended his hand, and the mist parted in a path to the gateway. The army of creatures halted their march, giving the boys a clear passage to the portal.

"Okay. Go, boys," Whit said, looking down at Junior. "You go through that portal and find Stephen's parents. They'll know what to do."

"But, Dada," Junior said.

"I know, Junior. But you can't stay here. You have to go. Stay close to Stephen and his parents no matter what. Be brave. Remember me and your mom. Remember that we always love you." Whit wrapped his arms around his son and squeezed him tight.

"I love you, Dada," Junior said.

"I love you too, kiddo. Always remember."

Junior nodded and sobbed into Whit's shirt. Whit held his son as long as he could, then he placed a hand on Junior's back and ushered him forward. Junior and Stephen bolted to the mouth of the spiraling black hole, then turned and waved to Whit. Whit waved back. Stephen steadied himself and leapt through the gate. Junior lingered a while longer, looking at his father's face one last time, then turned and dove in after Stephen.

CHAPTER 71

Bob and Sarah fanged it through the hollows chasing the murder of crows. Bob peeled dirt around a curve in the road and saw the crows circling above the vacant patch of gloam where the spire of Dr. Moore's widow's walk had once pierced the sky.

Sarah angled her head toward the crows and said, "It's gone. Dr. Moore's house is gone."

"That can't be good," Bob said, gunning the engine.

Bob was leaning into another curve when the seismic shock wave hit, scudding the car into a spinout. He took his foot off the gas and steered into the slide, but it was no use. The car skidded off the road and slingshot into a pine trunk. A cat-gray cloud of mist hissed from under the hood.

"Sarah, you okay?" Bob said.

Sarah rubbed her neck. "Yeah," she said. "We'll call the chiropractor tomorrow. I hear sheriffs get great benefits. Now let's go."

Bob turned the key. The engine didn't fire. "We're gonna have to hoof it," he said.

Sarah and Bob got out of the car and nashed for the trailhead. The ground rumbled beneath their feet, surging and skittering beyond the trees. They kicked to the mouth of the trail and stopped dead.

Scores of the pale nightmare creatures were catapulting from the mouth of a black hole hovering inside the ruins of Dr. Moore's house. The creatures seemed to materialize from thin air as the maw spewed them into the world, howling as they cavorted toward the business district. Crashing sounds, car alarms, and screams clamored through the streets.

When the last of the creatures crawled from the portal and swarmed into the strip mall across the street, Bob said, "Honey?"

"Yes, dear," Sarah said.

"Did you just see a bunch of monsters pop out of a black hole and run off to destroy the town?"

"Yes, dear," Sarah said.

"Oh, good. I thought I might have gone insane."

"Well, I'm sure your new sheriff's job comes with mental health benefits too, but by the look of things I'd say the town is short one shrink."

"At least there's that," Bob said.

Sarah looked up at the circling crows. "I thought the boys would be here," she said.

"I know." Bob wrapped an arm around Sarah's shoulder.

"Do you think maybe…" Sarah said and tilted her head toward the black hole.

"Only one way to find out," Bob said.

Sarah and Bob stepped to the edge of the black hole. They looked each other in the eye, held hands, and strode into the maw.

As Bob and Sarah crossed the horizon, Junior and Stephen sprang from the disk, barreling into them and knocking them to the ground.

"Mom, Dad!" Stephen said, dogpiling on top of Sarah and Bob.

Junior pulled himself to his feet. Dust and tears smeared his cheeks.

Still on the ground, Bob squeezed Stephen. "Hey, kiddo," he said.

Sarah kissed Stephen on his grimy forehead. "I'm so glad you boys are safe," she said.

"Junior," Bob said. "Do you know where your dad is?"

Junior nodded, sobbing. He pointed at the black hole. "He's in there," he said. "He's going to die."

CHAPTER 72

Whit turned to face the Other and his servant. The creature watched Whit, emptiness and despair in its eyeless gaze.

"I'm sorry, Adam," Whit said and waved a hand. The creature's neck snapped. It fell dead on the ash-covered ground.

"I think you've got it all wrong, Whitman," the Other said. "This is not an end. It is a beginning. The beginning of a pure and perfect world, unspoiled by man. Unspoiled by his greed and war. Unspoiled by his destruction of the natural world—the very world upon which his own survival depends. And in our new world, you shall be a king. A god."

"I don't care about being a king," Whit said. "I don't care about being a god."

"Then what do you care about, my boy?"

"Can you bring her back?"

"I'm sorry, lad," the Other said. "But I can neither bend time, nor raise the dead. Look around you." He swept his hand to indicate the lone withered tree and the wasteland. "My whole world is dead. But yours—*ours* is still alive."

The Other placed a hand on Whit's shoulder. "And though I can't bring your wife back," he said, "there may be something else I can do for you and your boy. There is another world where you can be together forever."

"What do you mean?" Whit said.

"Look into my eyes," the Other said. "Look into your perfect world."

Whit looked into the Other's eyes. Into black reflective pools. He felt himself drifting into another portal, falling into a memory that never was.

CHAPTER 73

The motion sensor light clicked on when Zelda and Jim entered the stairwell. Zelda leaned on the handrail, and they made their way down to the next floor. *Click.* The motion sensor light on the next floor flickered to life. They hobbled downward, descending another floor. *Click.* Only three more floors to go before they reached the parking garage. *Click.* Two more.

Halfway down the next flight of steps, Zelda lost her footing. She gripped the handrail and righted herself. She bit her lip and placed her hand over her stitches. Jim leaned against the opposite handrail and tried to catch his breath. "You okay?" he said.

Zelda nodded and gave Jim a thumbs up. *Click.* The stairwell motion sensor lights droned awake on the landing below. Scuttling claws climbed upward. *K-tchikitikitik. K-tchikitikitik.* Jim and Zelda crept back up the flight of stairs and pried open the hallway door. The scuttling claws climbed nearer. *K-tchikitikitik. K-tchikitikitik. K-tchikitikitikitikitikitikitikitik!*

As Zelda and Jim turned to shut the door behind them, the creature rounded the corner of the stairwell. The void hollows of its eyes peered up at them from the bottom of the flight. Jim and Zelda slammed the door and scrambled across the hallway toward the other stairwell, dodging overturned hospital equipment and mangled bodies. An elderly woman had somehow survived the carnage. She paced back and forth muttering to herself. They reached the far end of the hall just as the creature battered through the stairwell door behind them. They flung open the other stairwell door and sped down to the parking garage. "There's my truck," Jim said, pointing to his blue Chevy. They put on a final, terror-cranked charge for the truck. Jim fished his car keys from his pocket and—

K-tchikitikitik. The clacking echoed through the parking garage. One of the creatures crawled from the shadows behind a concrete support pillar. Then another emerged. And another. The creatures stalked forward and circled their prey.

CHAPTER 74

Whit sat in the bleachers and watched the pitch. The batter laced a single to center. The runner rounded third and slid into home. The umpire spread his arms. Safe. Whit, Alice, and Junior stood up and cheered. Fireworks shot off in the warm night beyond the stadium lights. Junior gave Whit a high five, and Alice gave him a big hug and a kiss. Whit chugged a gulp of beer from a plastic cup and looked out at the green grass of the baseball field. Then he looked at the smiling faces of his family. If this wasn't Heaven, he didn't know what was. He could stay in this moment forever.

"But you can't," he heard Alice's voice say. The stadium lights switched off and Whit was standing in darkness.

He stared into the darkness for what felt like a very long time. Then he saw a tiny light flutter in the distance. The light flew toward Whit. "Hey, sunshine," it said. "Think happy thoughts."

"I was," Whit said.

"No." The light twinkled in front of his face, then flickered. And there she was. "Real happy thoughts," Alice said. "None of this is real, sunshine."

"Maybe not," Whit said. "But it's better than anything real I can ever have again."

"Because I'm gone?"

Whit bowed his head.

"Well," Alice said, "I'm here with you now. And our son, your *real* son, is out there in the real world. And he needs his father. You have to snap out of this dream and get back into the real world before it's gone."

"But I already opened the gate," Whit said. "I let the Other into our world. It's too late. How can I stop it?"

"I already told you, silly," Alice said. She flickered and turned back into the tiny fluttering light. "Think happy thoughts. Now follow me, sunshine."

The tiny light flitted though the darkness and Whit followed. She zipped into a bright white tunnel and faded away. Whit stepped through the tunnel after her.

His eyes sprang open. He was standing beneath the withered tree. The Other was watching him.

"You should not be awake yet," the Other said. "Was your dream not to your satisfaction? In your mind, I read that this was your idea of Heaven."

"It is my idea of Heaven," Whit said. "But it's only an idea. It's a fantasy of what was but can never be again. It's not real."

"Reality is overrated, lad. At least at the moment. Besides, you can live in both worlds. I can let you escape into your perfect fantasy any time you like, while we shape a perfect reality out there." The Other pointed at the portal.

"You mean *your* perfect reality," Whit said.

"Of course."

"And the prophecy? Your means to that perfect end, I presume."

"Written in the stars by mine own hand."

"Well, that's poetic," Whit said. "But a bit hackneyed for my taste. Besides which, it's total bullshit." He scanned the horizon with his eyes and spread a hand to encompass the wasteland. "You once had a world. A beautiful world. Now that world is gone. Only a memory. Because of you and your prophecy. Well, I once had a world too. A beautiful world. And now that world is gone. Only a memory. Because of you and your goddamn prophecy. So fuck you and the prophecy you rode in on."

"My prophecy cannot be rejected," the Other said. "It is the truth and the word. Every part of it has come to pass."

"All except one," Whit said. "Aren't I supposed to join you and lead your army?"

"Yes, my boy. And you shall."

"No," Whit said. "I won't. You see there's one thing you failed to take into account: free will. I have to choose to join you for your prophecy to be fulfilled. And I would prefer not to. I choose to end you and your bullshit prophecy. I choose to fight you until you're dead, and so am I. And then I choose to fight some more."

"You are decided, then?" the Other said.

Whit squared up to face the Other. "Written in the stars by mine own hand," he said.

The Other shook his head. "Pity," he said. "Very well, then. Let's see what you've got, lad."

Whit reached into the well of rage burning inside him, extended his arms, and pushed at the Other. The Other careened backward into the decaying tree and ricocheted, face down, into its gnarled tangle of roots. He climbed to his feet, smiling.

"Impressive," the Other said. "You are more powerful than even I imagined. That anger inside you. I've never felt anything like it." The Other raised his head, looked upward, and sniffed the air. "And there's something else beneath that anger. Something even more powerful. It reeks, but it's so powerful. It's a shame you won't have the chance to hone it. Oh, the worlds we could have conquered together. Ah, well. My turn."

The Other circled Whit. He clawed his hand in the air, gripped Whit by the throat, and dashed him into the tree. Whit scudded to the ground on his hands and knees. He pulled himself to his feet and brushed himself off. He stared into the Other's eyes.

"You can take a hit," the Other said. "I'll give you that. But the time for testing is over. Now, Whitman, it is time for you to die, though it does pain me, my boy."

"Round three," Whit said. "Fight."

Whit and the Other dug in their heels and extended their arms in unison like mirror images of one another. They pushed against each other, straining and growling. Their eyes went black and their bodies burned white.

The Other's feet slid backward beneath the force of Whit's will, carving a trail in the dirt. He sensed the deeper well of power that Whit channeled beneath his anger again. He smelled it in the air once more. *What is it?* he wondered. And then he knew.

A tendril from the tree lashed out and wrapped around Whit's neck, pulling him off the ground. Whit dangled from a crooked branch, choking and gasping for air. He clutched at the tendril and kicked his feet.

"You don't wind up the sole survivor of a millennia-long war without picking up a few tricks," the Other said, looking up at Whit as he twitched his death throes. "Training and experience beat raw power every time. Ah, and that raw power in you." He sniffed the air. "That reek. It's grief. It's even more powerful than anger. But alas, I cannot experience it. I cannot draw on its power. But you..."

The Other shook his head. "So much grief. So much power. Such a waste."

The Other crooked a finger and the tendril tightened around Whit's neck. Whit flailed against the hangman's noose, then fell limp and closed his eyes.

The Other watched Whit die.

CHAPTER 75

The creatures tightened the hangman's noose, circling closer to Jim and Zelda. Jim stepped in front of Zelda, shielding her from the advancing monsters. "Take these," he said, handing Zelda the keys to his truck.

"Jim," Zelda said. "I can't."

"It's the only way, kid. I can't hold 'em off for long. Maybe a few seconds, so you gotta be quick. When I jump, you jump. Get into the truck and go. Get as far away from here as you can."

Zelda nodded and took the keys.

"Ready?" Jim said.

Zelda nodded again, blinking away tears.

"On three," Jim said. "One. Two. Three." He roared and charged the creatures. The creatures answered his roar and pounced on Jim. Zelda shot toward the driver's side door. One of the creatures sprang from behind the hood of the truck, blocking her way.

Jim screamed as three of the creatures dragged him to the ground. They plunged their claws into his sides and chest, then sank their teeth into his flesh.

The creature that had Zelda cornered whipped its arm, flinging her against the side of the truck. She clanged off the door and crumpled to the pavement. The creature hunched low and skittered on top of Zelda, its eyeless face bearing down on her. It drew closer and peeled back its shriveled lips. Ropey tendrils of blood and saliva dripped from its fangs. The creature unhinged its jaw with a wet crunch. It bellowed its death howl. And struck.

CHAPTER 76

Whit drifted in the abyss. In the pure darkness of the nothing. And then there was light. A warm and beautiful white glow that washed over Whit, filling him with a peace he had not known in a very long time. He opened his eyes to the light. And there she was.

"Hey, sunshine," Alice said. She smiled at Whit and stroked his cheek. They stood in front of a towering ash tree, its sturdy roots shooting into the depths of the cosmic well. "You're early. It's not your time yet."

"But I want to be with you," Whit said.

"I know," Alice said. "I want to be with you too. More than anything. But it's not your time. This is not your fate. You have so much more to do. You have to raise our son. He needs you even more than I do. The world needs you out there. You have to fight now."

"I did fight," Whit said. "And I lost. I can't beat the Other. He's too powerful."

Alice shook her head and smirked. "And you think I'm stubborn," she said. "Whit, you're the most stubborn person I've ever met. And the angriest." She raised an eyebrow. "But that anger can blind you sometimes, Whit. The Other said you have a power beneath the anger. A greater power."

"Grief?" Whit said.

"And why is grief stronger than anger?" Alice said.

Whit shrugged. "I don't know," he said.

"For such a smart man, Whit, sometimes you can't see the forest for the trees. Because grief comes from the most powerful human emotion of all. It comes from love. That's why it's a power the Other can't tap into. He's not human and he feels no love. Love is the power you need to use to beat him."

"How?"

"Don't you know yet, silly? Think happy thoughts. I'll show you."

Alice leaned in and kissed Whit. Whit closed his eyes and felt a pure white light eclipse him. A light that was the opposite of the flame of anger he had used to stoke his powers. This light was warm and welcoming. It soothed Whit's troubled spirit and filled him with peace and purpose. He opened his eyes to that white warmth.

Whit looked out across the wasteland of the Other's world. He dangled from the withered tree, its gnarled tendril wrapped around his neck. He reached into the white light within him. The light that he drew from Alice and Junior, and all those he loved. The light radiated through his body, and the tendril burned to ash. Whit dropped from the branch and landed on his feet.

The Other backed up, jaw hinging open. "That's impossible," he said. "You were dead. I saw you die."

"I've died before," Whit said. "Not my first rodeo."

The Other thrust out his arms and pushed against Whit with all his power, all his anger.

Whit didn't budge. "That doesn't seem to work on me anymore," he said. "Your prophecy is ash and dust. And so are you."

Whit raised his arm. The white light flowed from his hand, rushing over the Other, consuming him in its flame, searing the flesh from his bones. Whit closed his hand and the Other shattered to ash and dust. The ash drifted in the wind and disappeared into nothing.

As the Other died, so did his army. The creatures who rampaged through Rockwell, slashing and devouring, crumbled to ash with their master. The creature clutching Zelda disintegrated as its fangs plunged toward her neck, coating her face and clothes in fine gray particles. "Eww, gross," she said, spitting and swiping at her face with the back of her hand. "Monster cremains."

A seismic shock wave convulsed the ground again. Whit sprinted across the wasteland toward the portal. The black hole sun was collapsing. The door was closing. Whit put on a burst of speed and vaulted into the imploding maw as it snapped shut behind him. He cratered to the earth and rolled onto his back, sucking wind and gazing into a crystalline sky.

"You never told me you did your own stunts, Whit," Bob said.

Whit grinned and picked himself up. Junior and the Rockwells stood huddled together, staring at Whit as if he'd slept for a thousand years.

"Dada, you're alive!" Junior shouted and flung himself into Whit's arms.

Whit wrapped his arms around his son. "I'm working on it, buddy," he said.

CHAPTER 77

Whit set the cardboard box in the trunk of Alice's car and hinged the lid shut. "That's the last of it," he said, resting a hand on Junior's shoulder. He tilted his head at Bob, Sarah, and Stephen, then handed Bob the keys to Allan Coe's house.

"I'll pass these to Gary," Bob said.

"I'm still not sure you can trust a realtor named Gary," Whit said. "But if you say he's solid, I'll take your word."

Bob chuckled and said, "Well, Whit, it's been one hell of a trip, but it was great seeing you again, brother."

"And don't you dare be a stranger again," Sarah said.

"No, ma'am," Whit said. "I won't. But next time, why don't y'all come up to the city and stay with me and Junior? Maybe catch a baseball game and check out the zoo."

"Mom, Dad, can we?" Stephen said.

"You bet, kiddo," Sarah said.

"Yes!" Stephen said and gave Junior a high five.

"Awesome!" Junior said.

The sun dipped low and red on the horizon.

"Well," Whit said. "I guess we better get rolling before dark."

"Give her a minute," Sarah said. "She'll be here."

"Yeah," Bob said. "Stand awkwardly with us in the driveway a little longer."

Sarah swatted Bob on the arm.

A yellow Gremlin rounded the corner and pulled up to the curb. Zelda smiled out the window and jogged up the drive holding a shopping bag.

"I didn't think you were coming," Whit said.

"Sorry I'm running late," Zelda said. "I had to stop to pick up something." She handed Whit the bag.

Whit reached into the bag and pulled out a narrow rectangular box. He flipped it open. Inside was a green pen with 'O'Malley's Pub' inscribed along the side.

"Just in case," Zelda said.

"Thank you," Whit said, grinning. "It just so happens I got you something too."

"Really?" Zelda said.

"Yup. Just a sec." Whit popped the trunk of the car, rummaged around for a few seconds, then came back holding a camera box and an envelope. He handed the camera and the envelope to Zelda. "Look inside the envelope," he said.

Zelda opened the envelope and pulled out two slips of paper. Her eyes went wide. "No fucking way," she said and leapt into Whit's arms. She stepped back and stared at the slips of paper.

"That one on top is a first-class plane ticket to Tokyo," Whit said. "The one underneath is your reservation for the Hotel Gracery Shinjuku. You're booked for a whole week."

"Jesus Christ, Whit, you didn't have to do that."

"I was thinking about the conversation we had the other day. And I figured as long as the world's still there, you might as well see it. And take pictures like a big ol' tourist."

"Thank you, Whit," Zelda said. She hugged Whit again and buried her face in his chest. "Thank you, thank you, thank you."

"You go have a big adventure, Zelda," Whit said.

"Hey, kid," Bob said. "Save some of the big guy for the rest of us."

Zelda let go of Whit and kissed him on the cheek.

"Hey, wait!" Bob said, raising a finger. "Zelda, does that camera have a timer?"

Zelda scanned the back of the box. "Yep," she said.

"Perfect," Bob said. "We can snap a family photo. Everybody hold on while I get my tripod out of the closet. Two seconds."

"Alright," Whit said, slinging his arm over Junior's shoulder. "Let's make a new memory."

EPILOGUE

Whit sat in the red wingback chair in his study. He looked at the twin music box ballerinas on his desk and poured a glass of the Yamazaki 12 he saved for special occasions. He took a sip and settled in to finish the epilogue of his new book— or the epitaph as Alice liked to say. He picked up the pen Zelda had given him when he left Rockwell, pressed the tip against a yellow legal pad, and wrote:

And he drifted through the warm radiance of the tunnel. Into her radiance. He let it wash over and through him. They were together again at last, after all the years.

They wrapped their arms around each other once more.

"And what did you do for the rest of your life?" she said.

"I missed you," he said.

Whit set down his pen and gazed into the mirror on the wall. He leaned back in his chair and closed his eyes. The melancholy chimes of the ballerina's music box twinkled in the air like starlight. He felt Alice's arms encircle his neck. He felt her cheek press against his.

"Hey sunshine," she said.

THE END